The Quill
Conspiracy

Joseph R. Mullen

Copyright © 2022 Joseph R. Mullen
All rights reserved
First Edition

NEWMAN SPRINGS PUBLISHING
320 Broad Street
Red Bank, NJ 07701

First originally published by Newman Springs Publishing 2022

ISBN 978-1-68498-791-7 (Paperback)
ISBN 978-1-68498-792-4 (Digital)

Printed in the United States of America

For Mom, Jean, and Linda. Thinking of you always.

1

The war came. The war that nobody wanted. The war that everyone knew was coming. The war that nobody did anything to try to prevent. The war that would change everything. It came. It was merciless. It was devastating. It was far-reaching. It killed hundreds of thousands. It injured millions. It was still raging on. No one knew where they came from. No one knew what they wanted. No one remembered how the name Quill came about, whether it was from the media or the military, but it was the name given to the invaders. Earth had fought back and regained the space out to Jupiter and, in the process, constructed a series of forts that were meant to protect the inner planets. Saturn and beyond still remained in enemy hands. Tales of what went on in that area ran rampant on Earth and her colonies. They weren't pretty. Fighters sometimes went in, and once in a while, a ship would come out, but the pilots never saw the light of day again.

Karl Cregg was a middle-aged man with a military-style haircut composed of white and black colors. His muscular build stood just under six feet. He was sitting now in the realty office of his friend Kevin Base. Kevin was a year younger than Karl, but the two had become lifelong friends in high school. This was the first time in nearly twenty years that they had any physical contact with each other. Karl's work and Kevin's homelife had kept the two limited to voice mail only. Now Karl had the time, and Kevin had agreed to help his old friend. He had found Karl "exactly what you have been looking for," he said.

Kevin, at the moment, was in the other room, conversing with another client. He had informed Karl that he would be with him in a few minutes and told him to make himself comfortable. Karl sat at the huge desk and sipped at a bottle of water that he had taken from the small fridge that sat at the opposite side of the desk from him. He listened somewhat to the conversation in the other office while looking around at the main office. On one wall, neatly displayed, were the various awards that Kevin had won in his career. Another wall held the pictures of his beloved family: his wife, parents, children, as well as close friends. A third wall held pictures of the properties that he had sold. These consisted of homes, businesses, empty lots, and islands. The final wall held pictures of places and countries he and his family had visited. There weren't as many of them on this wall, but every one that was there showed him and his family having a wonderful time.

Kevin Base strolled in wearing a light-blue suit with a navy-blue tie. He motioned for Karl to remain seated as he passed him and patted him gently on the back, then took his seat opposite his longtime friend. A large smile came to his face, and he seemed to light up more than normal.

"How long has it been, Karl?" he asked, leaning back in his oversized chair.

"Too long, Kevin. How's the wife and children?"

"The oldest is getting ready for college. The middle one is entering high school, and the youngest is getting way too old too fast. She'll turn twelve in October," Kevin stated with pride. His eyes momentarily left his friend and drifted to the family pictures. He stared at the wall and couldn't believe how old each of them had gotten. It seemed it was just last week that he and his wife, Angela, had married. Karl had been his best man. "How about you? Anyone in your life yet?" Kevin inquired, leaning forward onto his forearms.

"Work was my wife. She and I just got a divorce. When there is someone new, you'll be the first to know," Karl replied with a small laugh.

"What happened?" Kevin demanded in a loud voice. "You two were inseparable. You were together for over twenty years. You were one of their top people. What on earth are they thinking?"

"They claim I'm not needed anymore. I'm a relic from another time. Nothing has happened out there for over a dozen years. They thought I was just stoking fear by constantly claiming that the Quill would return. My superiors felt it was long past time for a change," Karl told his friend before taking another sip of water.

Kevin leaned back in his chair and looked at his friend. Karl had been responsible for helping drive the enemy back. His planning had been crucial. He was a strategist. One of the best the Service had. Now suddenly, the Service had let him go. It wasn't right. Something about this smelled wrong.

"When did all this happen?" Kevin wondered.

"Last week. Tuesday. No warning. It was a normal day," informed Karl, relaxing slightly.

"So that's why you contacted me. You want a place to get away from the world for a short time. Recharge your batteries. Reflect on your possibilities," Kevin said, rising from his desk and beginning to walk around his office. He stopped when he came to the wall of properties that he had sold. He looked at them with pride. They always brought a smile to his face.

"Something like that. Basically I just want a private little place to forget what's happened. I knew if anybody could find that place for me, it was you. What about it? Was I right?" Karl asked with a smile.

Kevin turned away from the wall and looked at his friend. His smile grew bigger as he winked at Karl, then returned to his desk. He picked up a small hand computer and touched the screen. He moved toward the wall with his awards on it and motioned for Karl to follow him. A small island appeared, floating in midair. It was mostly covered with trees, with no buildings visible.

"Just over eleven acres. No wildlife except for the occasional birds that roost there from time to time. There is a freshwater lake that covers four acres. Several fruit trees and berry bushes. A cave or two, plus plenty of woods. The nearest land is sixty miles away. You would not be on any of the shipping lanes. What do you think?" Kevin explained enthusiastically.

"It's perfect," Karl stated, looking at the floating picture with his eyes wide open. He found himself starting to reach out and try to touch it but caught himself before he could lift his arm enough, and looked at his friend. "What about the other one? Did you find something in that area that I was looking for? Is it as good as this one?"

"Have a peek at this," Kevin said while touching his palm computer. The scene shifted to what looked like an arctic view. The three-dimensional picture floated in midair, and both men stared at it. "Smaller than the other one, just under nine acres, with four acres of fresh water, a small cabin that overlooks the lake, no running water, no electricity, woods cover more than three acres. Good fishing. Located off the coast of Alaska. Nearest neighbor is two hours by boat. No landing strips. If you take a plane, you have to land on the ocean."

"Beautiful," Karl stated, studying it hard. "They both have what I'm looking for. Both will fit into my plans perfectly. Put me down for the two of them," he said with a smile that appeared to almost mock his happiness. He reached out a hand to Kevin and waited for his friend to reach out his.

"Both?" Kevin questioned, not believing what he had just heard. His initial thought was that Karl would take one or the other. He never thought his friend would take both. "You want the two of them?"

"That's what I said. I want both. I have big plans. These two will fit perfectly."

Kevin slowly put his hand out and shook Karl's hand. Then the events fell into place in his head, and the handshake became more vigorous. Soon he put his other hand on his friend's hand and smiled ear to ear. He could almost see and hear the money flowing into his account.

"This is great, Karl. I'm glad I could find you two such places that fit you to a tee. These will look fantastic on my wall," he said cheerfully. He felt like dancing.

"Opposite ends of the spectrum. Maybe you should put them on opposite ends of the wall," Karl suggested with a chuckle. He gestured with both hands to where he thought they should go.

"I love that idea," Kevin said with a broad smile as he looked from one end of the wall to the other. They would be fine additions to his collection. He touched his hand computer once again, and the arctic island vanished. Turning, he made his way back to his desk and sat down in his chair. He motioned for Karl to take his seat. "When would you like to take possession?" he asked.

"Can you make it all happen today?" Karl asked, sitting down and crossing his legs.

"Absolutely!" Kevin said, flashing an even bigger smile. He looked at the instrument in his hand, and his fingers gracefully glided across the screen. When he was done, he handed it over to Karl, who took it and started to read what was on the screen. "All you have to do is thumbprint each page at the bottom. There are forty-three pages. They cover everything. When you're done, you will be the proud owner of the two islands. One in the South Pacific and the other just off the coast of Alaska. One for summer, one for winter," he said, laughing out loud.

"They're what I need, buddy," Karl said as he read and thumb-printed the pages.

Kevin rose from his chair and started to pace his office. He studied his longtime friend. He went over things in his head. Questioning what was really going on. He knew better than to ask Karl; he would only get a smoke screen of an answer. He was nervous. Concerned. Something wasn't sitting right. Something was out of place. What it was he couldn't say. He also knew Karl wouldn't tell him until he was good and ready. If it was trouble, Karl wanted to keep his friend as safe as possible.

"Here you go, Kevin. Think I got them all," Karl said after some twenty minutes as he handed the small palm computer over to its owner.

Kevin took the computer and began to check the pages over one by one. As he did so, he put his thumbprint on the opposite side of the page as his friend. He reread each page, making sure the *I*'s were dotted, and the *T*s were crossed. He knew his job. Knew it better than most. If only one comma was out of place, the deal could fall through, and they would have to start all over on another day. The delay could end up costing millions, plus his license. When he was satisfied everything was in order, he touched the screen on the last page that sent the contents up the ladder to the next level. He was never quite sure who received it, or where they were, but they knew their job since all of his transactions were certified the same day, and his bank account got fatter first thing the following morning.

"You want to tell me what's really going on, Karl? What your plans are for two islands?" Kevin asked, looking at Karl, who was still seated crossed-leg, rubbing his hands together as if they were bothering him.

"Someday," Karl said slowly. "Someday they will come for me. They're going to need me again. I need a place to rest and to plan. Two places mean it will take them that much longer to track me down. When the day comes that they locate me, I'll be ready for them."

Kevin stood near the pictures of his family and friends. He stared at the one that had been taken of the two of them years ago. He in his suit and Karl in his uniform. Both of them looking ahead to bright futures. He couldn't remember Karl ever speaking this way. Couldn't remember a time when he would hide, let alone plan a meeting with those that had crossed him. He knew Karl. Knew him well. Knew what he could do to those who crossed him.

"You all right, Karl?" he asked in a low voice as he moved away from the wall and back to his desk. He never took his eyes off his friend.

"Yeah. Fine," Karl said, smiling as he rose from his seat. "So do I get keys or something for these places?"

"By the time you get back to your hotel room, a paper copy, plus a digital one, will be waiting for you. You could leave here first thing in the morning and be there by lunch, moved in by dinner. They're both yours," Kevin explained as he walked behind his desk and rested his hands on the top of his chair.

"Beautiful," was all Karl could say as he made his way toward the door.

"What's your next move, Karl?"

"See a man about a boat. I ordered it a while ago. Should be completed by now. Then I can take it and visit my new homes," Karl said, smiling and winking at his friend. "Thanks for everything, Kevin. You outdid yourself."

"Thanks. Glad I could help. Maybe in the future, Angela and I could come and visit you in your tropical paradise. Maybe swim in the ocean."

"Yeah. I would very much enjoy that. I'll let you know when a good time is," Karl said in a low voice with a small smile on his face as he walked through the door to leave. He held his head high and walked briskly through the outer office, leaving Kevin standing near his desk.

Kevin remained standing at his desk, watching his longtime friend walk out the front door. He worried for him. He also worried for himself and his family. Karl had told him people would come looking for him. He knew the people Karl worked with. Knew what they could do. He had to take precautions. He looked at his wall and imagined the two new pictures being put up, but not too soon. Not until Angela and himself could swim in the ocean. He knew Karl well. Knew that day would come.

*****

A short time later, Karl found himself standing on the corner of a semibusy street, staring at the traffic as it passed by, paying him no mind. The whirl of the hover cars didn't bother him. He had his mind set on one thing, and nothing was going to distract him. His attention was focused on the large brown building down the street. With all his years in the Service, he had learned how to study one thing while appearing to be looking at something else. His eyes covered the building from top to bottom, front to back. His head never moved. His eyes did all the work. He studied who came and went. Memorized their faces and mannerisms. Committed their vehicles to the back of his mind for future reference.

His gaze wandered to the surrounding buildings. He needed to know everything about this area. A corner grocery store, a small restaurant with a bar, a manufacturing plant all lined the opposite side of the street. People walking the street paid no attention to the brown building. After a few minutes of looking things over, Karl made his way forward. His steps were deliberate. His eyes never stopped moving, always looking things over, making sure everything was in order. He was cautious. Perhaps too cautious, but he didn't think so.

It took Karl almost three minutes to walk from the corner to the front door of the brown building. Stopping in front of the building, he read the small sign over the door, "Jameson Naval Construction." He knew the name. He'd known it for most of his life. His father had been lifelong friends with the founder, Thomas Edward Jameson, but he himself hadn't been here since high school. He knew from press releases that Thomas had passed away a few years ago, not long after his own father. Amber Marie Jameson would be the one running the business now. He hadn't seen her since her father's funeral.

Stepping inside, he waited for the secretary to answer the automatic bell that had gone off, notifying people of his arrival. It was a small waiting area with pictures of the different ships the company manufactured. Everything from small personal vessels to the big corporate transports. No job was too large or too small for the Jameson Company. He found himself paying so much attention to the pictures that he failed to notice the middle-aged woman that appeared.

"You don't look much like a strategist," she said with her arms crossed across her chest and a small smile on her face. She was leaning against the door she had just come through, with her legs crossed.

"And you don't strike me as much of a shipbuilder," he replied without turning to face her.

"Well, if you would look at me, you would see one of the top five shipbuilders on the planet," she said in a raised voice.

Karl turned from the wall and spied the woman. She stood just short of six feet, with long black hair that was pulled back in a ponytail. She wore a sleeveless blouse and blue jeans that were covered in mud. Old work boots that were also covered in mud adorned her feet. Blood had pooled on the left side of her face from a cut that went from her top lip to her ear.

"I won't say I'm surprised at that fact since your father taught you everything you know. If you had fallen out of the top five, I wouldn't be here right now. Someone else would be getting my business. The place does look like you're doing quite well. He'd be proud of you, Amber," Karl said, stepping forward and stretching a hand out.

"Thanks," she said, grasping his hand and shaking it. She motioned for him to be seated at a small desk and then sat opposite him. "I wasn't expecting you for a few more months. What moved you up?"

"Lack of employment. Seems the Service had no more use for me and terminated me last week. Out there is suddenly safe again," he said, motioning with his right hand toward the heavens.

"They were never the smartest. Couldn't find their heads if they were attached. What're your plans now?" she inquired, leaning back in her chair and looking Karl over. She had a crush on him years ago, but since he left Earth and joined the Service, she had put that on hold. She hoped, someday, to renew her passion but knew she would have to stand in line and wait a long time. She was prepared to do both.

"Not much of a plan yet. Just get away from everything for a time. Recharge my batteries, you might say. Rest, relax. Enjoy life for a time," he explained with a forced smile.

"So that's what brings you here. You want to know about your purchase. It might interest you to know that it's done and waiting for you. Been done for a few days now," she said with a laugh.

"Just like your father. Always ahead of schedule. Good to see you kept that."

"Thank you," she whispered. "Tell me where to ship it to, and it will be waiting for you when you get there."

"Why don't we take it down to the ocean, and I'll take it from there? Save the shipping charge, which, if I remember correctly, your father never charged. Bad for business, he would say," Karl said, standing up and looking Amber in the eyes. He gave her a wink and a nod of his head. He knew she would understand.

"We could do that, yes. But how would you be sure we didn't mess something up? Maybe we didn't build her to the right specs? Something might be out of order. You would find it in a few days and come back and sue me. That wouldn't do my business any good either," she said with a smile. She was positive the job was done correctly, but she liked having him around, if only for a short time. She wasn't sure when he would be by this way again, if ever.

"Don't trust your people to read blueprints correctly, Amber?" he asked, stepping closer. "Or maybe, you just don't want me leaving and never coming back again."

"You know my people know their jobs. I trained them. I just want you to be happy," she said, stepping forward and coming face-to-face with Karl.

"Then show me. Let's have a look at her, and I'll wager everything is as it should be," he said with a smile. He knew the game. Knew there would be nothing wrong. Knew everything would be as he asked or even better. Knew this would protect her reputation and make her happy, and he was all about both.

Amber Jameson pulled a drawer open on her desk and revealed a small built-in keypad. Gently she touched one of the buttons, and a 3D picture of the boat appeared before them above the desk. Karl began to look it over as the picture rotated, revealing every aspect of the vessel. Amber studied it harder, taking pride in her people's ability. She studied it for any defect that might have gotten past them. At length, she smiled and sat down in her chair and quietly patted herself on the back. Everything appeared perfect. Karl kept looking it over. Studying it. Flipping it over in his head. It looked better than he had hoped. His only concern was the trip ahead. Would this sixty-foot vessel be able to make the trip to the South Pacific, as well as up to Alaska, and keep going?

"Looks beautiful, Amber. Perfect even. Will she hold up?" he asked, still studying the ship.

"Better than what anybody else would build. She'll last," Amber informed him. Her smile faded and curiosity set in. He hadn't told her a lot about why he needed a ship like this. One that was able to sail around the world a few times if needed and still be comfortable. She was beginning to worry about her friend. Something wasn't the same with him. He had changed a lot since the last time they were together; at first, she had suspected his release from the Service, but now it seemed much more. Slowly she stood back up.

"What is it, Karl? What's going on?" she asked softly.

Karl turned his attention from the picture and faced her. His face had suddenly lost its happiness, and turned serious. He put his two hands on the desk and let his face fall so he was looking at the desktop. He failed to see her reach into the drawer and touch another button that removed the ship from their view. Standing up, he walked away from her and faced the door through which, only a short time earlier, he had entered. He put his hands on top of his head and stretched. Amber could hear his back crack slightly.

"It's not over, Amber. They will come back. I'm positive of it," he said flatly and turned to face her again. He took his hands and put them on his hips and opened his stance slightly. "I know my job better than my superiors know theirs. The Quill haven't gone back home. They're out there, waiting. Planning their next move. Building up their forces. Their next assault will be even more devastating than their last one. I know it. Every fiber of my being knows it. Yet my superiors think this war is over. They only believe what they can see, and they haven't seen anything in years."

"You don't trust them anymore, do you?" Amber inquired, moving out from behind her desk. She knew him long enough to know that when he gets a feeling about something like this, he is usually correct. The Quill hadn't been seen in years. True. No fire had been exchanged between the two races in over ten years, but when Karl says they are still there, still planning, you could take it to the bank.

"No. Things are going on in Earth Force Headquarters. People are being moved around, shuffled. People are being retired or fired. The ones that are coming in were still in diapers when this all started. They have no clue what to expect. All they know is what headquarters tell them. They can't think for themselves," he explained, walking around the room slowly. He knew he was sounding like a madman, like someone who had an axe to grind because he was one of the ones that had been fired, but he knew his job. He could think for himself. He could see the picture, bigger and brighter than anyone else. It was a gift he had been given at birth. He had insight that no one else had.

"What are you going to do?" she asked, not really expecting the truth. She knew he had to hide some things from her. He had a lot still on his plate, and he didn't want anyone else to get hurt when things finally went down.

"Do? I'm going to do nothing. At the moment. I'm just going to take my new boat out for a cruise on the ocean and relax. I'm going to enjoy myself for a time. Work on my tan a little. Maybe find myself a girlfriend and sail the world," he said with a smile and a wink.

Amber stood there and stared at him and started to laugh softly. The only girl he had ever been genuinely interested in was standing right in front of him. They had known each other for years, and he had made no secret about his desire to retire with her to some exotic place and live the rest of their lives sitting on the front porch, holding hands and drinking drinks with umbrellas in them. It had all sounded real good years ago, and to Amber, it still sounded really good.

"You'll make the necessary withdrawal from my funds, I assume," Karl said to her, stepping closer and taking her hand in his.

"You can bet on it," she replied while squeezing his hand and putting her other one on top of his. "You'll be careful out there? I still look forward to our time together."

"When this is all over, I'll sweep you off your feet the way I should have done years ago. I'm sorry about all that has passed. I promise to make it up to you," he said, leaning in and kissing her on the lips.

"Not your fault. The war got in the way. But I will hold you to your word. You *will* make it up to me."

"Talk to you soon," Karl said and kissed her one last time and headed out the door. He hurt inside. Deep inside, he hurt bad and knew the reason but also knew he had to keep her as far from himself now as he could. She could get killed if she was too close to him at the wrong time. She would be safer here, not knowing where he was and what he was up to. If they came for her, she wouldn't know anything. Even their brain scans would show that. She was safe for the time being.

"Talk to me when you can. I'll be right here," she said aloud.

She stood by her desk and watched him walk out of her life again. She knew it was for the best. Knew he had her best interest in mind. It hurt, though. Really bad. She was in love with him, and too much time had passed already. More than twenty years had already passed, and she wasn't sure how much more time would go by. But she knew him well enough to know if he thought she would be safer here without him, then she would be safe. He wouldn't have to worry about her safety that much. He could concentrate on what he had to do to ensure victory.

Karl walked slowly back up the street the way he came. His head was faced toward the ground, but his eyes continually swept the street back and forth, searching for something that he suspected was there, but as yet, he hadn't seen. He could feel the presence. He wasn't afraid of it, but he didn't welcome it either. It was too soon. He wasn't fully prepared for the meeting. He needed more time. This was not the place either. Too close to friends. Too close to civilians. The casualty rate for a meeting here would be way too high for his liking. He had to get further away and take the Trackers with him. They would follow; he was sure of that. He just had to make sure they followed him right away and not go to where he had been. She was safe, but she could never be too safe.

The walk to the ocean was a short one, and he welcomed the walk. He still felt their presence. Still knew they were there, but at the ocean was better than back at the shop. His boat came into view. She reflected the sun brilliantly. She was sixty feet long by twenty-five feet wide. Her blue metallic paint with six-inch-wide red stripes made her stand out slightly against the other vessels that were moored in the harbor. The engines were idling softly. An old man stood on deck with a smile on his face, waiting for Karl. In his hand was a small palm device that he would use to transfer the title from Amber's company to Karl, and he would be free to leave at his leisure.

"Hello, Mr. Cregg. It's been too long this time," the old man said, stretching out a hand.

"Hello, Ben. Way too long a time. What do you have for me?"

"Need just a thumbprint on this page, and she's all yours. Anything I should know?" Ben asked, handing over the palm device.

"Being followed, just not sure by who," Karl said, putting his thumbprint on the page and handing the small device back. "Can I drop you anywhere?"

"No. They won't bother me. I'm too old for them. All I am to them is the final person in this purchase. I've done this for hundreds of others, and I'll keep doing it. I will alert Amber, though. She'll take the proper precautions," Ben informed him while shaking his hand. As he was walking down the dock, he turned and waved goodbye to Karl before walking out of sight.

Karl knew what he meant. The wave was more than a wave. It was his signal that Karl had been right. He had been followed. Whoever it was, was close by and would stay within sight of Karl until he sailed away. Ben never waved goodbye. He believed in saying it and nothing more. More was unnecessary. Waste of time. It was a signal that had been worked out years before. Everyone knew how dangerous Karl's job was and knew every precaution had to be taken. This was one of them. Karl now knew Ben was safe, and Amber would be safer. He could proceed now with his plans. Revving the engines, the little boat moved forward, and he steered it out into the harbor. He didn't bother looking back. He kept his attention on the open water. What was behind him was behind him, and the only thing he wanted to concentrate on now was what was in front of him. Behind was the past. In front was the future.

2

Fort Patton was a floating military base that bordered the disputed zone between Earth and the Quill. The fort was some ten miles in width and three miles high and five miles deep. It was free floating. Small emergency thrusters kept it from moving out of its orbit around the sun. Fort Patton was part of an elaborate set of military forts set up in the early years of the war to defend Earth. There were five in each sector and ten sectors overall.

Colonel Ruth Dewey was a career officer in Earth Force. She had gone to the Military Academy before the war began and had graduated in the top ten in her class. Now in her late fifties, and with her once-jet-black hair turning grayer by the year, she was closing in on retirement. She was the senior officer onboard Fort Patton. She had been posted here for the better part of the last six years and knew almost every man and women serving onboard. Colonel Dewey wasn't tall, barely five feet, five inches, but her mannerisms and her knowledge of both the post and the enemy demanded respect, and everyone under her command respected the colonel.

"Good morning, Colonel," the tall lieutenant said as Colonel Dewey entered the command deck of Fort Patton. He was in his late forties, with brown hair and a muscular build. "I trust you slept well," he said as the colonel came up and stood by his side.

"As well as I ever sleep," she responded with a chuckle. "Anything happening over there?" she questioned, pointing to the view screen that took up one whole wall of the command deck.

The room itself was larger than most on the station. It was fifty by sixty feet with one whole wall dedicated to a view screen that took in the entire disputed zone. Rows of desks and workstations were placed opposite the screen and were manned twenty-four hours a day by highly trained men and women, whose only task was to keep an eye on the zone and report to the senior officers of anything that was out of line. No one had reported anything out of the ordinary in the past ten years. No one working here had been present the last time something was out of line out there.

"Nothing to report, sir. Same as yesterday and the day before and the day before that. The whole sector is quiet," he said, looking at the view screen. He was tired of it all. Tired of the waiting. Of the not knowing when something was going to give and a whole lot of excitement would come his way. He wanted, needed, a change. Unfortunately change would not come for another six months, and then the Service could tell him to stay put.

"Word has it, Lieutenant, something will happen soon. Scuttlebutt says soon, Earth Force doesn't think so, but I tend to believe scuttlebutt before command. They're still out there. They haven't gone home or gone somewhere else. They're out there," she said, moving toward the screen. When she was in front of it is when the true size of the screen could be admired. It dwarfed her. It was a David-and-Goliath comparison that few would ever forget.

"How can you be sure, sir? Earth Force is claiming they've gone home. We gave them so much grief that they had to return to their home planet and rethink their strategy. What makes you think they're wrong and that the Quill are still hiding out there?" he asked, walking toward her.

"Ethan, I've been around long enough to know when Earth Force isn't telling the whole story. When they're trying to convince you of something because it benefits them. This is one of those times. I can't explain it any farther. You'll just have to trust me for now," she said calmly.

"Sir," he whispered so that only the two of them could hear his words. He leaned in closer so that he was only inches from her face. "I'm behind you. Always have been. If you say they are still out there, then that's good enough for me."

"Thank you, Ethan. Time may come when that will be put to the test," she whispered back, then turned and headed back to her spot in the room. She headed to what was one of the largest desks anyone could remember seeing. At over ten feet in length and six feet wide, it took up a good piece of real estate on the command deck. She stood at one end, and Lieutenant Ethan Merkel came back from the screen to stand at her right side.

"Anything from the other forts in this sector, Lieutenant?" she asked out loud for all to hear. Time had come for her to act out her part in all of this. She needed everyone on the command deck to know and understand that she alone was in charge here. She gave the orders. All others just followed.

"Just some small matters, sir. Fort Pershing reports that a Lieutenant Jason Lee has tendered his retirement effective at the end of the week. Lieutenant Annabelle Bishop will replace him. Lieutenant Lee was in charge of First Defense for the fort. Lieutenant Bishop will hold that job now," he reported calmly.

"I don't think I know either one of them. Anything else?"

"Lieutenant Lee is only twenty-four years old. Fresh out of the academy. He only reported to Fort Pershing three months ago," he said in a lowered voice to hide his concern. To retire at that age meant something was wrong. He knew it could be any number of reasons, such as health or a family illness. It just wasn't sitting right with him. He knew it could be something else that could put their safety, and the safety of others, at risk.

"Who's in command of Fort Pershing?" she asked, turning to look out at the command deck personnel that were busily working. It appeared as if no one was paying too much attention to either one of them, but she had to be sure. It was easy to pretend to be working and paying attention to something that was none of their business. She needed to be certain that no one was paying too close attention. Times were dangerous.

"Major Malcom Blishman, sir. He took over two years ago. Since then, more than a dozen top people have either retired or been replaced. Their readiness still reads high, though," the lieutenant reported in a military-style voice.

"I don't like it," she said harshly. "Too much turnover in such a short time can't be good. He could be fixing the reports somehow."

"You thinking he's a political plant? Only there because of friends in *real* high places?" questioned the lieutenant in a lowered voice.

"Could be. Keep an eye on Fort Pershing. Let me know of anything else that happens. No matter how small."

"Yes, sir," he responded firmly. He didn't like the possibilities that were going around in his head. There had to be a reasonable answer to all that turnover, but the colonel was right; there was too much turnover in a short period of time. His training told him to keep an eye on it; now his CO was telling him the same thing. It all wasn't sitting well.

"Colonel Dewey, message coming in from General Schmidt," the voice announced from everywhere. It was a woman's voice, sounding like someone in her late fifties. A little rough but soothing at the same time. Like a mother who had raised several children and was now sitting the grandchildren. She could be firm and soft at the same time.

"I'll take it in my conference room, Eve," Colonel Dewey responded, turning from the table and heading toward the rear of the command deck. There she walked over to a corner that was opposite the only entrance to the deck. Once there, walls immediately formed and kept prying ears and eyes out. This was her conference room. The place she needed to conduct high-ranking military business.

It was a small room, only six feet square. The walls went from the floor to the ceiling, and an electronic net blanketed the area to keep prying ears from hearing secret meetings. There was a table and one chair in the room, and Colonel Dewey immediately sat down and touched the console that was built into the table. A low hum sounded, and she knew the net was operating. She was alone. The outside couldn't hear her, and she couldn't hear the outside. Touching another button, the bust of General Schmidt appeared opposite her. She was a black woman in her early sixties with graying hair. She was one of the top generals in Earth Command. The only person higher than her was the president of the planet, Wilbur Hoss.

"Good morning, General," Colonel Dewey said cheerfully.

"Store it, Colonel," the general said firmly. "You've heard by now of the replacement of Lieutenant Lee at Fort Pershing, I trust," she said in a gravelly voice.

"Just this morning, sir. I have my Lieutenant Merkel keeping an eye on the fort for any more moves," she said quickly.

"Good," General Schmidt commented, nodding her head. She closed her eyes for a second, as if trying to get the words right in her head before saying them. When she opened them, she stared at Colonel Dewey for a few seconds before speaking again. "We don't have a lot of time, Colonel. We have to move quickly and as quietly as we can. They have ears everywhere. You need to contact the majors of the other forts and get a plan of attack put together. Leave Major Blishman out of it for now. I believe he is working on the wrong side of the fence. You and the other three majors put together a plan of attack and defense at the same time. Defend yourself from within, attack the Quill. My time here is short. I know they're coming for me even as we speak. President Hoss may have appointed me to this position, but some of his underlings, without his knowledge, are going to remove me before the day is out. You need to be ready. Once you think you have a plan, contact Cregg. He'll go over it with you and make changes for the better. We will have no more contact between us. Am I clear?"

"Yes, sir," Colonel Dewey answered, straightening up and casting a salute. She had suspected this day would come but never expected it this soon. She had heard the rumors, but that's all they were. Now to hear it from the general's own lips sent shivers down her spine. Traitors, high in the military tree, were opening the door for the invaders to come in. She felt sick to her stomach.

The general faded, and Colonel Dewey was left standing there alone. Never in her life had she felt this alone. This vulnerable. She let her head drop so she was looking at the desktop. She studied it for a moment, trying to figure out her next move. She ran over the names in her head. She knew which ones she could trust and which ones to stay away from. She knew most of her crew was loyal, but she wasn't naive enough to think all of them were. The fact that Karl Cregg would help her out in the planning made her feel somewhat better, considering the fact that he had just been forced to retire. She would have to find him to get him to help, and she had no idea where to even begin to look for him. Her stomach felt queasy. She closed her eyes hard and tried to picture her next move.

"Eve, get me the majors of the other forts. Not Major Blishman. Just the other three, please," she said aloud without opening her eyes. She reached behind herself and found her chair. Pulling it in, she sat down and waited for the others to join her.

"Acknowledged," came the computer voice.

Colonel Dewey sat there, in silence, getting her thoughts together in order to tell her subordinates what was happening. She knew she would get only one chance. She had to get it right. If General Schmidt was being removed, she suspected it wouldn't be long before they came for her. Not today. Maybe not tomorrow nor next week. But they would come as early as next month. She had to make plans. Prepare. She knew the first thing she had to do after this meeting was to find Karl Cregg. It was a big solar system out there, and he knew it better than anyone. He knew where to hide. She would have to figure it out somehow and find him.

"Colonel," came the deep voice.

Opening her eyes and lifting her head, she came face-to-face with the image of Major Jackson Wright. A black man in his late forties, he was the youngest of the majors. He had graduated near the top of his class and had attained the rank of major by the time he was forty-three, fastest in the history of the Service. Now he was one of her closest allies.

"Hello, Major," she said softly, trying to smile. "The others will be with us shortly, then we can begin."

"Fine, Colonel. How've you been? Been a long time," the major said, returning her smile with a nonforced one.

"Okay, I guess," she said, not being honest.

"What's going on, Colonel?" he asked, suddenly turning serious. He was worried now. He had never seen his commanding officer, his friend, like this. Nothing usually bothered her, but now she seemed concerned.

"I'll tell you when the rest get here. I thought they would have been here by now. Something must have delayed their arrival." She tried to put on a better face, but it was proving more difficult than she expected. She hated this. Feeling weak. It wasn't like her. She was usually confident. That was the way the Academy had trained her; but now it was all changing, and she was more than a little scared.

"Sorry I'm late, Colonel," came the high-pitched female voice.

"Morning, Major Vorr," Colonel Dewey offered.

Major Maria Vorr was a woman in her midfifties, with long black hair that she liked to pull back into a tail. She wore shaded glasses due to an eye disease she had developed as a child. No surgery could fix it, and the only way to ease the headaches was to wear dark prescription sunglasses. To the ordinary person, she looked like a blind woman, but to those that knew her well, she was one of the most observant people they had ever met.

"Apologies," came another voice as her image appeared next to the other two majors.

"Nice of you to join us, Major Huntsmann," Colonel Dewey said with more than a little agitation in her voice. She liked her people to be punctual. That was the way the Academy taught them. Tardiness was never tolerated.

Major Velera Huntsmann was in her early fifties. Her short reddish-blond hair was neatly pulled back to expose her freckle-covered face. A small scar could be seen from below her left eye to her left ear, the result of an accident at the Academy that could have been much worse if not for her quick actions. A training accident that left the other cadet nearly expelled.

"Once again, apologies, Colonel. Fort matters demanded immediate attention. Seems Command wants to transfer some of my fighters to another sector. I was on a call with General Hingis when your call came in. Apologies," Major Huntsmann explained quickly. She hoped her short explanation would calm the colonel somewhat, and the incident could be forgotten. It had the opposite effect.

Colonel Dewey looked up, and her facial expressions changed to one of even more concern. She eyed Major Huntsmann hard and ran the explanation over in her mind more than once. She tried to tie it into her call with General Schmidt earlier. The retirement of Lieutenant Lee and his replacement, Lieutenant Bishop. The relocation of fighters from one fort to another, no matter how small, wasn't a good sign. It happened on occasion, but not often and never without all fort commanders being informed. This was highly unusual.

"How many fighters, Major? And where are they going?" she asked quickly.

"Forty, sir. They are to be sent to Fort Raleigh. No explanation was given, even after I protested. They merely said it was a matter of security and to let it lay there. The more I argued, the angrier they got till it got to the point where they said that I could be relocated as well. I don't like it, Colonel," she said in an agitated voice. The more she explained the whole incident, the angrier she became, and the louder her voice got. Her face had even begun to turn color.

"Anybody else receive orders similar to Major Huntsmann?" inquired Colonel Dewey.

The general answer was no, but the other majors seemed just as appalled as the colonel. They could be seen checking their messages in case new orders had come in in the past few minutes. Their expressions turned from curiosity to alarm. To move 10 percent of a fort's fighters to another sector altogether was nothing to laugh at. A huge hole had been opened up in this sector, and if more orders came down similar to this one, the result would be nothing less than catastrophic.

"For now, it appears that only Major Huntsmann has received this order," Colonel Dewey said trying to calm the others down and get herself back to the business she had summoned them for. "General Schmidt and I talked earlier. Things aren't looking good. The general is going to be relieved of her duties soon." A gasp could be heard from the majors. Each was on good footing with the general and respected her. To hear she was being replaced sent shock waves through the three of them. "Major Blishman, in her eyes, can't be trusted, which is why he isn't here. According to the general, high command is insisting the Quill have turned tail and headed home. They insist the war is over. The danger has passed. General Schmidt and I are in total agreement that the danger is still out there. She has ordered us to come up with a plan of both defense and attack. We have to defend ourselves from our own people and plan a surprise attack on the Quill at the same time. What I need from each of you, whom I trust with my life, is that plan. I need you to get together with your top people, people you trust, and come up with a plan. I want that plan ASAP. I also want to know who each of you trust. I'll inform you of who I trust. Together, hopefully, we can defeat two enemies at one time."

"Colonel," Major Wright said louder than he intended. He caught himself almost immediately and raised both his hands to show he was slightly out of line with his vocals. "Do we know how high up this goes? How high these orders are coming from?"

"No. What we do know is that they are very deliberate. We could see an order today, like Major Huntsmann has received, and not see another one for weeks. They are taking their time and being very deliberate. They're trying not to draw too much attention to themselves."

"Colonel," Major Vorr began. She pushed her glasses up onto her forehead and squinted slightly at the light. "Who do we trust? Aside from our own people and you, who do we put our trust in? How do we communicate with one another and not draw too much attention to ourselves?" she asked before letting her glasses fall back into place.

Colonel Dewey walked around the desk and sat herself on the edge of it and gripped the desktop with both hands. She stared at the floor for a second, as if something down there had caught her attention suddenly, then raised her head and looked at the three images in front of her. From one to the other, she looked, as if trying to size them up separately. She knew them well, better than others would know them, but she knew what she was asking was a lot, and she was giving them so little to go on.

"Trust one another. No one else. Increase your communications only slightly so as not to draw too much unneeded attention. Keep up your communications with Major Blishman. You don't want him to get suspicious. Increase your communications with him also. Don't divulge too much information with him. Act normal. Don't ask too many questions of him. Give him only the answers to questions he asked. Don't volunteer information. Keep one eye on the stars and the other eye on Earth. Question everything and everyone," she explained. It was a lot to take in in a short period of time. She knew they would have more questions in the future, and she just wasn't sure she would be here to answer them.

"What about you, Colonel?" questioned Major Wright. He was worried. Maybe more worried than any of the others. His friend was in trouble, and he wasn't sure what he could do to help her.

"If anything happens to me, you'll be the first to know. I'll get a message out to you somehow. If not from me, then from Lieutenant Merkel. If you hear from Lieutenant Merkel, you can be sure that you're on your own. Seek out Karl Cregg. He'll know what to do next. I'm just not sure where to find him. He was let go last week, and I haven't heard from him. All I know is he is somewhere on Earth," she said in a somber tone. She knew it wasn't much to go on, but it was all she had. She couldn't help them anymore.

"Colonel," began Major Vorr.

"That's all I have for you right now," Colonel Dewey said, interrupting the major. "I can't tell you any more than that. If I'm still here in forty-eight hours, I'll contact you. If not, you'll know about it, and the three of you must get together and go over whatever plans you made. I know the planning will take longer than that, but at that time, we'll go over what you have. For now, dismissed," she said and stood up and walked back around the table. The images of the three majors vanished, and she found herself alone in the small office.

Colonel Dewey sat down and put her head into her hands. Her breathing was short and labored; her heart was beating faster than normal. Sweat had appeared on her brow. Her hands shook slightly. She knew her legs wouldn't hold up under her weight. She was a colonel in the Service and had seen action years ago in this war, but never had she felt the way she felt now. She was being left out in the cold. She was slowly having her friends and defenses stripped away from her. She knew it was just a matter of time before someone came for her. Her only hope rested with the three majors she had just spoken to and the one man she knew had already been relieved of command and was somewhere on that vast blue ball below her. Karl Cregg was out there, somewhere, and she didn't know where, but she needed to find him.

"Lieutenant Merkel, come to my conference room, please," she said. The words echoed all around the command deck. Moments later, Lieutenant Merkel walked through the made-up wall and took his place opposite his commanding officer.

"You wished to see me, sir?" he asked, more than stated.

"You said earlier you had my back. Is that still true?" she asked without looking up.

Lieutenant Merkel stiffened his back and stood as tall as he could. He threw his head back and pushed his chest out. He came to full attention without being commanded to do so.

"Absolutely, sir. All the way to hell and back if necessary."

She lifted her head and looked at him. She felt better inside but not 100 percent. She felt something. Something small was in the way, but she wasn't sure what. She wasn't even sure if there was something. It was just a feeling. She stood up and walked around to his side of the desk and took up a place next to him. She remembered her time at the Academy when her DI did the same thing to her. She remembered the feeling. The feeling of being small. Insignificant. That he could squash her like a fly.

"I hope so, mister," she said in a whisper. "If I find out that you don't have my back, you'll wish you had never met me." With that said, she returned to her chair and sat down. She continued to look at the man in front of her. "I need absolute loyalty now more than ever, Lieutenant. I'm going to ask something of you, and I need to know that you'll do it without asking any questions. Without running it up the line of command. This is something that will be between you and me and just a handful of other people. Am I clear?"

"Yes, sir," he replied quickly. Without so much as blinking an eye. He stood there, perfectly still. Not blinking.

"Good," she said. "Things are going on that aren't sitting right. You know of people being moved around or forced out. Now there are reports of equipment being moved from one fort to another with no explanation. Holes being left in our defenses. Something big is going down, and I don't know what it is, and I don't like it. I've been in the Service too many years to just let things slide. What I need from you is your word that you'll contact the majors of the forts in this sector if anything should happen to me. Notify them of what happened. They'll take care of the rest. Do you understand?"

"Yes, sir. Anything happens to you suddenly, I'll contact the majors and explain to them what happened. They'll take it from there," he said flatly, as if he was responding to a normal order. He knew it wasn't normal, not even close, but he also knew that times were changing. His role on this fort was changing. His role in this sector would never be the same.

3

General Jordan Schmidt sat behind her large wooden desk in her spacious office, staring at the man that now stood in front of her. The expression on her face told the whole story. She was having none of what he was selling. He was her superior officer in every sense of the word except for the fact he wasn't actually in the Service. He had been hired by the Service to "trim the fat," as they said. He had fired or retired more people in the past year than the Service had enlisted. He was responsible for all that was going on. People moving around, being retired, drummed out, equipment suddenly leaving one fort and going to another. This was the man. The only people above him were the president and vice president. No one else controlled him. No one else pulled his strings. Now he was here.

"There is no danger out there, General," he said sharply. "The only danger is in your head. The Quill have gone home. We bloodied their nose, and they whimpered home to lick their wounds. They won't be back. At least not for an awfully long time."

"So you say, Mr. Shaw. I believe, as many in the Service believe, that they are still out there. Just past Saturn. Waiting. Biding their time. Studying us to see what we are doing. Once we drop our defenses, they'll pounce," she said firmly. Her back stiffened. She clenched her fists and wanted only to plant one in his face, but she couldn't. She wanted to, but regulations prohibited it. She knew the consequences of such an action. She had to hold back.

For his part, Devlin Shaw stood there and looked down on his next opponent. She was the highest-ranking Service member to date that he would retire or fire. He preferred to retire her—it was a lot less messy—but he was prepared to fire her. Either way, she would be gone, and he could put his own person in her place. He wasn't an impressive-looking man. Average height, gray hair, just north of fifty years of age, glasses. He wasn't impressive, but what he had done to date more than made up for it.

General Schmidt stood up and pulled at the sides of her uniform coat in order to get the wrinkles out of it. She cleared her throat and then leaned on her desk so she could look this man in the face. She felt the anger welling up inside her. She wanted nothing more than to throw him out of her office and give orders that he should never be allowed to enter it again. But she couldn't. She would get her revenge, but not here, not now. She would have to be patient. Wait for the right time. The right place. It would come, she knew it. For now, though, she would do the thing that bothered her the most. The thing that made her sick to her stomach. She wanted, and felt, like vomiting on the desk and the man opposite it.

"I would like to stay till the end of the day in order to clean out my office," she said softly. It made her sicker. It went against everything she stood for.

"Very well," Devlin Shaw said in a slightly happy voice. Too happy for the general, but that didn't bother him. "But no orders will go out from this office. A guard will be posted outside your door until the end of your shift, when he *will* escort you out of here and off the base. I do hope you won't cause any problems for him. He's really a nice man, but if you do anything to set him off, they won't be able to identify the remains. Is my meaning clear, Ms. Schmidt?"

Ms. Schmidt. It started to sink in. She wasn't in the Service anymore. She had been retired without any fanfare. Without a going-away party. Without being afforded the opportunity to say goodbye to her people. Ms. Schmidt. The sound of it was foreign to her. She hadn't been called that in her entire life. Her parents, friends, teachers, coworkers, no one had ever called her Ms. Schmidt. She knew it would take some time to get used to.

"Your man will have no trouble with me, Mr. Shaw. By four o'clock this afternoon, this office will be empty, and I will be on my way," she said in the same tone she had used when she asked for the day to clear the office. She didn't much like this man or what he stood for, but she didn't want to upset him. Not here and now anyway.

"I'm glad we understand each other, Ms. Schmidt" Devlin Shaw said as he turned to leave. His face was set in a smile, and he looked forward to his next mission. He was more than happy to see the old guard being put out to pasture. His people would begin to change everything, slowly at first, then as fast as humanly possible. The human race could get on with its life. People could once again begin to live without fear. He exited the office, then proceeded to the front door of the building. Upon opening it, he breathed in the fresh air. His steps grew faster and lighter. Another brick had been removed, and he liked the idea.

Inside the office, General Schmidt slowly sank into her chair. She had a lot to do and not a whole lot of time to do it in. She looked around the office and realized she really didn't have all that much that had to be packed up. She had never married, so no pictures of the husband, children, grandchildren adorned either the desk or the walls. She was never into plants, so those things weren't busy growing in this place. There really wasn't much to show that she had a life outside of the Service. There were a few pictures she would pack up. There was the one of her family. Her parents and her sister, Marie. The picture of her and her top officers. The one of her and Karl Cregg. That one meant the most. He had been a true friend over the many years. He had stood by her in good times and in bad. He was part of the reason she had been promoted to general. He carried a lot of weight with the senior command. Now, though, even he was gone.

"Do you need anything, General?" came the voice from the open door.

Turning, she saw her aide standing there. A young enlisted woman she had seen one day and had talked to for only a minute, but in that minute, she had seen something in her. She was sure that she could be someone she could trust. Someone that would tell her the truth no matter how much it hurt. They had been together a little less than a year, yet she had come to think of this young woman as family.

"You know what's going on, Corporal?" she asked.

"Mr. Shaw relieved you of your command and basically threw you out of the Service," the corporal said, stepping into the office and moving toward the desk.

"You now answer to someone else. I'm no longer your boss. I hope my replacement is as nice to you as I have tried to be," General Schmidt said, reaching a hand forward.

"I have no complaints, General. I've enjoyed my time with you," the corporal stated and shook the general's hand. When she was done, she held onto it and put her other hand on top of it. She leaned in slightly and smiled. It was a strange smile. An odd smile. The kind of smile you would give when you had something mischievous planned. "He did say you have until the end of the day," she whispered.

"That he did, but no orders will go out from this office," General Schmidt replied.

"You could 'ask' for something to be done. Ask me, and I'll do what I can. I want to help."

"Corporal Lindsey Russ, do you know what you are saying? Do you know how much trouble you could get into for this? They could court-martial you. You could get twenty years in a Service prison," General Schmidt cautioned. She took a tighter grip on the corporal's hand and pulled her slightly down so she could look into her eyes. She was afraid for the corporal. The kind of talk she was doing wouldn't sit well with the new senior command. She wanted better for her aide. "Think about what you just said."

"I have thought about it, General. I see what's going on, and I don't like it. I want to be a part of the solution. I want a piece of action. Me and several others. We want to help. All you have to do is give the word, sir," she whispered.

General Schmidt studied her face. The corporal was like family. Like many families, she had secrets. The general didn't even know that she had friends. Corporal Russ spent so much of her time aiding the general that General Schmidt just naturally assumed she had no friends. Yet here she was, offering her help, plus the help of others that she knew next to nothing about. She was beginning to get that warm feeling one gets when they realize that the bottom of the pit has been reached, and all that was left was to climb out and dust yourself off and move on. A grin appeared on the general's face, and she released the corporal's hand and rested back in her chair.

"First thing is that this is between you and me. No one else is to know about this. Yet. Second is to contact the majors in Colonel Dewey's sector and tell them that I have been retired. Nothing else. *Nothing!* The only thing you know is that I have been retired. They'll know what to do. Third is to locate Karl Cregg. He'll have gone underground. It will take a lot to find him, and we don't have a whole lot of time."

Corporal Russ listened to her and made mental notes. She was disappointed that it was only going to be the two of them for now, but she knew this is the way it had to be. She knew that at some point in the future—she wasn't sure when—her friends would be needed. She also knew that they would be ready and willing to help.

Corporal Russ stood up straight and turned to leave. She had her orders, though she knew they carried no weight with the Service. She would have to explain her actions as just following through with helping a friend. The first person that she would have to hide things from was waiting for her in the outer office. He was the guard that Devlin Shaw had sent to make sure that General Schmidt left on time and left nothing behind and gave no orders. The man who could make life extremely difficult if crossed. She knew she was about to cross him and hide the things from him that would eventually lead to a change in the senior command. Looking at him as she entered the outer office, she had seconds thoughts, if only for a split second.

"Can I help you?" she asked as she took her seat behind the desk. The question wasn't necessary; she knew why he was here, but the thought of just asking it, delaying him for a second or two, gave her enjoyment. She flashed him a smile that hid so much.

"My name is Lincoln Jacobson. I was sent by Devlin Shaw to make sure that Ms. Schmidt leaves the premises on time. Also to make sure that no orders go out of this office. Failure to comply will result in actions that neither of you will appreciate," he said in a harsh tone. His face was cold and showed no sign of warmth. No smile crossed his face. His physique gave the impression that nothing was beyond his ability. At over six feet in height, he dwarfed the young corporal.

"I can assure you, Mr. Jacobson, that no orders will attempt to leave this office today. *General* Schmidt will leave here today as she has promised to do. I have work to do, so if you don't mind waiting outside…" she said, trying to equal the harshness of his tone but coming up short.

"My orders are to wait in here and make sure of everything. You can go about your business. I'll just take a seat over here and watch over everything," he said, taking a seat near the door and keeping an eye on the corporal. He trusted no one. He was suspicious of everything. His eyes drifted from Corporal Russ to the office of Ms. Schmidt. His ears listened to every noise that came from the two offices.

Corporal Russ touched a button on her desk console, which caused the guard to jump to his feet and rush over to the desk and slap her hand away. Too late. The images of three majors appeared off to the side. They saw everything and heard the hard smack of his hand against her skin. Before they could say or do anything, she hit him in the middle of his chest with her other hand, and he stumbled back a step but recovered quickly and moved against her again. His anger boiling up.

"You told me I could go about my business. *This* is my business. I have to inform the majors of what went down today so they know who they are taking orders from," she said in a loud voice. She braced herself for his next assault on her. She may have been young and small in size, but she was trained by the Service, and that training was extensive. If she needed to, she could cripple, or even kill, Mr. Jacobson.

"Corporal Russ, who is that man, and why is he there?" demanded Major Wright. His voice was raised, and everyone heard the anger that went with it.

"His name is Lincoln Jacobson. He was stationed here by Devlin Shaw due to the retirement of General Schmidt this morning," she answered, taking her seat again and keeping an eye on her opponent.

"Does that stationing mean assaulting a member of the Service, Mr. Jacobson?' asked Major Valera Huntsmann in a stern tone.

There was silence for what seemed like a few minutes. Lincoln Jacobson backed up to his seat and took it once again. His breathing was short and heavy, and his eyes had turned red in anger. His full attention was now on the young corporal who had dared to assault him. She had guts in doing it, but no brains since she did the action. He knew he had her and that Devlin Shaw could now fire her.

"You were asked a question, Mr. Jacobson," Major Wright called out in an even louder tone than before. "I suggest, for your sake, you answer it. You just assaulted a Service member, and we don't take too kindly to it. Answer the question. Does your job include assaulting a Service member for doing her job?"

"She was informed no orders go out of here today. She violated that information by contacting you," he said, keeping an eye on the corporal.

"She has a job to do," said Major Blishman. "If you think differently, then may I suggest you get in touch with Mr. Shaw and ask him. Until then, I suggest you keep your hands to yourself and let her do her job, or I will make sure you are looking for a new one by the end of today. Am I clear, mister?"

"Crystal," replied Lincoln Jacobson, refusing to look at the images of the three majors. Instead, he kept his eyes glued to the corporal, who simply sat there and smiled at him. She knew a lesson had been given, and the lesson had not been well liked.

"Report!" came the voice of Colonel Dewey. Her image appeared mixed in with the other three, and she wanted to get caught up as quickly as possible. "Corporal Russ, who is he?"

"Lincoln Jacobson, sir. Stationed here by Mr. Shaw. Major Blishman was just informing him of some future employment possibilities should he continue with the course of action he had just taken. General Schmidt was relieved of her duties this morning and retired. She will be leaving the office for the last time this afternoon. She asked me to contact all of you and inform you of this happening. I have no further information."

Colonel Dewey studied the young corporal for a few seconds before turning her attention to the man sitting opposite her and refusing to take his gaze off of the corporal. She wasn't happy with the news of the general's retirement, and she was beginning to get equally annoyed at the actions of Mr. Jacobson. She knew there was more to the story than the corporal had told her, and she was determined to get to the bottom of it all.

"Major Wright, what can you tell me about all of this?" Colonel Dewey requested. She knew Major Maria Vorr would be of more use, but as yet, she had not reported to the meeting.

"The corporal here was assaulted by Mr. Jacobson and responded in kind. Mr. Jacobson was not happy with the response and wished to take the situation further until it was explained to him that he would be looking for a new job before the day was over, sir."

Colonel Dewey turned her full attention to Lincoln Jacobson. Her anger began to build. She could feel her face turning redder by the second. She knew that if she had him with her, he would not walk out of the office. She also knew that the corporal was well versed in how to handle herself in hand-to-hand combat. The Service was very thorough in its training. She could see the smile on the corporal's face, but she could also see the anger on Mr. Jacobson's face. Something would have to give, and she was the person to see to it that it gave.

"Mr. Jacobson, please stand and approach us," the Colonel began. She waited a second or two for her request to be understood. Then she took note of Mr. Jacobson's moves to rise from his seat and turn his attention to the images of the four officers. Slowly but with head held high and his back stiffened, he approached them. "Mr. Jacobson, I am only going to say this once, so pay attention and understand my words. If you so much as raise a hand toward Corporal Russ or anyone in the Service, from now until such time as they plant you in the ground, I will forget my oath to the Service, resign my commission, and hunt you down like the animal I'm beginning to think you are. You will find no hiding place either on Earth or in space. I *will* find you, and I *will* kill you. Do I make my meaning perfectly clear?" she said in a tone that was both firm and harsh. Her face was, by now, the color of the sun.

"Crystal clear, sir," he said sheepishly. He turned his attention from the officers to the floor under his feet and turned slowly to make his way back to his seat. He had heard all he needed to hear; he knew how thorough the Service could be. He knew that if an officer told you that they were going to kill you, you had better say your prayers and make peace with your God.

"Corporal, how is General Schmidt doing? Is she okay?" asked Colonel Dewey, turning her attention from Mr. Jacobson to the corporal. She wished to change the subject back to the reason she and the majors had been summoned here. She hoped the incident with Mr. Jacobson was over, for his sake.

"The general is quite fine, sir. She's in her office, cleaning it out. Her plans are to be out of here at the end of the shift. After that, I don't know what her plans are," the corporal reported from behind her desk, switching her attention to the senior officers.

"Do you have any further information for us? Any last orders from the general?" inquired Colonel Dewey. She wasn't liking the situation much. The sudden retirement of General Schmidt wasn't sitting well with her. She had been made aware by the general that this might happen, but she hadn't expected it this soon.

"There are no last orders, sir. No further information to relay," the corporal said in a low voice. She knew she had much more to relay to them, but she had been forbidden to go any further. More information would have to come from the general herself when, and if, she saw fit.

"Corporal, may I speak with the general, please?" wondered Colonel Dewey. She knew the answer to that question, even knew who would answer it, but she put it forward, more to see the response she would get from Mr. Jacobson. She had heard stories of other officers retiring and the guard posted by Mr. Shaw refusing junior officers from conversing with the retiring officer. She wanted to see for herself if this was the case or not.

"I can't allow that, sir," Lincoln Jacobson snapped as he jumped to his feet. "Regulations state that communications between the retiring officers and junior officers under their command are forbidden," he stated, staring at the images in front of him.

"Very well, Mr. Jacobson. Have it your way. Majors, this meeting is adjourned. I will contact each of you later to get your input on General Schmidt's sudden retirement," she said as she looked Mr. Jacobson in the eye. "Mr. Jacobson, you will do well to remember my words. They weren't a threat against you, they were a promise to you." And with that, the image of Colonel Dewey vanished. A second later, the others vanished as well, leaving Mr. Jacobson and Corporal Russ in the room, alone with each other.

The two sat in silence, staring at each other. Wondering what the other would do next. Mr. Jacobson kept his eyes glued to the corporal. He was still smarting from the blow she had delivered earlier. Both his body and his pride had been hurt, and he was itching for a second chance at her. He remembered Colonel Dewey's warning, and it was the only thing that kept him from lunging at her now. For her part, Corporal Russ sat behind her desk and pretended to be reading various reports on her palm computer. In reality, she was keeping her attention devoted entirely to Lincoln Jacobson. She thought it might not be over, even with the threat of death, and she wanted to be ready.

"Corporal, a minute if you please," came General Schmidt's voice from the inner office. She had been absent from the commotion in the outer office. She had opted to keep a low profile during the assault on the corporal as well as the conversations with the other officers. Now she spoke, and her words still caused the corporal to come to her feet and enter the inner office as if nothing had changed.

"Yes, sir," she said as she entered the general's office and found General Schmidt seated behind her desk as if nothing had changed. The only difference from yesterday to today was the absence of the few personal belongings that the general had used to decorate the office.

"Corporal, did you relay my message to the others?" General Schmidt asked with a wink in her eye. She motioned for the corporal to take a seat opposite her and to keep her voice down.

"Done, sir. The only one I couldn't get in touch with was Major Vorr. She must have been busy with other matters. It was my impression that Colonel Dewey would contact her later and fill her in," the corporal reported, taking a seat and leaning forward to be closer to the general.

"Good. What of our friend out there? Will he give you any more trouble?" the general asked, motioning toward the outer office.

"I doubt it, but I wish he would. Colonel Dewey promised to hunt him down and kill him like a wild animal if he did anything. I suspect he would like to, but I don't know if he has the stomach for the fight," the corporal relayed in a cheerful voice with a smile on her face.

The two sat there and laughed quietly. General Schmidt thought it quite funny that the petite corporal that she had come to think of as family could kick the butt of a six-foot-plus guard. She would have given anything to have seen that happen, but she was involved with other matters that demanded her attention. She made a mental note to bring the topic up at a later date when the two could discuss the matter at length. She leaned forward and rested her arms on the desk and motioned the corporal to lean in as well. Her left hand came up to her face and covered her mouth. She knew the walls had ears, and that they sometimes had eyes as well. She suspected some of the other officers of eavesdropping on conversations that were supposed to be top secret.

"Corporal, I've run into a wall. I've been trying to use my contacts to find out where Karl Cregg has gone, but so far, none of them have any idea. The last any of them have heard about him was the day he left office. After that he seemed to drop off the face of the planet. No one can locate him. Do you have any idea where he might be or who could be of service in finding him?"

The corporal's face lit up. She sat back in her chair, and a smile filled her face from ear to ear. She had wanted to be a part of this operation, and it had offended her slightly when the general had told her to remain at her post and keep her mouth shut. She had connections in places where others couldn't go. She knew who to ask and when to ask. She knew some of the best hiding places on the planet. Now she was glad to be of real use to a person she considered more than a CO, a person she considered an older sister.

"I have connections, General. I come from an overly large family, and each of them has connections to someone who knows something about everything. If anyone can find Karl Cregg, it would be one of my relatives, and they would keep it hush-hush. I can find him for you," she whispered so the guard wouldn't overhear.

"When can you contact them?" the general inquired. She needed to talk to him fast. Tomorrow, to her, was too late. The sooner, the better for all.

"When we get off duty, I'll contact one of my brothers and see if he knows anything. He can spread the word, and by nightfall, I should have something for you," the corporal informed her old boss. She felt good about this. She was doing something that would lead to making things right. She knew the dismissal of so many top officers could lead to trouble. The Quill was still out there, somewhere, and she knew they were close and that Karl Cregg was their only real hope of winning this bloody war.

"Very good," General Schmidt said, leaning back in her chair. She was starting to feel better about the whole situation. It was far from the way things should be, but she was feeling better, and she let it show. Her face formed a small grin, and her eyes lit up a little.

"It's getting late. What would you say about joining me for an early dinner? We could go off base and get us some good homemade food for a change. Have a drink or two," the general suggested with another wink in her eye. She was formulating a plan and needed an assistant, and the young corporal would do splendidly.

"I don't get off till 1700 hours, sir, but I would be glad to join you," she relayed with a large smile.

"Then it's settled," said the general, rising to her feet and motioning the corporal to do the same. The two made their way toward the door, not trying to hide their conversation anymore. They wanted the guard to hear so he would think they had been just talking about making dinner plans the whole time. "How does Lexi's sound? I hear they have a wonderful special today, and I think I would like to try it before leaving the area."

"I always liked Lexi's, sir. I haven't been there as much as I would like, but the food never disappointed me," the corporal said joyfully as the two arrived at the doorway. "I get off at 1700 hours, where should I meet you?"

"At Lexi's. When I leave here, I'll stop at my place and inform the owners that I'll be leaving the area for good in the morning, then I'll head over to Lexi's and wait for you there. Maybe I'll even have a couple of drinks while I wait for you," the general explained in a more-than-cheerful voice.

"I'll be there, sir," the corporal insisted and returned to her desk to complete her afternoon work.

Corporal Russ was in a good mood for this late in the day. She had accomplished much and knew she would get a lot more done once she left the base. Her communications wouldn't be monitored once she was off the base, and she could speak freely to her brother, whom she hoped could help them get in touch with Karl Cregg. She hoped quietly that she would be able to accompany the general to Karl's location, but she knew that if she did, she would be classified as AWOL, and the whole of the Service would come down on her head. She had to come up with a plan to avoid that and to convince the general that she was needed for the operation. Her first problem, though, sat opposite from her by the door. Lincoln Jacobson hadn't gone anywhere. He still sat there, staring. Occasionally his eyes would adjust toward the inner office, but more often than not, they were focused squarely on her. He had a bone to pick with her, and she knew it.

"Mr. Jacobson," General Schmidt said aloud, walking into the outer office. "I need you to witness something for me, please," she said, waving a piece of paper around. "This here is a transfer form alerting one Corporal Russ that she is being transferred to Fort Washington, effective tomorrow at 0800 hours. Her transport will be waiting at the port at 0600 hours tomorrow morning," she said, slapping the paper down in front of Corporal Russ.

Corporal Russ sat there, stunned. Her eyes opened wide, and her mouth refused to close. She hadn't expected this. She had expected to stay with the general or at least on Earth and help fight the coming battles. To find out she was being transferred to one of the forts on the front lines with the Quill wasn't what she wanted. She felt she couldn't do any good there. Her expertise was needed here, on Earth, with the general.

"When did this order come down, Ms. Schmidt?" Mr. Jacobson inquired as he stood up and approached the corporal's desk. He was more than a little skeptical. He didn't trust the general.

"The same time that Mr. Shaw was alerting me to my retirement. Almost immediately after he left, I received these orders. I'm guessing he wanted this office completely overhauled. I'm retired, the corporal here is transferred off planet. Clean sweep," General Schmidt said, shaking her head.

"May I see the order?" he questioned.

"Certainly," the general answered, handing the paper over to him.

Lincoln Jacobson stood there, silently reading the order. He read it over once, then a second time. He silently questioned it, but it had all the correct names attached to it.

"I'll have to clear this with Mr. Shaw. Please hold on," he said as he stepped toward the door and took out his palm tablet. Touching one of the keys, he was soon face-to-face with Devlin Shaw, who seemed surprised to be hearing from him but curious just the same. The two conversed silently for a few minutes before he turned back to the general and handed the paperwork back to her.

"Mr. Shaw was under the impression that the corporal would be heading out to Fort Pershing, but he said he really didn't care where she ended up as long as the office was cleared by the end of the day," he said, handing the paper over to the general.

"Then it's settled, Corporal. Tomorrow you start your new assignment working for Major Vorr onboard Fort Washington," the general said. "Now, Mr. Jacobson, if you would escort me off the base. I have a dinner date I have to get ready for as well as some packing at home."

The general and Mr. Jacobson exited the office, leaving a bewildered corporal behind. She sat there, reading over her orders. They were signed by all the right people, from President Hoss on down the line to Mr. Shaw. The last signature affixed was that of Colonel Dewey, who was now the highest-ranking Service member in the sector that she would be serving in. She knew the colonel well, had met her face-to-face at least once in the past year. She felt she was a fair and capable leader. She secretly wished she could be serving directly under the colonel but serving under Major Vorr could have its own benefits.

She slowly, but silently, began to pack her things. Dinner would have to be a small affair now if she was to meet the transport in the morning. Drinking was now out of the question. Somehow she envied the general. No such restraint was placed on her now. She could eat and drink till the sun came up if she so desired.

4

Colonel Dewey sat behind her desk in her office, with the face of Major Blishman floating opposite her. She had felt a need to start with him. To talk things over with him before moving on to the other majors, who she trusted much more. Her feeling was that if he was first, then he would be less inclined to become suspicious of her and the others and run it up the line of command. This way she felt in control. She would be able to spend more time with the others.

"Colonel, I just don't see why they felt the need to retire General Schmidt. She was one of the top generals in the Service. Handpicked by President Hoss himself. Respected by Service members and civilians alike. To replace her is going to be next to impossible. To explain to civilians *why* she is being replaced won't be easy," Major Blishman was saying. He was a middle-aged man with glasses and a bald head. Right now, his glasses sat atop his head, and his eyes were wide open. He hadn't expected the retirement of General Schmidt at all. He respected the general, even if they did have disagreements over policy. She was his superior, and he knew his place. As a Service member, he received orders and followed them to the letter so long as they didn't violate the law. "This war is far from over, Colonel. The general knows that, and you know that."

"I know, Major. That doesn't change the fact that they saw a need for change. They felt General Schmidt was getting too set in her ways and wasn't responding to their calls for change. Now they can get that change," she explained, hoping to somehow settle her major down and get on with the next meetings she intended to have. This one was just a courtesy. She really hoped it would be over quickly, but it was starting to drag on.

"But at what cost, Colonel? General Schmidt knew the Quill better than anyone, with the possible exception of Karl Cregg, and they relieved *him* last week. Now there's nobody. How do they expect us to win this war if they keep taking away the players we need? Soon there won't be anybody left," he complained even louder. His face was turning to a darker shade of red, and he was losing his temper.

"Calm down, Major," Colonel Dewey said at the same time she raised both her hands and pushed forward in midair. She was trying everything she knew in an attempt to calm him down. She could tell she wasn't getting far, and she was a bit surprised at the loyalty he was showing General Schmidt. She remembered the general telling her not to trust Major Blishman, but she wondered what the general would say now if she could listen to the major talking now. "I'm sure that there's a reasonably good explanation for the general's sudden retirement. I do intend to get to the bottom of it as quickly as I can. For now, though, your argument is duly noted, and I will keep you in the loop. I'll contact you tomorrow at the same time and let you know if I find out anything new."

"Thank you, Colonel. I appreciate that. I'm sorry I came close to losing my temper with you, but this whole thing has got me and my crew a little testy. We all see things going down, and we don't exactly like it," he said in a voice that was indeed losing some of its anger. He forced a small smile to appear on his face, trying to calm the waters a little more.

"Think nothing of it, Major. We all see the activity that's going on, and trust me, none of us are happy about it. Trust me, I'll be looking into it deeper than anyone else, and I will find the answers. No matter how high up I have to go," she confessed. She wanted to say more, to start to trust him more than the general did, but her words kept running through her head. She bit her tongue and signaled him goodbye.

Major Blishman's image faded from the room, and Colonel Dewey rose from her chair and walked about the area for several minutes. She ran things over in her head. General Schmidt's warnings about the Service and Major Blishman. Major Blishman's anger at the general being retired. His opposition to fighters being moved from this sector to another sector. His whole reaction to it all didn't add up to what she had expected. Things were changing in headquarters, but they appeared to be changing out here on the front line as well. She wanted to believe that he was someone she could trust, but General Schmidt's conversation kept playing over and over in her mind. She felt more than a little confused but had to put all of it on hold as the images of the other majors appeared in her office.

"Colonel," they said in unison. Their greeting caused the colonel to jump, if only slightly. She had been expecting them, but she had been so deep in thought that she had actually failed to see them enter.

"Majors. Good afternoon. What have you got for me?" she asked as she returned to the desk and made herself comfortable. She wasn't expecting a lot, but she half hoped they had something to make her day a little better.

"Colonel, first let me say that none of us are taking this lying down," Major Vorr said in a raised tone. Her sunglasses sat on her face, but everyone could see the redness seeping into her appearance. "We intend to fight the retirement of General Schmidt. It wasn't right. She should have been allowed to continue with her duties and to pick her own replacement. What Mr. Shaw did is offensive to us all."

"I agree, Colonel," agreed Major Huntsmann. Her scar did a sort of dance on her face as she spoke. Unconsciously she rubbed her one hand over it. "Mr. Shaw should not have done what he did. General Schmidt was placed in that position by President Hoss. He, and only he, should have the power to remove her. What Mr. Shaw did is an affront to everything the Service stands for. He insulted both us and our tradition."

"Colonel, we stand with you more than ever," Major Wright said. "You have the authority and power to move on Mr. Shaw. We're with you. Tell us what you need from us. We can take him and his people out now, then turn our attention back to the Quill. We'll be stronger by that time."

"Easy, Majors. Settle down. Major Wright, I want you to understand that what you have just proposed is mutiny. Punishable by the death penalty. Mr. Shaw was appointed by the Senate, and only they can remove him. If I, or anybody else in Earth Service, moves against him, they will be tried and shot. The problem would still remain. Understand that," she explained, staring hard at the image of Major Wright. She took note of his sudden change. He sat back in his chair and let his head drop slightly. She knew her message had gotten across. She turned her attention to the other two majors. "I don't agree with what happened to General Schmidt any more than you do. But it happened. We have to live with it. I still need a plan for both defense and offense. We have to move on two fronts which, even in the best of times, is difficult to do. Time is short, people. Work the problems and forget the past few hours. General Schmidt is gone, there is nothing we can do about that now. The Quill is still a problem. Protecting ourselves from Mr. Shaw is still a problem. Work the problems."

"What about Major Blishman, Colonel?" inquired Major Huntsmann. "He's bound to get a whiff of something soon. What do we do about him?"

"Major Blishman is my problem. Leave him alone. Leave him out of your plans, for now."

"What are saying, Colonel? That you're actually thinking of trusting him?" demanded Major Vorr. She removed her glasses, if only for a second. The pain of the light demanded they be put back in place, but her message had gotten across. She wasn't liking what the colonel was saying.

"I'm saying, leave Major Blishman to me. He is my problem. Stay away from him," she responded in a stern voice. She believed in discipline in the ranks, and she was their superior officer. She had the last word. She gave them leeway when questioning her orders but knew where to shut them down. She was shutting them down now.

"Understood, Colonel," said Major Wright. He knew her well enough to know that this conversation about Major Blishman was over.

Major Vorr remained silent. She sat there, with her glasses perched on her nose, just staring at the colonel. She was simmering inside. She could feel the anger rising up inside her, but she knew when to stay quiet. When to hold her tongue. This was one of those times when it was best to remain silent and wait for another day. She wasn't liking it, but she wasn't here to like things. She was here to do a job. To do it to the best of her abilities and to trust her immediate superior officer. Colonel Dewy was that officer. If she couldn't trust her, then who could she trust? She would find herself out here in space alone, and space could be a deadly place to be if you were alone.

"Major Vorr, you weren't at the meeting this morning that Corporal Russ invited us all to. Explain," Colonel Dewey said, looking the major in the face. To miss a meeting like this, you had to have a really great reason. Colonel Dewey was waiting for that reason. She could think of nothing that could keep one of them away except for an attack by the Quill, and there hadn't been one.

"Colonel, my apologies for my absence. Duties most urgent kept me busy this morning. With your permission, I will come over in a shuttle and explain them face-to-face," Major Vorr explained. Her anger had died down considerably, and she knew disciplinary action against her might occur if her reason didn't sit well with the colonel. She needed a little bit of time to get things in order, to prepare her explanation.

"Very well, Major. When can I expect you?"

"Within the hour, Colonel. I just have to gather some stuff together, and I'll be on my way," the Major explained, letting a smile come to her face. She was excited that the colonel had accepted her request for a visit. The two hadn't been face-to-face for some time, and she was anxious for a visit. She didn't always agree with the Colonel, but the two got along like long-lost sisters. It was good to have friends like that. "Thank you, Colonel."

"That is all people. Stay alert. Keep an eye and an ear open. I'll be in touch tomorrow. Same time. Remember, work the problems," the colonel said, and the images of the three majors faded from view, and she found herself alone again.

She didn't feel as alone as she did earlier, but she was alone. She knew she could trust three of them. The fourth she wasn't sure of, but he had made overtures toward her. He had made it understood that he was as unhappy with senior command as she was. She was on the fence when it came to him, but for the time being, he was still on the wrong side of the fence.

"Flight deck," she called aloud.

"Flight deck here. Commander Kung speaking," came the reply almost immediately.

"Commanded Kung, there is a shuttle coming over from Fort Washington. Notify me as soon as it docks and escort the major to the command deck," she explained as she took her seat and wiped her brow of sweat.

"Acknowledged, Colonel."

The communications link went silent, and the colonel was alone once again. She began to run things over in her mind. Trying to find a reason for the absence of Major Vorr this morning and her sudden request to meet face-to-face. She seldom turned down the requests of one of her majors to meet this way, but these were dangerous times in more ways than one, and for a major to leave their fort, even for a short time, sent flags up the flagpole. She worried that people in senior command could take this the wrong way and start snooping around. It was too soon for them to be snooping here. General Schmidt had only been relieved today. Too soon for them to come looking at her and her command. It was already clear that they were looking in her direction, but she didn't need them zooming in. Didn't need them putting her under a microscope. She had things to get done and not a lot of time to do them. She needed to move about without being seen. Colonel Dewey rose from her seat and moved to the end of the desk. Stopping there for only a second or two, she looked around herself before moving toward the wall.

"Eve, exit," she said out loud, and the walls vanished, and she found herself on the command deck of Fort Patton. People were moving about, going about their business. Their duties. Her sudden appearance failed to draw attention. Everyone was used to it. They all knew where her office was and when it was in use. They steered clear of the area as much as possible. They had jobs to do, like she did, but she couldn't help herself and began to look around at everyone. She made mental notes of what each person was doing.

Making her way toward her station, she cast her eyes to the wall that held the screen that showed the disputed area of space. Nothing moved out there. Even the stars seemed to have decided to keep their distance from this war. She could see them in the distance. They seemed to just sit there. Watching. Waiting. Waiting for someone to make the next move. Yet she knew moves were already being made. Behind the lines on both sides. She didn't know what the Quill were doing. She wasn't sure what the senior command was up to. But moves were being made. That much she was sure of.

"Lieutenant Merkel, report," she said as she approached the station.

"All is quiet, sir. Nothing going on out there," the lieutenant reported. He gave her a look that said there was more to report but that it would wait until they were alone.

"Walk with me, Lieutenant," she said firmly and started off in the direction of the wall that offered a picture of a war zone. "Eve, magnify sector M-thirteen," she said aloud, and the screen changed to show the surface of Saturn close up.

They could make out the inner ring of the giant planet and the gaseous clouds that covered the surface. The clouds spun around like a top and moved from left to right and back again. The colors of yellow and orange seemed to form their own area and, in some places, mix together to form another color that wasn't expected. The gases, when added, changed everything. It was hostile-looking. One couldn't live there long without precautions being taken. Earth was just beginning to understand the giant when the Quill suddenly attacked, and everything changed.

Giant space cruisers used to come out this way carrying passengers who wished to experience life—if only for a short time—in space. These cruises would last anywhere from one to two months. They would leave Mars and head out through the asteroid belt. Then change course and head toward Jupiter. They would see Fort Patton on their right and Fort Pershing on their left. The cruisers would go past Jupiter and swing to within a thousand miles of Saturn before turning and beginning their way back home. That all ended when the war came. Unnecessary space travel was ended, and Earth Command took control of the cruisers to use for troop transport.

"What is it, Lieutenant?" Colonel Dewey inquired when they were far enough away from everyone and standing in front of the view screen. She stood there and faced the screen rather than her right-hand man so that the crew wouldn't suspect anything. They were loyal, but she wasn't taking any chances.

"Chatter, sir. Extensive chatter on the channels. Mostly from senior command. Nothing much to do with us out here, but a whole lot to do with back home. Someone is trying really hard to get something big done. I don't as yet know who or what, but it is something big and it is urgent," he whispered.

Colonel Dewey turned from the screen and faced her right-hand man. She trusted him. Knew she could trust him with her life. If he said something big was going on back home, she knew it to be the truth. If it was someone in Earth Force, anything could happen at any time, anywhere. She began to wonder how to prepare for that. She turned back to the screen and stepped closer to run her hand over the image. She needed the command crew to know that nothing was going on that was unusual. She needed to collect her thoughts. Her plan of action might have to be bumped up by quite a bit.

"Keep an eye on it, Ethan. Let me know if anything comes of it. Let me know if the chatter increases and where it's coming from. Something big could be anything, but the biggest thing is out here. If they have a plan to pull back for some reason, I want to know about it ahead of time. Why would anyone want us to pull back now? Nothing out there has happened in years. Why now?" she questioned.

Her mind raced over the events of the past two weeks, trying hard to tie it all together. From the retirement of Karl Cregg, through the moving of fighters, the replacement of Lieutenant Lee up to the retirement of General Schmidt. Too many things happening in such a short time. She was sure something was going on, and that something wasn't good. She started to run the names of various people through her head that she thought she could trust. The number she came up failed to make her comfortable. She winced slightly and closed her eyes.

"What's going on, Colonel? How far up the ladder does this go?" Lieutenant Merkel asked. He moved toward her but at the same time pointed to the screen like he was trying to get his point across. He knew the possible cost of the wrong person finding out what they were talking about. The whole senior command operation could be bumped up by months, and he and the colonel could be spending the rest of their days in a Martian prison.

"I wish I knew," she said in a low voice. "When I find out, I'll let you know."

The two stood there silently staring at the screen. Almost oblivious to the rest of the command deck. They stared at the screen, then turned slightly to face each other. Each one thinking they had an answer only to be overruled by their brain. They would then turn back and stare at it longer, as if expecting an answer to jump out of the screen. They were so involved that they almost missed a junior officer approaching them from behind. They turned at the last possible second and confronted him.

"What is it?" Lieutenant Merkel asked, moving toward the newcomer.

"Priority message, sir," he said, holding out a palm tablet.

Lieutenant Merkel took it quickly and dismissed him. Holding it up, he began to read the message that had just come in from Earth Command. His expression changed from one of confusion to one of sheer terror. The color went out of his face, and he reached for something to hold onto. His legs began to shake.

"What is it, Lieutenant?" questioned the colonel, stepping closer and taking the tablet from his hand.

"He's dead. The vice president is dead," he mumbled.

Colonel Dewey reached out a hand and steadied the lieutenant while she began to read the notice on the pad. Her face slowly lost color, and she felt herself beginning to grow faint. She summoned her strength and regained her footing. Looking around quickly, she made sure that none of her subordinates had seen her momentary lapse in strength. She was their commanding officer and felt the need to show strength at all times. Satisfied that no one had witnessed the incident, she returned her attention to the pad and began again.

> We are saddened to announce the death of Vice President Anthony Cologne. He passed away in his sleep last night at his family home in the northeast of Italy. He is survived by his wife of thirty years, Gina Pasinetti Cologne, and their three children: Marco, Venessa, and Dominick. He was sixty-seven years old. He will truly be missed by all who knew him.

"Do you think this has anything to do with the other events, sir?" the lieutenant inquired when he had gotten himself together.

"I don't know. I hope not," Colonel Dewey responded, handing the tablet back to her first officer. "I knew the vice president. Not well, but I had met him on several occasions and had come to admire him. To hear that he passed away, especially now, is disturbing. I wouldn't mind if he had passed away last year, but now, now is something different."

The two stood there silently for some time. Neither one wanting to talk. Both hoping the news was wrong. That somehow, somebody had gotten something messed up, but they both knew that the news was correct. That the vice president had passed away. That there was an opening at the top that no one had expected. They both knew Vice President Cologne was an okay man. Both understood that the next V.P. could be somehow tied to Devlin Shaw. Neither one wanted to be the first to state the obvious. Devlin Shaw had the ear of President Hoss, and both feared that the president would accept any vice presidential nominee that he put forth.

"Colonel, Major Vorr from Fort Washington to see you," the silence was broken by a wide muscular man dressed in a white jumpsuit. He had truly short black hair that was laced with strands of white.

"Very well, Commander Kung. Show her to my office and wait there for me," Colonel Dewey called back.

Commander Kung and Major Vorr were at the very rear of the command deck. They were some distance from Colonel Dewey and Lieutenant Merkel, who were still near the viewer that dwarfed both of them. They had been immersed in the death of Vice President Cologne that they had totally failed to notice the arrival of both the commander and the major. They had both wanted to continue this conversation, but Colonel Dewey had important duties to see to, and she turned and dismissed the lieutenant and started across the floor to her office. She kept a watchful eye on her people as she moved across the floor. She was looking for anything that was out of the ordinary. Anything that would assist her in seeing who was loyal and who wasn't. She saw nothing that disturbed her. Everything seemed as it should be, but appearances, she knew, could sometimes hide things.

"Eve, walls," she called out as she approached the two visitors. The walls went up, and she took her place behind the desk and motioned for the major to sit. "Commander, I need you to make sure all our fighters are fully prepared to go at a moment's notice. No exception. If a fighter is down, fix it. We'll start doing drills first thing in the morning and will stop when I'm satisfied. We are to be in tip-top condition. Am I clear?" she asked, staring hard at the muscular man before her.

"Yes, sir. Perfectly," was his answer without delay. He was a career man. He took orders and carried them out to the best of his abilities. "Will that be all, sir?"

"That's it. You're dismissed, Commander," she said, turning her attention immediately to her major. "Eve, doorway."

A doorway opened in the wall, and the outside world was allowed in for a second or two as Commander Kung exited the room. Without a word being said, the doorway vanished, and the wall took over, blocking all from peering in on the two women. Colonel Dewey waited for the wall to reseal before turning her anger loose on her subordinate. She still felt the anger of this morning when Major Vorr had missed a meeting. She wanted answers, and she wasn't going to take *sorry* for one.

"Explain your absence from this morning's meeting, Major," she said in a harsh tone. Her anger had boiled up, and she was as mad as she could ever remember being. One didn't miss meetings in her book. It wasn't the way she was trained, and she expected her junior officers to be the same way. "Make it good, Major."

"Yes, sir," replied Major Vorr, taking a deep breath. She knew the colonel, knew what could set her off, knew what it would take to calm her down. She had specifically asked for this meeting in an attempt to head off the anger, but now she saw that it had only built, and the colonel was ready to explode. "I was in a meeting with General Schmidt. While you were in a meeting in the outer office with the corporal, I was meeting with the general in the inner office. She had a favor to ask of me, and I wasn't about to let her down."

Colonel Dewey stood there for a second. She wasn't sure what to say. She had a speech ready about meetings and loyalty and punctuality, but all that had just walked out of the room. She had assumed her major had been derelict in duty, and she was ready to pounce. Now it appeared her major had done an end around and had met with the general while she had been keeping Mr. Jacobson busy in the outer office. Her hard looks evaporated, and a small smile crossed her face.

"You got some last-minute orders, didn't you?" she inquired. Sitting down, she leaned forward and put her elbows on the desk and folded her hands in front of herself. "You got some last orders when the general was forbidden to give any."

"Not much in the way of orders. More like a request," Major Vorr explained, leaning in to rest her arms on the desk and come almost face-to-face with the colonel. "Corporal Russ is being transferred to my command, effective tomorrow. The general has 'requested' that I take Corporal Russ and make her part of my command team. She would like for Lindsey to be a sort of go-between between yourself and the forts under your command. A silent messenger, if you will. That way all sensitive communications can be done using her. The corporal wants to help, and General Schmidt felt this was the perfect way to use her. She's young, new, and innocent-looking. No one would suspect her of being anything but a courier of normal fort business."

Colonel Dewey leaned back in her chair and allowed her smile to fill her face. She knew something was up, and she had been looking for a way to communicate with others without using the open channels. This was the general's way of helping her. A willing courier dropped on her lap that no one would suspect. She had received orders this morning, before the meeting, that Corporal Russ was being transferred to her fort, but now the orders had been changed, and the young corporal was going to be going between all five forts, and no one would be any wiser about the information that would be traveling with her.

"Brilliant!" was all the colonel could say in a low voice.

"General Schmidt thought you might feel that way. She hoped you wouldn't mind a little undiscipline in the ranks. My apologies if I did anything that you disapprove of. I didn't mean to make you mad or cause any hardship," Major Vorr said, pushing her glasses up off her nose and squinting her eyes to shade them from the bright lights.

"Nothing to apologize for, Major. I jumped to conclusions and read everything all wrong. It is I who should apologize to you. I'm sorry if I was a little hard on you earlier and if your ears had been ringing all day. I should have known better. I should have known one of my best majors, whom I am also friends with, wouldn't have skipped a meeting without a good reason. I'm sorry," Colonel Dewey stated, stretching her hand out.

"No need to apologize, sir," Major Vorr replied, grasping her hand and shaking it. "These are troubled times, and the need to be vigilant exists in all of us. I take no offense."

"The times got even more troubled recently. Seems Vice President Cologne passed away earlier today," the colonel said in a low voice.

"What happened?"

"All I know is he is supposed to have passed away in his sleep at the family home in Italy. That's all anybody is saying," informed Colonel Dewey in a somber voice.

"Has a replacement been named yet?" asked Major Vorr.

"Not yet. The president has thirty days to name someone from the Senate. Then the country the senator comes from has thirty days to name a replacement. As soon as I hear something, I'll pass it along. Hopefully the person is as good and upstanding as Cologne was,"

Colonel Dewey said, studying the major and trying to gain an idea of how she was taking it. "Did you ever meet the VP?"

"I never had the honor, sir. Came close on one occasion, but the timing was all wrong. How about you?"

"Yeah. We met. He was a good and honest man. Not a bad bone in his body. I'd trust him with my life. Hopefully whoever the president selects, I can say the same thing about."

"How much say do you think Devlin Shaw will have in picking the next vice president?" questioned Major Vorr in a cautious voice. She wasn't liking what she was thinking and wanted to know if her superior was thinking the same way.

"I'm not sure, but I know President Hoss trusts him. His voice might carry a lot of weight on the selection," Colonel Dewey told her in a voice that was more than a little scared.

The two sat there in silence for a few minutes. Both were concerned about who President Hoss would select to fill the vacancy. Neither one wanted to be the one that brought up the idea of someone loyal to Devlin Shaw being selected. Both knew what that would mean to the Service, and both of them were loyal to the Service above everything else. They had each taken a pledge and swore to stand by it till they either retired or died. Both hoped for the best but knew enough to plan for the worst, and a young corporal had just become a key tool to their plans. They both hoped quietly that she was up to the task.

5

Lexi's was a small Service-mainly restaurant and bar. Max capacity was two hundred, with additional seating on a rather large wooden deck that overlooked the nearby military base. The menu consisted of dishes from around the world with drinks to match. Uniforms of all the various branches of the Service could be seen gathered around the large bar. Most of the nearly thirty-five tables were taken by Service members and their families having dinner together. When retired General Schmidt entered the place, no one paid her any attention.

The general was dressed in civilian clothing, which consisted of a sweatshirt with black dress pants and black boots. She didn't look the same as she had earlier, and she certainly felt like a different woman. In a way, she was relieved she didn't have the responsibilities of the Service on her shoulders anymore, but in another way, she felt helpless. Things were happening, and she had no way of affecting the eventual outcome. She was torn between two worlds of existence and didn't know which way to turn. Looking around the place, she tried to find her friend but failed to see her. Shrugging her shoulders gently, she made her way to the bar and took a seat at the far end where she could keep an eye on the door so as not to miss anyone entering.

People came and went, and General Schmidt took notice of them all. Not much missed her trained eye. Forty minutes after taking her seat at the bar, she watched as the person she had come here to meet walked into the place and stopped to look around. It was the young Corporal Lindsey Russ. She was still in her uniform and looking as if she had just come from her desk. Her uniform was slightly disheveled, and her hair was messed up. In her hand, she carried her palm tablet, and she held this tighter than normal, as if her life depended on it. Gazing around, she quickly caught sight of the retired general and hurriedly made her way over to take a seat next to her friend and former CO.

"Your late, Corporal," General Schmidt stated with a smile. "Your new commanding officer won't put up with tardiness. Better get yourself a new alarm clock," she said while taking a sip of her drink.

"Sorry, sir. It won't happen again," the corporal said, taking a seat. "I have news. I had to verify it before coming to see you."

"Karl?" asked the general, using the same tone a child would use on Christmas morning. She was hopeful the corporal had found out something, anything.

"Mr. Cregg is rumored to have visited an old friend in the realty business. From there, it is said he visited the daughter of another old friend who's in the construction business. Boat construction to be precise. From there, unfortunately the trail goes cold. No one in my family can find any trace of him," the corporal said, handing over the tablet.

The general looked at the tablet and flipped the pages with a swipe of her thumb, reading everything on the page as quickly as possible and taking extra care to remember the high points. The names of the places he visited. The names of the people involved. The city where it all took place. These, to her, were the important things; everything else was trivial. She would remember it all, her training taught her that; the high points would especially stick out. At length, she looked at the corporal and managed a wide smile.

"How did you manage all this in such a short time, Lindsey?"

Lindsey. She had never called the corporal that. It was as foreign as being called Ms. Schmidt. Her life had changed today, and she knew deep inside, she would have to get used to it. To call the corporal by her first name didn't sit well, but to keep calling her corporal when she was no longer in the Service sat even worse. She would have to get used to new things, and the woman sitting next to her would be one of the hardest to get used to. Lindsey instead of Corporal. It would take time to get used to, but she promised herself she would.

"I told you I have a rather large family. Each of those members has a rather large list of friends and acquaintances. It was just a matter of time before someone came back with a friend of a friend of a friend having seen Karl visiting places where he knew the owner or someone working there. Money transfer is another matter. They are so closely guarded by the government that it will take a few more hours to get ahold of them. In the end, I suspect that we'll find he bought himself some land somewhere near the water and has retired to it."

"Sounds about right. Realty and boat construction. Makes sense. But I wouldn't rule anything out at this point. It could be near the water. It could be on the water. The water could be frozen or thawed. Anything is possible. I'm grateful. Thank you, Cor—Lindsey. I have to try to remember I'm not in the Service anymore and should call you by your first name," General Schmidt said with a small laugh.

"Then that means I should call you Jordan instead of General," Corporal Russ stated with a raised glass and a smile.

The two raised glasses and clinked them together, and both let out a hearty laugh. Things were different. Instead of commanding officer and Corporal, they were becoming like sisters. The way Jordan Schmidt had been thinking of Lindsey Russ for some time now. They were enjoying each other's company. Celebrating their liberation from the restrictions of the Service.

"Tell me something, Jordan," Lindsey said, setting her glass down on the bar and getting a serious look on her face. "Why was I transferred? I figured I would remain in my position for several more months before the Service relocated me. I never thought I would be sent to one of the frontline forts, not that I have anything against them. I also thought that I would eventually serve under Colonel Dewey, not Major Vorr—nothing against her either. I get along with both and respect both. Why was I transferred?" she questioned.

"I felt you were in danger here. I also knew that Devlin Shaw wouldn't let you stay here. He would move you somewhere else, and that somewhere else would be some out-of-the-way station that you probably never heard of, and we wouldn't hear from you again. You would be left there to rot. I couldn't have that. I contacted Major Vorr and explained the situation to her, and she suggested you should be moved to her fort for your own safety. We got ahold of your orders and changed them slightly. Everything is on the up-and-up. As far as Mr. Shaw is concerned, you are out of the way, never to be heard from again. As far as Major Vorr and Colonel Dewey is concerned, you are at their disposal to use as they see fit, and they will use you. Plans are already being put in place, if they haven't been already. You wanted to be involved—you are. Deeper than you could have ever imagined, Lindsey. Prepare yourself because nothing you have done up to now will compete with what you will do in the coming months and maybe years," Jordan Schmidt told her young friend. She was torn about her feelings for the young corporal. She wanted her to be safe but knew this new assignment was anything but safe.

"Thank you, Jordan," Corporal Russ said softly. She picked her cup again and took a long sip from it. Putting it back down, she looked at her friend. "I did want to be involved, as far up to my neck as possible. I suppose I should have thought it through a little bit more, but it appears too late now for that. I'm grateful that you felt a need for my safety, and by putting me in the front forts, I now have more people than I could have imagined looking out for me," she said, forcing a smile onto her face. "I promise I won't let you down. Whatever they need me to do, I will do it to the best of my abilities. Like the Service, and you, taught me."

"I've never known you to do anything else. You've never disappointed me, and I doubt you ever will," Jordan Schmidt said, casting a smile toward her friend. "One thing you have to remember, though, is that the Quill are still out there and still a threat. If they should happen to attack while you're out in space, there will be no one to keep you safe. You'll be on your own. The only help you'll get is from your fellow Service members. They'll have your back but only to a certain point. After that, you're on your own."

"I understand, sir," the corporal said, letting Jordan Schmidt's warning sink in. She was a bit more uncomfortable now than she was just a few minutes ago. The whole idea of death in space with no one around didn't give her a warm feeling. She squirmed in her chair slightly and tried to remain calm.

"Good. Now shall we order something to eat? I'm starved, and you have an early flight to catch," Jordan said, changing the subject and spinning her chair so that she was facing the bar. She knew she had made her friend uncomfortable, but she needed to do it. She needed the young corporal to understand the dangers, both of being stationed on Earth as well as being stationed in space. Neither place was safe now. Death was a constant companion from here on out. There could be no escaping it. Corporal Russ had to get used to that fact.

*****

Corporal Russ sat in her seat with her head in her hands. Her eyes were closed. She knew if she opened them, there would be an increase in the pain she felt in her head. Silently she cursed herself for having too many drinks and being out way too late. They both knew she had an early flight. Both knew it would be a long journey to the fort. Yet neither one of them was prepared to say goodbye to the other first. Eventually they did, but it was past midnight, and she had gotten little to no sleep before meeting the Service transport. Now she was at the beginning of her fifty-six-hour flight to Fort Washington, and she found herself alone on the transport save for the flight crew. The captain, one Benjamin Tanner, had introduced himself, plus the first officer, Olivia Manley, at the boarding gate. The navigator, Stacie Beck, introduced herself when she came aboard. They seemed like a capable crew, thought the corporal. Right now, though, all she wanted was to be left alone. She needed time for the pain in her head to recede. Time to get some shut-eye before they arrived at their destination. Time for all that had happened in the past few days to settle in.

"Can I get you anything, Corporal?" questioned First Officer Manley.

She was in her early fifties, with short blond hair. There was a tattoo on her right arm of the Earth Force logo with the Navy insignia below it. To Corporal Russ, she appeared to be somewhere between five feet six inches, and six feet. Her eyesight today wasn't quite working right. She did note that the first officer was courteous and seemed to have her smile permanently attached to her face, as if she was doing the only thing that really made her happy.

"A pillow and some aspirin would be great," Corporal Russ responded, forcing her eyes to open so she could return the courtesy.

"The best I can do is an old blanket from the storage locker and an ice pack," apologized the first officer. "We're only a freight transport and don't carry much in the way of comfort or medicine. Sorry."

"I'll take both. Thank you," said Corporal Russ, once again closing her eyes. She understood the first officer was doing her best, but she couldn't help but wonder why she was on a Service transport that didn't carry people. Shuttles were available; she had looked that information up before meeting Jordan last night.

Service transports were used mainly to carry food and supplies to the forts. Rarely, if ever, did they carry Service members being transferred. That was left to the shuttles. Shuttles were equipped for comfort. They came with an assigned sleeping compartment and three square meals a day. There was a main area for recreation. A small bar for refreshments. Windows to look out into space and see the stars or to wish upon one. But here on the transport, there were none of those things. She was basically a prisoner of her seat. There was no place to walk around to brag about. She could walk up to the door to the flight deck and back, but that would take only about ten seconds if she took her time. She could walk back to the hold, but that would take even less time. She was stuck here for the next fifty-six hours. No place to go, no stars to look at. Her head began to hurt even more. Silently she cursed her predicament.

At length, the first officer came back with an old blanket and an ice pack. She placed the blanket behind the corporal's head and laid the ice pack on her forehead. Then she knelt down next to the corporal and took hold of her hand. Corporal Russ opened her eyes and looked at the first officer. She wasn't sure what to expect. Had First Officer Manley found out about her? Was she prepared to move against her before her mission had even begun? Was First Officer Manley somehow affiliated with Devlin Shaw?

"We've heard about you, Corporal," First Officer Manley began softly. "We know what happened to General Schmidt, and we're sorry. She was a good officer. She deserved better. We assume you going to Fort Washington is the beginning of something. We're not sure what, but we assume something. The three of us are hoping it has something to do with ridding us of one Devlin Shaw."

"What do you know of Devlin Shaw?" questioned the corporal, suddenly waking up all the way and sitting up taller in her seat. Her head hurt for a brief second, but only for a second.

"He's no friend of Fleet. He's been moving ships around and replacing competent officers with ones that are loyal only to himself. Only a fool believes this war is over. We've seen signs of them out here. Signs that say they are still out there, watching. Returning pilots from the forts have told stories about seeing Quill ships on their screens. They sit out there at the end of our detecting capability. Some pilots have reported hearing the Quill giving orders to one another."

"Who's we? What kind of signs?" questioned Corporal Russ, suddenly interested in this conversation.

"The three of us here. And more. Many more. Fleet has no love for Mr. Shaw. He doesn't know tradition. Nor does he have any loyalties except to himself. He's put us all into great danger. Worse yet, he seems to love it. The more he messes things up, moves people and equipment around, the happier he gets."

Corporal Russ looked at the woman. Her tone indicated that she was frightened. She was scared. The corporal wasn't sure how she fit into their plans of getting rid of Mr. Shaw. They were officers; she was a lowly corporal with a few connections. Yet somehow, they were relying on her to help them out. To help all of the Service out.

"What do expect from me? I'm just a corporal. You're the officers. Why aren't you doing anything?" she exploded.

"We are. Behind the scenes, the same as you. What we need for you to know is that you're not alone. We need you to relay to your people that Fleet is ready to assist whenever needed. All we ask is that you keep us in the loop. Keep us up to date on what's going on. When the time comes, we'll be ready to act. More ships will come to your aid than will turn against you. You have to trust me on that. Inform your people, keep us in the loop. That's it," she said and rose to her feet. She had already committed treason for what she had said, but she didn't care. The Fleet she had served loyally for over twenty years was gone. It was now a shell of its former self, and she wasn't liking what was going on. She felt lucky to have been assigned to a ship where the flight crew felt the same as she did. Turning, she made her way toward the flight deck.

"Wait," called Corporal Russ, getting to her feet slowly. "How do I know this isn't a trap? That once I fall asleep, you won't throw me out the airlock. That once we dock, Mr. Jacobson won't be waiting for me."

"When you get to Fort Washington, Major Vorr will summon you to her quarters. Once there, and you find yourself getting comfortable, ask her about this flight crew. If her answer puts you at ease, then you'll know we're level with you. If you feel even more uncomfortable, then don't contact us again. It's that simple. For the rest of this trip, you'll see me, or one of the others, only once or twice. Should you feel the need to shoot us with your sidearm, remember, space is a very unforgiving place," she said and exited the compartment, closing the door tightly behind her.

Corporal Russ stood there looking after the first officer. She felt more confused now than when she boarded the transport. She, and all the supplies onboard, were needed at the forts, but she still wasn't sure how she fit in. Was she a bit player or one of the main actors? Was she bound for stardom or bound for failure? Was she the bait or the hunter? Her stomach felt queasy. Her head hurt even more. Reaching for her seat, she let herself fall into it and curl up. She pulled the blanket up over herself and placed the icepack back on her forehead and closed her eyes. The future was more in doubt now than when the day had begun.

*****

Corporal Russ sat straight up and looked around herself. She was still on the transport, but she swore she had heard a noise. Her hand rested on her sidearm, reflex. She knew there was nothing here that could cause her harm, but her reflexes were quite good. Many were the nights she would sit up and practice drawing her weapon in anticipation of the day when she would need to do so. She hoped and prayed it would never come, but she knew she needed to be ready. Now her hand rested where it needed to be, and her eyes roamed the compartment, yet she failed to see anything. The door slid open, and in walked a man in his late forties with short salt-and-pepper hair. His thick black glasses hid his face partially. From her position, she guessed him to be six feet, maybe taller. The uniform did nothing to hide the muscular physique beneath it.

"I'm Captain Benjamin Tanner," he offered in a deep voice as he knelt down on one knee next to her. "Thought I would come back and introduce myself so you have some idea of who's flying this crate," he said with a small laugh.

"Corporal Lindsey Russ," she replied, reaching out a hand.

"So I've heard," he returned while reaching out and shaking her hand firmly. "My first officer was back earlier filling you in on some things. Thought I might fill in some of the gaps she might have left and take you a little further into our world. I'm career. Been in Fleet since graduating high school. Been flying since before the war. Seen some things in my time. Saw some of my best friends and classmates killed in ways that a normal person should never witness. My instincts have gotten me out of more than one jam."

"And what are your instincts telling you now?" Corporal Russ asked.

"That I can trust you. That you are one of the good guys. Also that someone is trying to get you out of the way. Make you disappear. I don't know why or who, but someone wants you off of Earth in a big way," the captain said while staring at her.

"That would be Devlin Shaw. He retired General Schmidt, whose office I worked in, and I just didn't fit into his plans," she filled him in.

"Devlin Shaw. He's been doing things for some time now that most of us disagree with. He's a danger to us and to Earth, but someone high up loves him. He's protected," Captain Tanner said, standing up and moving around the compartment.

"Who?" asked Corporal Russ, following him with her eyes.

"Can't seem to find out. I put feelers out, quietly, but they keep coming back empty. Can't even get any suspicions. Every time I think

I have it narrowed down to two or three, another one enters the picture, or one of the other ones go away, and things keep on changing. I thought about Vice President Cologne, but then he died, and this morning we got new orders that don't make much sense."

Corporal Russ stood up quickly. Her face told the story of someone who hadn't yet heard the news of the vice president's passing. She had been totally blindsided. "What happened to him? When did he pass?" she asked in a shaky voice.

"According to reports, he passed away yesterday at his family home in Italy. No details were given about what caused his death."

"What new orders were received?" she questioned, stepping forward to meet him in the middle of the floor. She understood he was a captain, above her in rank; she was just a corporal, but he had started this, and she was determined to get as much information as possible from him before they reached the forts.

"Fleet has been ordered to relocate the battleships *Constellation*, *Churchill*, *Horatio*, and *Kennedy*. They've been ordered back, close to Earth. It makes no sense. Where they are now is where Fleet command claimed just last year is where they are needed. To move them to the rear makes the whole disputed zone more vulnerable to attack. If the Quill were to advance once these battleships are in their new designated zone, this whole sector would fall within hours. The only thing standing between the Quill and Earth would be the forts, and I know they have gotten orders recently to relocate some fighters."

"General Schmidt has talked to Colonel Dewey about that. I'm not privy to those discussions, so I don't know how the forts are responding. I do know that neither one of them was comfortable with those orders. Both feel the same way that you do," Corporal Russ explained.

Captain Tanner stood staring at Corporal Russ for a second or two. He unconsciously reached up to his chin with his right hand and began rubbing it. He let his head dip down and let his eyes roam around the floor by his feet. His mind was going over everything he had heard and everything he knew. He was weighing everything. Thinking of his next move once he docked at the forts. He knew he could trust most of the Service members there, but he also knew that he couldn't trust them all. Some would turn him in as a traitor. Caution had to be observed.

"Corporal," he began slowly. "I think I can trust you. I want to trust you. You'll have the ears of the majors once you get to the forts. I would appreciate it if you could see your way to somehow keeping me in the loop on what's happening at the forts in your sector. I need to know who I can trust in these trying times."

"Meaning no disrespect, sir, but you know I'm only a corporal. I really can't do much without getting permission from my superiors, and I don't know how they'll take it if I was to ask for permission to pass on information," she explained, stepping forward to stand toe to toe with the captain.

"Quite right, Corporal," stated the captain with a smile. He turned and took a step away from her, then spun back to look at her again while he rubbed his chin unconsciously with his right hand. "I suggest that when we dock at the fort, and you report to Major Vorr, that you ask her about this crew. See if she is aware of who flew you there from Earth. See how she responds. It might surprise you," he said. Then he turned and exited the cabin, returning to the flight deck. Leaving the corporal to stand there, alone, and think back on their conversation.

He had taken a chance on bringing her into their plans. She had never met him before this flight nor had she ever heard of him. She was Infantry. He was Fleet. The two worked together but seldom ran in the same circles. She found herself thinking back on everything the two had said to each other. She wondered if she could trust him. If he really trusted her or if it was a trap. She could find herself in a Mars penal camp for treason if she wasn't careful. If the two could trust each other, then what did he want from her? She was a nobody. There were plenty of other people with higher ranks that could get things done easier than she could. They were the ones that moved about without having to explain themselves. She needed proper paperwork just to go home at night. It all made truly little sense to her, and she found herself sitting back down and holding her aching head again. It took a little work, but she soon found herself falling asleep and hoping it could last the rest of the trip.

It was several hours before Corporal Russ awakened. She felt more rested than before and found her head didn't hurt as much. She stood and stretched and began to walk around the small compartment. As she walked, she ran things over in her mind. Everything from the retirement of Karl Cregg to the conversation between herself and Captain Tanner. The relocation of the battleships and fighters. Her sudden transfer. She tried to piece it all together. To make sense of it all. To see how they all fit together and went hand in hand. She shook her head to clear it some more and continued her trek around the compartment. She silently cursed it for being so small. If she had been on a regular ship, there would be trails she could walk that could take up to an hour to complete. Here, on this transport, it took only a matter of seconds.

The door slid open again, and Captain Tanner stepped back into the compartment. His appearance caused Corporal Russ to cease her walk and stand in the middle of the floor. She straightened her back in an attempt to stand as tall as possible. Captain Tanner did the same before approaching her. When he was as close as possible without touching her, he stopped. He looked at her, then around the compartment, then back to her again. He cleared his throat and ran his right hand over his chin. He was searching for the right words.

"You wanted something, Captain?" questioned the corporal.

"We intercepted a message destined for Fort Bradley. They are to transfer a squadron of fighters to Fort McHenry. At the same time, we were informed that the battleship *King George VI* is being recalled to Earth for what is being called a refit. The King George is only eight years old and not set for a refit for another seven years," he said without looking the corporal in the eyes. His eyes never rested on any one thing; they seemed to be constantly moving. His feet never settled down either. He constantly shifted his weight between one foot and the other.

"How long until we reach Fort Washington, Captain?" she asked in a low voice. She was scared but didn't want to show it. Her training was kicking in, and she gave a small prayer of thanks to all her trainers in boot camp.

"We dock in less than forty hours," he informed her.

"When is the King George supposed to leave for Earth?"

"The King George was ordered to leave no later than forty-eight hours from now."

"So once we dock, we have eight hours to find out what they know. We'll contact them from Major Vorr's office and see what they have to say. While we're doing that, we'll contact Colonel Dewey and see what she can tell us. This whole thing seems to be going down faster than General Schmidt thought," she said in a low voice, as if she was only talking to herself. Captain Tanner stood there and looked thoughtfully at her. His attitude seemed to change in an instant.

"You're in this, aren't you? Up to your eyeballs," he said, getting as close as possible.

"I'm loyal to the Service, Captain," she replied in an elevated tone. "What Earth Force is doing out here to the forts and the Fleet isn't in our best interest. This whole thing is wrong, and I want to be a part of the team that turns it all around and takes out the people who are putting us, and everyone on Earth, in danger."

Captain Tanner stood there looking at her. He had his doubts earlier, but now they were gone, and he was beginning to feel glad that she was on his side. Now there were at least three other people he could trust. He knew they had other people they could trust, which meant he could trust them as well. It suddenly came to him that a small army was working inside Earth Force Command to right what was being wronged. To fix things before they got so far out of hand that millions more would perish in a needless war.

"We'll be docking in less than forty hours, Corporal. Make yourself as comfortable as possible," the captain informed her, then turned and walked out of the cabin and closed the door behind himself. Leaving the young corporal to wonder what all was going on. Who could she trust? To wonder if this flight crew was on her side or setting up some kind of trap to spring on her and her friends once they docked at Fort Washington. She was alone and had no way of contacting anyone at the fort. Her heart pounded while her pulse raced. She was scared. Things were happening faster than even

General Schmidt had suspected, and she had no way of knowing how it was all going to end or when.

*****

Corporal Russ found herself being escorted down one of the massive hallways of Fort Washington by Commander Miguel Hernandez, a forty-something career Service member who had been stationed on all of the forts in the sector at one time or another. He had extensive knowledge of each fort and its major. He could tear apart a fighter or shuttle and put it back together again with his eyes closed. At nearly six feet tall, he towered over the corporal. He led her down each hallway without speaking a word until they came to the command deck.

"Major Vorr," he called in a stiff voice, so loud that everyone turned to see why he was here. Rarely did he venture onto the command deck, preferring instead to stay below on the hangar deck and fiddle with one of the vehicles that had already been deemed unflyable, only to make it fly once again.

"Commander Hernandez," came the voice of Major Vorr over the speakers. "Bring our guest to my office, please."

The two turned and proceeded down another short hallway, only to be met by an electronic wall. Within seconds of their arrival at the wall, a small doorway opened in it, and the two entered the office of Major Vorr. It was small, measuring only ten feet by fifteen feet. A desk, three chairs, and a potted plant that sat in one corner were the only furnishings of the office. On the desk sat a picture of the fort, plus another one showing all the forts in this sector floating in space, with a battleship flying in the background. Major Vorr was seated behind the desk with her glasses folded on top of the desk. The lighting in the room was slightly darker than that on the command deck.

"Thank you, Commander. I'll take it from here," the major said and gave a small salute to the commander, who in turn returned it and exited the room. "Eve, wall please."

The two were alone in the small office. A junior officer facing her new superior officer. A desk the only thing coming between the two. Corporal Russ stood there silently, waiting for her superior to speak first. It was something she had been taught at the academy—don't speak unless spoken to first. For her part, Major Vorr sat there, taking in the corporal. Trying to size her up. She knew what had to be said, and the order in which to say it, but she wanted to see how the corporal would react to silence for an extended period. She knew her from General Schmidt's office, but that was all. She had never spent time alone with the young woman. After several minutes, she knew what she felt she needed to know about the corporal and decided it was time to break the ice.

"Have a seat, Corporal," she said, pointing to a chair.

"Thank you, sir," Corporal Russ said as she pulled the chair out and sat down. She was now directly across from the major and not sure if she was going to like this new assignment. She gave a thought as to what she could do when her contract with the Service was up, and she was handed a new one with the stipulation she serve a few more years serving under Major Vorr. She knew the major only from meetings; she had never met her face-to-face until now. She didn't know what to expect.

"You're probably wondering if this was a mistake on your part. To come here. To serve beneath me. You're wondering if you should have tendered your resignation back on Earth and followed General Schmidt in search of Karl Cregg. Let me tell you, for the record, that would not do. I need you here. *We* need you here. Your part in this is extensive, though it will seem minor. Your connections back home, and the ones you will make here, are badly needed. What you will be asked to do here is desperately needed. If I have made you feel uncomfortable with my silence a little while ago, I apologize. It was necessary so I could see what kind of character you have. At times, there will be orders given to you that will make you feel even more uncomfortable, but they will have to carried out. Am I making myself clear, Sergeant?" she asked with a stiff tone. She had to be as tough as possible with the young Service member. Things could be much worse for her out there.

"Crystal clear, sir," was the response. Then it hit her. Hard. She had never had something hit her so hard and not create any real pain. "Sir, no offense, but my rank is corporal. Not sergeant."

"Congrats, Sergeant Russ. As of now, you carry the rank of sergeant. That rank will be needed for where you need to go. A corporal could not get into everything needed. But a sergeant, a sergeant can easily access every area of a fort. Of every fort. Nothing is off-limits. Orders went out some time ago to allow Sergeant Russ to have access to every inch of every fort. I'm going to ask this once, and only once, so think about it before you give me your response. If you have second thoughts, now is the time for them. Now is the time for questions. Now is the only time you will be given to back out. No one will think the less of you, and you will serve out the rest of your contract here, with me, with your new rank. That is earned and will be kept. Remember, think before you answer. This mission could prove deadly. Hazards lay around every corner, in every person. You can't take anything for granted. Space is unforgiving. Are you sure, Sergeant Russ, that you wish to continue with this mission? Think before you respond," Major Vorr said, then she rose from her seat and started to walk around the small office. She stopped at her plant, which was almost the same size as her, and picked the small water container up from the floor and proceeded to water the plant. She spoke softly to it, but Sergeant Russ couldn't make out the words. Putting the container back in place and running one hand over the plant, she returned to her seat and stared at the woman sitting opposite her. She already knew the answer, but she had to ask the question and had to wait for the response. Everything had to be done by the book.

"As I have told Captain Tanner on my way over here, my loyalties are to the Service. Whatever it takes, I want the Service to continue. I want the cancer that has taken it over at the top to be cut out. Whatever I am asked to do, I will do or die trying. Someone has put Earth and her people in danger, and that person, or persons, must be removed. This war isn't over by a long shot," Sergeant Russ said, rising from her seat and stiffening her back. She pushed her chest and her chin out in an effort to make herself looker stronger and more determined.

"So you've met Captain Tanner and his crew. They are as loyal as you and me. Trust them. If we are to get through this, we are going to need more people like them, and according to Captain Tanner, there are hundreds of them in Fleet. The more we have, the more comfortable a lot of us here are going to feel. Take your seat, and I'll fill you in on what is expected from you. From this minute forward, you answer to me and only to me. Your orders will come with my name on them. Nobody else's," Major Vorr informed her. The two sat across from each other, and Major Vorr began to speak, and Sergeant Russ sat there in silence and took it all in. She already had one question answered, but there were still a lot more to be asked, but she understood this wasn't the time for asking, this was a time to listen. She nodded her head now and again, but kept her mouth shut. She had so much to learn and just a little period of time to learn it in.

6

Jordan Schmidt stood on the sidewalk across the street from the building she had been told Karl Cregg had had business in several weeks earlier. It was early morning. The sun was just beginning to climb past the mountains in the distance and light everything up in its glory. She was dressed in civilian clothes, like she had been these past weeks since being retired by Devlin Shaw unceremoniously: black pants and a tan button-down blouse that she was still trying to get used to. She was more comfortable now in these clothes than she had been on the first day of retirement. The first day in them was like the first day in boot camp—scared and uncomfortable. Now she felt she was fitting in them better. A few more weeks, and she knew they would become second nature. The same way her uniform had become second nature.

Something moved across the street. The lighting for this time of day was really quite good, and she didn't have to struggle hard to see that it was a man. He was well dressed and seemed to be in no big hurry. She followed him with her eyes, not wanting to turn her head for fear he would see her and catch on to what she was about. He walked steadily down the street till he came to a doorway, then stopped and fumbled in his pocket for something. She saw the small palm computer light up and watched as he touched the door with it, and it opened to admit him. A second later, he disappeared inside.

She waited for moment. She had to be sure he wasn't followed. She had to be sure she was the only one out at this hour that was interested in the gentleman and what he had to offer. As she stood there, she noticed the lights being lit in the building and, in turn, the sidewalk lighting up. She saw his shadow on the walk as he went from one side of the office to the other, then watched as it disappeared from view, and she assumed he had gone into some back room to start his day. That's when she gave the street one last look in all directions without moving her head and began moving in the direction of the building. Her footsteps echoed softly; she was careful not to step too hard or move too fast. She didn't want to alert anyone that she was here. She stopped when she came to the door that she had seen him unlock and enter. She gave the street one last glance. A hover car was approaching, but it was still two blocks away. A worker was returning to his home after having completed his shift at a nearby hospital, his scrubs swaying softly with each step. A delivery truck went through the nearby intersection without stopping. Satisfied no one was following or watching her, she reached for the door and gave it a gentle push. It opened softly, and she stepped inside.

Once inside she looked about to find the man she had seen. She found herself in an outer office with a reception desk and four chairs that lined one wall. Pictures on the wall were of the common kind that one could purchase cheaply enough at the corner store or online. Small flowers decorated the desk, nothing fancy; you could purchase them at the same store you bought the pictures. Property fliers lay neatly stacked on the desk. The man she was after wasn't in the outer office. She turned and made her way slowly to the doorway that led to the inner office. She stopped suddenly when he appeared from around the corner and stood in front of her. The doorway being the only thing that separated them.

"If you're here to rob the place, I have to tell that you are now surrounded by a level 5 force field that will prohibit you from leaving. If you attempt to shoot your way out with an energy weapon, the weapons energy will only bounce off the shield and be returned to you. Any conventional weapon will be just as useless," he said in a flat tone, never taking his eyes off of her. "So tell me, why are you here at this hour of the day? We don't open for another hour and a half."

"So why are you here at this hour?" Jordan Schmidt asked, reaching for a chair and pulling it over so she could sit down.

"I own the place. Kevin Base at your service. I always come in early to check my accounts and see if any new listings have been dropped into the system. Have to stay on top of things, you know," he said with a smile. "You haven't answered my question. Why are you here?"

"Looking for a man," she replied, not offering any more than that for the present time.

"You found one, but I'm sorry to disappoint you. I'm married," he said holding his left hand up so she could see the ring on his finger.

"Friend of yours, I think. My sources tell me he bought some property from you within the last few months. I need to talk to him, and I was hoping you could send me in his direction. The matter of my business with him is personal, so don't waste your time asking me why I need to see him."

"This supposed friend of mine have a name?" he asked, shifting his weight from one foot to the other but never taking his eyes off of the woman in front of him. He knew who she was looking for, but as yet, he wasn't sure if she was a friend or an enemy. He had to protect both himself and his friend. Had to give Karl time to recharge and set up a new battle plan at any cost. This woman could have come alone, or she could have an accomplice with her that could create real trouble for himself and for Karl.

"Karl Cregg," she said flatly, checking to see if the name had any effect on the man before her. "My sources tell me you and him go back quite a ways. I'm sure you know either where to find him or someone that can send me in the direction of him."

"And who are you?" he asked, reaching into the other room.

Jordan Schmidt saw the move and immediately pulled her sidearm from beneath her jacket. She fell to the floor and aimed it at him before he could complete his move. She lay there and watched as he pulled a chair into the area and sat himself on it. It was only then that she stood up and replaced the weapon out of sight and took her seat again.

"Sorry," was all she said after sitting back down.

"You forgot about the field. You could not have hurt me," he said.

"Service weapons are capable of going through level 5 fields, for your information. If I had fired, you would not be here right now, and I would be back to square one in my search. Next time take some time to enlighten yourself into whom exactly you're talking to. My name is retired General Jordan Schmidt. I'm here as a friend. I need Karl's help," she said, looking him in the eyes to detect anything that would give him away. She knew how to push buttons on a person and have them give away more than they intended. "Can you help me or not? I don't have a lot of time."

"Good advice. All I was reaching for, though, was a chair so I could sit down, and we could have a pleasant conversation in comfort," he said, pulling the chair closer and sitting himself down. "There was no need to worry on your part. Next time, give a man a chance."

"In my former line of work, giving someone a chance can get you killed. Now do you know where I can find Karl or do I have to keep looking? As I said, time is short."

"Karl mentioned you a few times in his letters. Said he trusted you more than anyone else in the Service. Told me that if anything should happen to him that I should find you, and you would give me the true story. Never thought that you would come here, to me, looking for him. What happened?" Kevin Base asked as he touched the wall in front of himself.

"They retired me. I need Karl's help in figuring out what's happening in Earth Force. Something smells, and I'm sure he can figure it all out before it's too late," she said, standing up and moving forward. "I know something about force fields, and I'm assuming you turned yours off."

"Quite correct, General," Kevin said, getting to his feet and stepping forward to meet her. "No need to keep it on anymore. Seems we have a mutual friend, but I'm not sure how much help I can offer. He purchased more than one property and failed to tell me which one he was retiring to. Come on in, and I'll show you," he said, reaching one hand out.

Jordan Schmidt reached out her hand and took hold of his and followed him into the inner office. She took note of the pictures hanging on the walls. Her eyes quickly moved from the awards to the family photos to the property photos. She was surprised at how many there were and stepped closer to get a better view. She allowed her eyes to take them in one at a time, starting at the top and slowly working her way down. She could tell Kevin was one of the best in his line of work.

"You sold all these?" she asked, still going through them all.

"I did. Years' worth of hard work. That's why I come in so early. My parents always told me that if I wanted to succeed, I had to put work into it. I had to push myself. They did also warn me that if I pushed too hard, I would miss out on too much. So I always made time for other things, as you can see. Family and vacation are just as important to me as my work, and even more gratifying," he informed her as he made his way around his desk and sat himself down. He looked at the pictures with pride, and a smile came to his face. It stayed for only a second, then he remembered why she was here. "He's in trouble, isn't he?"

"We all are," Jordan Schmidt said, turning from the wall and walking over to a chair. Sitting down, she faced the man that she hoped could help her in her search and decided to put it all out there. Tell him everything he needed to know, but nothing more. "What I am going to tell you has already happened and is common knowledge to some people, but not all, and those people who know it don't know the whole scope of what has happened. Command has been shifting people, fighters, and battleships around out there. At first glance, it appears to be normal housekeeping business, but when you go beneath the covers, you start to see things that don't add up. Top people being removed or relocated. Fighters being taken from the front lines to the rear. Battleships being moved from one sector to the rear for what is being called a 'refit.' Then the vice president of the planet passing away suddenly. Put them all together in one basket, and it smells bad. Right now, there's a hole in our defenses out there. If the Quill were to launch an attack in that sector, they would make it to Mars before we could even set up a defensive line. They would be halfway to the moon before we could even launch a counterattack, and as many as four of our forts would be destroyed in the first hour. Hundreds of thousands would be dead and millions more wounded. Earth would fall within three days. I need to find, and speak, to Karl before matters really get too far out of hand. Right now, you are my best hope for that."

Kevin Base sat there and let it all sink in. He had known Karl for longer than either cared to admit to, but he couldn't remember Karl ever painting a picture so dark as this one. He knew things were getting rough, rougher than even Karl would admit to, but he had no idea that it was this bad. He wanted to help. To point her in the right direction. But Karl hadn't told him where he was going. All he had was an idea. One of two places. He wasn't even sure that they were the only two places. What if Karl had contacted other Realtors? How many places could he hide if he didn't wish to be found?

"I would like to help you, Ms. Schmidt, I really would, but Karl didn't confide in me as to where he was going. I sold him a pair of islands in the Pacific, but that was all I did. He paid for them, then we said our goodbyes, and he was gone. I have no idea where he went or how to contact him. When this was all over, he was supposed to contact me, and we would go swimming together like in the old days," Kevin confessed.

Jordan Schmidt felt the life go out of herself. She let her head fall into her hands. She felt defeated. She had not only let the Service down, but she felt as if she had let all of Earth down. She had come so far only to be stopped by someone she thought she knew. She knew that Karl would always leave one thread open. One line of search open if someone wanted to find him badly enough. Earth meant too much to him to close himself off from it altogether. Yet here she sat, with the last person she thought could get in touch with him, and he just informed her that even he couldn't contact Karl.

"So that's it then. All is lost. Earth has no hope of surviving if the Quill relaunches their offensive against us. The one man who could see the battlefield and make plans as the battle is being fought, the one man who could wipe away defeat and replace it with victory, the one man most of Earth Force trusts can't be found or reached. Earth, as we know it, will come to an end," she said without even lifting her head up to look at Kevin Base.

Jordan Schmidt stood up and extended her hand to Kevin Base. It was over. She had done all she could and was now prepared to go back to her home and contact her friends and allies and tell them the bad news. She saw no way out of this. She shook his hand and turned to leave. She glanced at the pictures of the properties one last time, still amazed at how successful Kevin was. She shook her head and walked into the outer office, prepared to exit the building and call it a life.

"*Wait!*" Kevin called before she could open the door to the street. "Ms. Schmidt, wait one moment, please. I know I can't help you, but there might be someone that knows Karl even better than you and me put together."

"Who?" she asked, turning around and walking back to where Kevin was standing in the doorway between offices.

"An old friend. Going back to when Karl was just a boy. They have known each other for more than a quarter of a century. Her crush on him goes back almost as far. She might have an idea of where he was headed. As far as I know, the two of them don't keep too many secrets from each other. He may have told her where to reach him in case of an emergency."

"Can you contact her now and set up a meeting with me?" Jordan inquired, suddenly feeling life come back into her body.

"Don't need a meeting. I can take you there right now if you would like. Her place is open almost twenty-four hours a day. She's always there. She lives there. The only thing she loves more than Karl," Kevin said with a slight laugh. He took hold of Jordan's hand and led her to the door. After locking his place up, he led Jordan down the street toward the Pacific Ocean.

It wasn't long before the two of them were standing on a busy street corner, looking down a side street that housed a restaurant and a manufacturing plant. A brown building stood across from them that seemed to be deserted. People were moving about but paying no mind to the brown building. It looked as if it came from another time. It somehow didn't fit in with the rest of the block.

"Jameson Naval Construction," Kevin said, pointing at the building.

"I've heard of them. Just never knew where to find them. Never had a need for a boat," Jordan commented as she stepped forward to make her way down the street.

"The Jameson family and Karl go way back. Karl's father used to come here. He was good friends with Amber Jameson's father. That's how Karl and Amber first met. Which was years before Karl and myself met. If anyone can help you, it would be Amber Jameson."

The two walked hurriedly down the street and stopped in front of the old building. A small sign told of the business inside. To Jordan, the sign didn't quite fit the reputation of the company inside. She had heard stories of just how good these people were at their craft. She marveled at how well their ships held up under use. Service members were always bragging about how good a Jameson ship was compared to others. She even knew some members who refused to board any vessel except a Jameson. At one point, she had tried to model her office after the Jameson Naval Construction company, but she could never get the quality of people she needed. She tried to get the best, but even these couldn't measure up, and she ended up deciding it wasn't worth the effort.

The two walked through the door at the same time and found themselves in a small reception area. One desk with a chair behind it and two more chairs for customers were all the furnishings the area held. No pictures on the walls. No signs that anyone worked here could be seen. An overhead light illuminated the small room. A door that led to another room was closed.

"No one was expecting us, I see," commented Jordan Schmidt as she took a seat.

"I'm sure she's here. She has no other place to go," informed Kevin Base as he walked around the room.

The door opened, and a middle-aged woman in blue jeans, an old shirt, and work boots walked in. Her face was covered with grease, and her hair was pulled back out of the way. She stood silently in the doorway, studying the two people that were in her office.

"Kevin Base," she said softly, eyeing the man up. "Long time. How's the wife and children?"

"Family is doing great, Amber. Thanks for asking," he replied, stepping forward and extending his hand.

"Glad to hear it," she answered and reached forward her hand. The two shook hands for a second, then she pulled him closer and gave him a hug and a kiss on the cheek. "*Too* long," she said out loud, pushing past him and walking over to where Jordan sat. "Amber Jameson. And you are?"

"Jordan Schmidt," Jordan claimed, standing up and stretching out a hand.

"General Jordan Schmidt?" questioned Amber Jameson, shaking her hand. "*The* General Schmidt? General Jordan Schmidt?"

"The one and only," claimed Kevin Base, moving across the floor to stand by the two ladies.

"I've heard of you. Karl mentioned you on more than one occasion. He admires you. Thinks the world of you even. What brings you to my little humble shop?" Amber asked as she moved around the desk and took a seat. Once seated, she motioned the other two to sit also.

"We need your help, Amber," Kevin said. "Jordan here needs to find Karl. I can't help her, but I thought maybe you would know where he went."

"It's a matter of life and death, Ms. Jameson. The world is at risk," Jordan put forth.

"Call me Amber. Everyone else does," Amber replied with a smile. She pulled an old rag out of her pocket and began to try to wipe her face clean. When she finished, she laid the rag on her desk and sat up straight in her chair. She looked first to Kevin, then to Jordan. "I'm afraid the two of you have come here for no reason at all. I have no idea where Karl went after he left my place. Yes, he did order a ship here, but he sailed away in it. We didn't ship it to him. He insisted on that even though we don't charge a shipping fee. And he hasn't been in touch with me since."

"He didn't say anything about where he was headed?" questioned Kevin in a somber voice.

"The only thing he said was that he was going to work on his tan and that he would contact me later. He never told me anything about where he was going or how he would make contact," Amber said, leaning back in her chair.

The three of them sat there in silence. No one wanted to be the first to say it. No one wanted to be the first to say everything was over.

Time was up. The Quill had won. Earth was lost. No one wanted to admit it to the others. They sat there. Not even wanting to look at the others. Their eyes looked to the floor, then to the walls, then back to the floor. Each of them felt defeated. Then Kevin jumped to his feet and let out a loud cry. His eyes were opened as wide as they would go. His hands went to his head and started to slap it.

"Stupid! Stupid!" he said loudly.

"What is it?" questioned Jordan, looking at him as if he had lost his mind.

"Yeah. What has gotten into you?" asked Amber, standing up and moving out from behind her desk.

Kevin Base stood there and smiled the biggest smile he could remember making. His hands left his head and drifted slowly down on each side of his face. He turned and walked over to the wall and gently bounced his head off of it. He started to laugh, the kind of laugh that told the others that he had something fantastic to tell them. He turned from the wall and continued to laugh as he got hold of himself and looked at the others. He nodded his head up and down.

"Don't you get it?" he asked, looking at their blank stares. "He's going to work on his tan. *His tan!* He's gone to the tropics to work on his tan. One of the properties I sold him was an island in the South Pacific. He can work on his tan there," he said.

Amber and Jordan suddenly came back to life. They understood. His actions were all making sense now. They no longer thought of him as a madman but as somebody who held the key to the chest of knowledge. He was now the wise old man.

"Where in the Pacific is this island that you sold to him that he could retreat to in order to work on his tan?" Jordan asked in a jubilant voice. Her eyes were open as far as they could go, and her mouth remained opened after asking the question. She no longer felt that everything was coming to an end. She now felt that everything was given a second chance and that they stood a chance against a Quill second attack should it come.

"The South Pacific. Way out there. The only way to get there is by boat," he replied.

"How long will that take?" questioned Amber, suddenly stopping her celebration and coming to realize that it may take days to get to where Karl was.

"Shouldn't be more than a couple of days," Kevin informed them. The thought of taking a few more days to find his old friend didn't seem to bother him. He was still relishing the fact that it was he and not one of the others that had figured out Karl's single thread. He had put all the clues together and came out with what everyone hoped was the correct answer. He alone had done it, and he was celebrating that fact.

"You don't seem to get it, Mr. Base," Jordan said with more than a hint of anger in her voice. "We might not have a couple more days. Things out there happen a lot quicker than things down here. It could be by the time we get to where Karl is, the Quill would have launched an attack and are halfway to Mars. And what happens if Karl isn't where you think he is? Then we would have to waste even more time trying to figure out exactly where he is. This is not the time to be patting yourself on the back. What you should be doing is gathering up everything you'll need for the trip, plus all your records on sales to Karl and meeting Amber and myself by the ocean so we can leave as soon as possible."

"Then, oh smart one, you can inform us as to how we are going to get to that island in the South Pacific. It's too far to swim," Amber said, staring at Kevin hard. She knew the answer, but she just had to ask the question. She wanted to see if he was as smart as he thought he was.

"By boat, of course," he said, looking at her in a questioning way.

"Where do you suppose you can get a boat that can take the three of us to that island in such a short period of time? We need one today, not next week," Jordan said.

"Amber owns the best boat-building company on the planet. She should have one sitting around that we can rent for a few days," he said, pointing at his old friend. "Don't you?"

"All the boats at my place are for customers. I don't have a spare one 'lying around' just for me to take out and cruise the Pacific," she informed him in a harsh tone.

"You have to do it," he said, stepping over to her and trying to intimidate her.

"Back off, buddy," she said, pushing him away. "If I borrow one of those boats, I could lose my license. If I lose my license, then I lose my livelihood. I could even end up in some Martian prison, never to see this planet again. You better think twice about what you're asking me to do. If I have to put my ass on the line, you had better be prepared to do the same."

The two stood there, face-to-face, waiting for the other to make the next move. Kevin knew she was right, on more than one issue. He understood that she had more to lose than he did. She was the only shipbuilder he knew, and she was a longtime friend. To ask her to put more on the table than he was prepared to do just wasn't sitting well. He had to come up with something else and come up with it fast. Time was wasting, and time was the one thing they were sure they didn't have a lot of.

"I'm sorry, Amber. I should have known better. I just got caught up in the celebration that I forgot about what you could lose and what could happen to you. If I could come up with something else, another way of getting us there, I would, but I'm stumped," he confessed, walking slowly back to his chair.

Amber looked after him, then turned her attention to Jordan. She hadn't said too much lately. Amber wasn't sure how Jordan felt about the whole borrowing-a-boat thing and possibly ending up in a Martian prison cell. Now she wondered if Jordan had something else to say about how the three of them can get to Karl's island. Jordan saw the look in Amber's face. She knew Amber was right. Amber could lose everything. Jordan knew her well enough to know that the thought of spending the rest of her life in Martian prison wasn't resting too well with her.

"We need something, Amber," she said softly. "Right now, you're the only person we know that has access to either a boat or someone who owns one that we can borrow for a few days. You hold the last card."

Amber looked at the two people in front of her. She liked the one and was beginning to like the other. She hated the thought of letting either of them down; also the thought of Earth being overtaken by the Quill wasn't sitting well with her either. She wasn't sure what would happen if she ended up in a Martian cell, and the Quill took over Mars. It was up to her to come up with a solution now. Kevin had figured out where Karl was living, now it was up to her to find a way to get there.

"I do have a boat at my place that could get us there. It isn't much, barely room for the three of us plus supplies. The customer called this morning and told me he wouldn't be able to take possession of it until four months from now. Some kind of business deal he had going on that would keep him overseas. We could take that one, and I could start my people on building a new one for him," she informed them. She really didn't like the idea, but it was the best she had at the moment. And she figured if the Quill did suddenly launch an attack, she could always claim it was damaged in the fighting.

"How much?" Kevin suddenly asked.

"How much what?" Amber questioned.

"For the boat. I don't want to see you get in any trouble. If he can't take it now, must mean it's up for sale. I'll buy it from you. Angela and I have talked about getting a boat to get away on for some time. This one sounds like a winner. How much?" Kevin explained with a smile.

"Looks like we're on our way to Karl's tropical paradise," Jordan said as she turned away from the others and headed toward the door. A smile slowly came across her face, and she realized all was not as lost as she had believed. A small glimmer of hope still burned.

7

"Message from Earth Force, Major," the young lieutenant said, handing over a small palm computer to Major Jackson Wright.

Major Jackson Wright was a young black man who was the commanding officer of Fort Bradley. He had been in high school when the Quill first entered the solar system. He hadn't yet graduated when all-out war broke out. At seventeen he enlisted, but his superiors soon took note of his high IQ and sent him to Officers College. There he excelled in almost every course offered and graduated at the top of his class in only three years' time. With the war raging on, he was sent to the frontline forts and put under the command of Major Jordan Schmidt. It wasn't long before she came to rely on him completely and made him a captain, over the objections of almost no one. When the Quill attacked the fort that he was stationed on, the major—one Major George Hanover Collins—was killed in action. Major Schmidt gave him temporary command of Fort Bradley, and he had been in command ever since. He enjoyed his command. Enjoyed the responsibility that came with it. When the Quill left for whatever reason, he was promoted to major and turned every other promotion down, preferring instead to stay at his post and wait for what he knew was coming someday.

"What's it say, Lieutenant?" he said without even looking in the direction of the lieutenant. He preferred to stand at his post and stare at the view screen.

"Fort Pershing is to transfer one squadron of fighters plus three shuttles to Fort De Gaulle within the next four days," he read. "That is all, Major."

Major Wright stood there, his arms folded across his chest and his eyes never blinking. He took a deep breath and held it for a few seconds. Then he closed his eyes and said a silent prayer. He knew what the orders meant. More fighters, and now shuttles, being moved from this sector, which, for the next couple of months, were in direct sight of Saturn. Someone was playing chess, and he didn't like the way the game was going. These forts were the closest to the action. All others would get their chance, but not for several more months, and Fort DeGaulle had just come off of being the closest. They wouldn't need additional fighters for years. No, he wasn't liking this at all. In fact, it was turning his stomach.

"Thank you, Lieutenant. Return to your post," he told the young man.

While the young lieutenant walked away, Major Wright went over in his head all his options. He didn't have many, and he knew time was running out. He still couldn't bring himself to completely trust Major Blishman, but right now, he was glad he wasn't in his shoes. To lose that many fighters, plus a couple of shuttles, would leave Fort Pershing in a dangerous position. He was sure the other majors had received the same message at the same time. Colonel Dewey would be calling a meeting at any moment to discuss how best to cover Fort Pershing should war break out again.

"Message from Colonel Dewey, Major Wright," Eve called out over the speakers. "She requests a meeting with her majors," was all Eve would say, but everyone knew what it meant.

"Eve, walls," Major Wright said as he turned and made his way to the rear of the command deck. He walked past several rows of desks and computers. Several rows of people, his people, watching him out of the corner of their eye to see how he was reacting to the news. He trusted them. Most of them anyway. They had served together for some time now, and he had come to know them all. Now he could feel their eyes staring into him. Wanting to know more than they already did, but he wasn't ready yet to fill them all in. The time would come when he would tell them everything, leaving nothing out, but that time wasn't now. Right now, other things had to be taken care of. Other plans had to be made.

Major Wright entered his office, and the walls filled in behind him. It had taken him several months after taking command of the fort to get used to the feeling of being separated from his command deck. It still wasn't second nature to him, even after all this time, but he was getting more comfortable with it. He enjoyed being among his people. He enjoyed their company. In here he felt alone. Too much alone. The weight of command bore down even harder in this room. Especially when he was in conference with his superiors like he was going to be now. In front of him appeared the bust of Colonel Dewey. He could tell from her image that something was terribly wrong. He sucked in as much air as possible and prepared to speak.

"Hello, Major," the colonel said, beating him to the punch. "By now you are aware of the order for Fort Pershing to transfer more fighters, plus a couple of shuttles, to another sector. I have already filed a protest with Earth Command, but I don't see them doing anything about it. I have, therefore, asked the other majors to join us in this little meeting of ours to discuss plans on how we are going to compensate for this loss. Major Blishman *will* be a part of the meeting, and I expect everyone to be on their best behavior. I still don't trust him, and I know the rest of you don't either, but it is his fort that is losing the fighters."

"I can't speak for the others, Colonel, but I will obey your order. Like you said, he is the one losing equipment, not me. May I ask how he's taking the order?" Major Wright said as he sat behind his desk, waiting for the others to appear.

"Like anyone would, I suppose. He's hotter than I've ever seen him. He's lost fighters before, remember, this only deepens his loss and ineffectiveness should the Quill decide to hit us here," she said. Her face began to turn a shade of red, even as she was talking about the loss. She was long past beginning to dislike her superiors. She was now nearing hatred for them.

"I understand, sir. Whatever I can do to help out Major Blishman, I'll do. I just hope he doesn't travel the other side of the street," Major Wright said. He wasn't sure the two of them were on the same page in the overall picture, but for now, he was on the same page as Major Blishman and knew his help was needed for the security of this sector of space.

As he finished speaking, the images of Majors Vorr and Huntsmann appeared alongside Colonel Dewey. Major Blishman was still absent, and Colonel Dewey wasn't taking it in her usual way. She liked punctuality, but now it seemed she was giving the major a little more time. She sat up straighter in her chair and looked around at the small group of Service members in front of her. They were her people, and she trusted them with her life. She cleared her throat and began to speak.

"I haven't asked Major Blishman to join us yet. I needed to talk to the three of you first," she said, still looking around at them. "A few weeks ago, I ordered the three of you to come up with both a defensive and offensive plan. One to deal with Major Blishman, the other to deal with the Quill. Sergeant Lindsey Russ is part of that defensive plan. She's currently running between the forts collecting information on the sly. Up until now, she was the only part of that plan. Now we need something better. The four of us have to have one another's back, but we have to keep an extra eye on Blishman. We have to watch him, but we have to help him as well. We have to cover this sector of space with everything we have, including his fighters. When he gets here, I expect a battle plan that includes him and us helping him. Am I clear?"

"Yes, sir," Major Huntsmann said. "Can we transfer some of our fighters to his fort?"

"Earth Force will see it on their screens and immediately begin to ask questions," Major Vorr injected.

"We have to find a way around their screens then," Major Huntsmann countered. "There has to be a way for us to do it without them seeing it."

"If we can get some of our fighters over to Fort Pershing, then our pilots can keep an eye on Major Blishman," Major Wright suggested.

"The thing, people, is how do we get the fighters over there without Earth Force seeing them?" Colonel Dewey said. "Or should we let them see?"

She turned away for a second and appeared to touch something on her desk. The others couldn't see what she was doing, but they had an idea. When she turned back, she sat silent for a second, then the image of Major Blishman appeared. His face was still red, and they could see the anger in him. He made no attempt to hide his frustration. He sat at his desk, and his two fists were spotted with blood. Blood could also be seen on his desk.

"Yes, Colonel," he said in a tone that indicated he was holding back his anger and trying to be civil to his immediate superior.

"Major, good to see you. We think we have a plan to help out Fort Pershing, but we need your help. We want to move some of our fighters to your fort, but if Earth Force sees it, they'll come snooping around, and things could get worse for all of us. My thought is to let them see the fighters being moved. Do you have any input as to how this could happen?" Colonel Dewey inquired.

"Short of a flight deck mishap, *no*," he responded with the emphasis on the *no*. "I appreciate any help you can give me, but the only way Earth Force is going to let this happen is if something were to happen to a flight deck, and even then, only one of you will be able to send fighters over."

"Not necessarily," offered Major Vorr. "According to regs, if a flight deck is rendered out of commission, the other forts in the sector must immediately render aid. As many fighters and shuttles as needed to maintain fighting ability must be transferred as soon as possible to the nearby forts."

"Major Vorr, how long do you expect your secondary flight deck to be out of service?" questioned Colonel Dewey. "I hope nobody was hurt in the accident this morning," Colonel Dewey said, looking toward Major Vorr, and then to Major Blishman, with a smug smile on her face.

"Medical reports only minor injuries, sir. All personnel should be back to duty status tomorrow. The flight deck, however, will be unusable for some time. Repair teams say they'll know more later today. Permission to offload some fighters to the other forts for the foreseeable future."

"Major Blishman," Colonel Dewey said in a louder-than-normal voice. "How many of Fort Washington's fighters are you able to give shelter to?"

"I have room for two squadrons, sir. Whenever Major Vorr would like to send them over, I'll have the room for them and accommodations set up for her pilots," Major Blishman announced, suddenly feeling better about his position.

"Sounds like a plan to me," offered Major Wright, standing up and walking around to the front of his desk. A smile was on his face from side to side. "And command will be none the wiser. The rest of us are in a far better position to protect one another. Major Blishman was the only one that had been seriously crippled by the orders, yet I still think it is only a matter of time before they come for the rest of us, and their hand is shown. Something big, really big, is going on back home. Problem is, we have no one on the inside to keep us updated."

"Colonel, what progress has General Schmidt made in finding Karl Cregg? Has she reported in recently?" questioned Major Huntsmann.

"Last I heard, she was on her way to some South Pacific island where she believes Mr. Cregg is working on his tan. That was several days ago. I can only speculate that she is nearing her destination and that I should be hearing something soon," Colonel Dewey answered in a low voice. "We better get some good news soon from Earth. Morale is beginning to be a problem. We need a little pick me up."

"Colonel, won't Earth Force expect some kind of report on the secondary flight deck of Fort Washington?" inquired Major Huntsmann, as if she were having second thoughts about this part of their plan.

"I can handle that," quickly replied Major Vorr. "I'll send a report as soon as we're done here and attach a few pictures showing the damage. I'll claim a chemical spill and that we're sending two squadrons to Fort Pershing temporarily as a precaution. They'll have some questions for Major Blishman and myself, but nothing we can't handle."

"Anything else, people?" Colonel Dewey asked. She waited a minute, then decided the meeting could be adjourned. "Then I will talk to each of you tomorrow, one at a time, to see how all this is playing out and to see if any new news has come our way. In the meantime, this stays between us, except for the secondary flight deck accident and the moving of fighters from one fort to another in this sector. I don't trust Earth Force that much, and I trust the Quill not at all. Caution and common sense, people. Till tomorrow," she said, and her image faded. Seconds later, the images of the other three faded as well, and Major Wright found himself alone again.

He sat there and let it all sink in. He didn't like it all. The fact that Fort Pershing was losing fighters. The fact that Major Blishman was in their plans. The fact that Fort Washington was sending two squads to Fort Pershing, and the pilots were being instructed to spy on Major Blishman. The fact that this sector was being torn apart piece by piece. None of that sat well with him. He was career, and he never expected the Service to suddenly turn against him and his colleagues. It sickened him. The speakers tore him back to the moment, and he was forced to deal with daily matters once again.

"Major, Sergeant Russ is here to see you," called his first officer.

Major Wright rose from his desk and walked to the far wall. His steps were slow, and his head hung the same way. His mind was still on the meeting, but he would have to shake that fast enough to deal with this new matter. It wouldn't take him long to move from one incident to another; he was used to it, and if the situation was right, he actually thrived on it.

"Eve, doorway," was all he had to say for the computer to create a doorway that Sergeant Russ could use to enter his office. Once inside, the doorway closed without a word being said. The two Service members stood facing each other. He in his command uniform, and she in her flight suit.

"Afternoon, Sergeant," he said, shaking her hand and motioning her to sit. He walked back around his desk to once again take his seat. He forced himself to forget the meeting he had just come from so that he could be here to hear what she had to say. He sat straight up and rested his folded hands on the desk.

"Afternoon, Major," she began. "I've just come from Fort Pershing. The news is bad over there. Two squads are being moved out within days. People suspect the Quill will attack at any minute and that they won't be able to put up a good fight. They suspect that senior command is aiding the Quill in their attempt to take over

Earth. Someone high up is getting a kickback from the Quill. They expect their fort to fall faster than any of the others."

"What is their opinion of Major Blishman? What are they saying about him?" questioned Major Wright. He already knew what she had just told him, but now he needed to know more about the major. He had to somehow put his mind either at ease about his fellow major or elevate his suspicions of the man. There was no in between. He had to trust him or suspect him as General Schmidt had done.

"They're loyal to him. They believe Earth Force is working to weaken him so that they can replace him, then to return the fighters that they transferred. Apparently in their eyes, he's a thorn in Earth Force's side. Whoever is at the heart of the matter, they don't like Major Blishman. His people have vowed to get to the heart of this and set the record straight," the sergeant informed him.

Major Wright leaned back in his seat and placed his hands on his lap. He hadn't expected this. He and the others had been told that Major Blishman was working with Earth Force to weaken this sector. Now he was being told the exact opposite. He had expected the crew to be angry at the major, but now he was hearing how loyal they were and how far they would go to protect their leader. He needed some time—not much, just a little—to figure this all out. He didn't have it at the moment, but he would in a few hours. Once off duty, he could sit and take it all in and plot a course of action. He did know he would have to alert Colonel Dewey in the morning.

"Is that all, Sergeant?" he asked.

"There is something else, Major. I spoke with some Service members who had just arrived at Fort Patton from the Mars base, and they suspect something big is going to happen soon. They claimed to have heard rumors of another big retirement coming in the next few weeks, but they weren't sure who. They also heard that President Hoss is expected to name a new vice president in the next few days, but they haven't heard any names yet."

"That alone could be fatal out here. The wrong person in that office could prove deadly. Some of the senators don't really have any use for the forts anymore. The war's been over for years according to them. We can only hope that President Hoss selects one of them that still believes like we do," Major Wright said in a hopeful voice.

"I agree, sir. I'll keep my ears open, and if I hear anything else, I'll immediately let you and the others know. If there isn't anything else for now, I'll be on my way. My next stop is Fort Patton. Any news for Colonel Dewey?" she asked as she stood to leave.

"Nothing for the colonel, but there is one more thing for you. Please remain seated," he said as he rose and walked around the desk and sat on the edge of it, close to where the sergeant was seated. "Eve, doorway," he said aloud, and a section of the wall faded, and a doorway appeared, showing a Service member waiting for his turn with the major. "Enter, Lieutenant Lee."

The middle-aged Lieutenant Jason Lee entered and immediately saluted his superior officer, while Sergeant Russ stood up swiftly from her chair and saluted the lieutenant. The whole affair was more than too formal for Major Wright, and after returning the salute, he showed the lieutenant a chair and watched as Lieutenant Lee saluted the sergeant and took a chair next to hers.

"Sergeant Russ, this is Lieutenant Jason Lee, late of Fort Pershing. He was retired several months ago by Mr. Shaw. I've brought him here to ride shotgun with you on the shuttle. Things have been getting pretty hairy out there from the reports I've been getting, and I thought you could use the help just in case. Jason Lee here was the First Defense leader for the fort and had a stellar record. He's agreed to report to you directly regardless of the rank difference because of the extenuating circumstances. I have the utmost confidence in him, as well as with you."

"No disrespect to the lieutenant, sir, but I've been doing just fine on my own. Why do I need the help now?" she asked in a slightly agitated voice. She had been doing the run for some time now and hadn't had a single incident that could draw attention to herself. As far as she knew, Earth Force saw her as someone just running regular maintenance runs. To hear that she needed someone now both confused and agitated her.

"You heard about the shuttle incident last week near Mars? That was a regularly scheduled maintenance run, the kind you regularly run. We lost three people in that incident. We haven't been able to find out where the other ships came from or where they went. They appeared out of nowhere and disappeared the same way. None of us need a repeat of that. Lieutenant Lee's job is to monitor space and take immediate action if anything like that should happen in the space you're flying. The two of you might not survive, but the rest of us will have some kind of warning and will be better prepared to launch fighters and to track them to their base. Our main objective here is to keep you flying. We think they're working for senior command, but we can't be sure. They could be part of a bigger conspiracy. They could eventually lead us to the top people," he said as he walked around the office, never taking his eyes off of the two people in front of him.

"If I could, Major," Lieutenant Lee said. "Sergeant, I have no intention of taking command of the shuttle from you. It's yours. I don't want it. As far as Earth Force is concerned, I'm retired and on my way somewhere to spend my golden years with someone I haven't met yet. My job here is to be another set of eyes for you. Someone to monitor the screens for any anomaly and alert both you and the forts. That's it. That is my entire life right now. If they lead us in some way to figure this whole mess out and help get Earth Force back to what it should be, that justifies my being with you. My rank, for now, is honorary. Mr. Shaw retired me, and when this opportunity arose, I jumped at it. Rank meant nothing. Colonel Dewey insisted I retain my rank only for the sake of show. In the shuttle, you are in command. I take orders from you. I don't give them. You have my word on that."

Sergeant Russ sat there silently, looking at the man at her side. She knew he had been retired, and that prior to that, he was one of the best FDLs in the Service. He had received numerous awards for his service and praise from almost everyone in Earth Force. Which was one of the reasons it came as a shock when he was retired. He was respected. From superiors as well as subordinates. No one, as far as she could tell, had a bad thing to say about him. She even respected him, and she had never met the man until now. Now he was apologizing for being a superior. Her respect for him grew in that moment, and she began to look forward to being by his side in the shuttle.

"Works for me," was all she could say. Words were failing her.

"Great!" Major Wright said as he turned and walked over to the two. "I'm glad we could come to this agreement. It's best for all parties. Now once you two are out there, keep an eye open, now more than ever. Things are getting dangerous in more ways than one, and I would hate to have to notify your families. I would also hate to have your deaths on my conscience. Notify me and the others if anything—I mean anything—should happen. No matter how small. If it's just a blip on the screen that appears for a second, notify us. It could lead to something more. Am I clear?" he said, returning to his side of the desk.

"Yes, sir," they answered in unison.

"Dismissed then."

Lieutenant Lee raised his arm to salute, while Sergeant Russ simply turned away and headed toward where she knew the door would be. Major Wright saw the arm going up and waved it off. He preferred to keep things informal when it came to the three of them. Saluting was just a waste of time right now.

"We're a little informal around here, Lieutenant. Lose the formality. It will be better in the long run. Eve, doorway."

As the two Service members left his office, Major Wright sat in his chair and thought about what had just occurred. He was sending two members out into space to face the regular dangers of space plus the added dangers of hostile forces from Earth bent on destroying the Service, plus the dangers of the Quill launching an all-out attack at any time. These were just some of the dangers he could think of right off the top. He knew there were many more, but he didn't have the time nor the luxury of thinking of all of them at the present time. Things were happening and happening at an accelerated rate. He had to move fast and try to move faster than the dangers that were out there waiting for all of them. He needed Cregg, but as yet, that man hadn't been found. He and the others would have to make do for the time being without their most celebrated strategist. Rising from the chair, he forced himself out of his office and down to the aisle to his station.

"Eve, end," he said as he exited the room, and the small room disappeared as if it had never been there. No one took notice.

Everyone did wonder about the new lieutenant that had just left with the sergeant. Something was going on, and everyone wondered silently what it was and how it would affect them.

8

Fort Grant was situated in between Forts Patton and Bradley. The smallest of the forts in this sector, it was considered, at the time, an afterthought. It was completed and delivered just before the war started and wasn't even fully functional until almost eight months into the war, yet she left a mark on the Quill. The first Quill battle cruiser was taken out with fire from Fort Grant. Her fighters racked up more kills than any other fort in the sector. Her battle scars could still be seen from the neighboring forts. Repairs had been made years ago, but the major had wanted the outside to stay the same. "A badge of honor," he had called them. He was gone now, retired of his own will, so were two other majors, and Major Valera Huntsmann now commanded the fort.

Major Huntsmann's family had a history of military service that could be traced all the way back to before the American Revolutionary War. Two of her ancestors fought in that one and died for the freedom of the United States. Three more served during that country's Civil War, two in the south and one in the north. Five more served during World War II; none of them ever returned home. The first female Huntsmann to serve came during the Vietnam War. She was a doctor who was awarded the Purple Heart. Other Huntsmann women served during the Second Gulf War in the midtwenty-first century. One receiving the Medal of Honor, the other the Silver Star. It was a military family that once again answered the call when this war came. Now Major Valera Huntsmann commanded one of the most advanced forts ever constructed and was trying desperately to live up to her name, plus the man the fort was named after.

She stood on the command deck, surrounded by almost one hundred of her people who were doing their job and not paying her any mind unless she spoke to them first. She studied the wall screen, trying to find any sign of life out there past Saturn. She hated this. The waiting. The waiting was the worst part of the job. She would rather be involved in an intense firefight than to be standing here waiting for something to happen. She itched for a fight. Casually she lifted her arm up and ran her hand across the scar on her face. It was an unconscious thing. A bad habit she wanted to quit but knew she never would.

"Reports coming in from the other forts, Major," came the voice that brought her back to the present.

"Anything special, Commander?" she asked, turning to face him.

Commander Anthony Viscully was in his midforties. Standing just under six feet in height, he stood almost a half-foot taller than his major. His forearms were barely concealed by his uniform. In his spare time, he would weight lift in his quarters to eliminate the stress of the job. The smile on his face seemed to be painted there. He loved his job, and he loved the people he served with.

"Nothing out of the ordinary, Major. No fort has received new orders for several days now. Things seem to be settling down. Sergeant Russ is on schedule and should be here sometime this afternoon. All appears to be quiet," he said in a matter-of-fact style.

"Which means all hell will break lose at any minute. I want our fighters to be in top fighting condition. Coordinate with the CAG and run some drills after Sergeant Russ docks. Keep them running until she leaves. I want our people to be ready. I don't want them soft. Get with the flight deck commander and make sure every fighter—and I mean every last one of them—is in flying condition. I can feel it. Something is headed this way, and I don't like the feel of it," she said, turning back to the wall screen. "It has been quiet way too long. It's coming."

"I'll make it so that as she is touching down, our fighters will be lifting off. It will be seamless. She's scheduled to be here several hours. The drills will end just as she is lifting off. We'll have the best launch time anyone has ever seen," Commander Viscully said proudly.

"Better than Lieutenant Lee when he was flying?" asked the major.

"No one can ever be *that* good. He was one of a kind. We'll give him a run for his money, though," answered the commander with a smile and a small chuckle.

"I want to know when the shuttle lands. I want Sergeant Russ brought immediately to my office," Major Huntsmann said, still facing the large screen. She was still staring at Saturn, looking for something that she didn't even know if it existed. This was all that really mattered to her at this time. The Quill were still out there, and her scar was telling her that now more than ever. It itched badly when they were around, and it was almost killing her now.

"Understood, Major," he replied in a serious tone. He knew when to be serious, and he knew when to be relaxed. Her tone had told him this was a time for seriousness.

"And, Commander…please join us at that time. I may need you," she whispered and turned to face him. She said nothing more, but her facial expression told the story. She was expecting something, something big, and wanted him there for a witness.

"Understood, Major," he replied once more, then turned and went back to his station to await word from the flight deck that the shuttle had landed.

As Commander Viscully resumed his duties, and Major Huntsmann continued to stare at the screen, the lights flashed red, and a siren blared overhead. It brought everyone into action, and people scrambled and voices sounded out, getting louder with each second. Major Huntsmann turned and ran from the screen to be next to Commander Viscully, who was still trying to understand what was happening. She stood there, silently waiting for confirmation of Quill activity. Commander Viscully knew his job well, and he knew his major even better. He knew she wouldn't say anything until he informed her of just what exactly was going on. All around them service members were shouting commands and counter commands in an effort to find out where the alarm had originated from. What sector of space had the Quill begun to launch their attack? Was it really the Quill or had some kind of attack been launched by hostile forces from Earth?

"No one seems to know where they are, sir," he said quickly to his major. He was still listening to the information coming from his earpiece. He was still trying to sort it all out. "Some are saying from in front of us, while others seem to think it's a rear attack, but the forts in that direction aren't detecting anything. It's unclear what exactly is going on."

"Launch all fighters now. I want everything we have airborne in the next two minutes. I want eyes out there looking for them. Arm the defense grid and prepare to repel borders. Security alert all decks," she yelled as she turned in a small circle to see her people operating. They were still trying to sort everything out, and the sight and sound of their major barking orders calmed them somewhat. She was in command, and she knew how to do it, and they took comfort in it. "Eve, get me the other forts!" she yelled even louder.

Within seconds, the images of the other majors, plus Colonel Dewey, were in front of her. It was a rare sight to see the five of them together on the command deck. Onlookers could tell that the other four were going through the same events that Fort Grant was currently going through. Their images were cloaked in red lighting, and sirens were sounding. They could see Service members scrambling about, trying to put it all together and figure out where the attack was coming from. They could see Major Huntsmann's mouth move as if she was speaking, but the sound of the siren blocked out what was being said. Colonel Dewey answered as best she could, but from her facial expression, members could tell she was just as confused as Major Huntsmann. The fort suddenly jerked, and the roar of engines could be heard as squadron after squadron launched from all the docks. Hundreds of fighters took to the sky in an attempt to block the Quill attack. As Service members turned their attention to the wall screen, they could see the fighters filling the sky between them and Saturn, yet they couldn't make out a single Quill ship in the area.

"Does anyone have a visual on them?" questioned Colonel Dewey in an anxious voice. She could be seen turning around on her command deck, giving orders both there and on the command deck of Fort Grant. She was trying to be in two places at once and was somewhat successful. She was receiving information from both decks and could be seen taking a brief second to put it all together. She had to get this right. Lives were depending on her. Decisions had to be made, and she was the one that was going to make them. "All forts, launch everything. Arm all defense grids. Security alert status red. I need a squadron to protect Sergeant Russ's shuttle. She's closest to you, Major Huntsmann. Send one squad in her direction and make sure she lands safely. Once onboard, that squad is to continue patrolling."

"Squad on the way, Major," Commander Viscully reported before Colonel Dewey's words could be completed. "Gamma wing has them on their screens and is radioing them our status. It will be some time before they rendezvous with them and at least another two hours after that before they dock."

"Damn shuttles! Why couldn't Earth Force put the new engines on them when they were putting them on the fighters?" Major Huntsmann complained out loud. She slammed her fist into the desk, and the resulting thump caused most heads on the command deck to turn. "Tell them to do the best they can. I want that shuttle powered up to full speed. Check the log when it docks, and this thing is over," she ordered in an angry voice. "Does anyone see the enemy yet?"

"Negative," came a reply from one of the other majors. Major Huntsmann wasn't sure who had replied, but she nodded her head to acknowledge the reply.

"Best anyone can tell, there is nothing out there," came the voice of Major Vorr.

"My people tell me the same thing," agreed Major Blishman. "Nothing but the black of space out there."

"Then what triggered the alarm?" demanded Major Huntsmann.

No one had an answer for her. She slammed her fist into the desk again and turned to face the others. Her face was as red as anyone had ever seen it. Her anger was boiling over, and everyone knew it. She glanced at them quickly, then turned her attention to the view screen and watched as the fighters flew their courses in search of the enemy that she knew had to be out there. On the far corner of the screen, she could just make out Gamma Squadron as it headed toward the shuttle. Nothing else was even close to them. Looking at the remainder of the screen, she watched intently. She listened as each fighter contacted its leader, then the leader contacted the fort. It seemed everyone out there was just as confused as the rest of them. No contact could be seen or heard. She let her head sag slightly, but not too much so as to alert the crew, then she stood tall and shook it all off.

"Suggest we step down from red to yellow, Colonel," she said without looking in Colonel Dewey's direction.

"I concur," responded Major Blishman quickly. "Seems nothing is moving out there now."

"Something set off the alarms, people. I want it found. We'll go to condition yellow, keep two squadrons from each fort out there, rest the others. But I want that something found, and I want it found quickly. This could be the first step in the next phase of this war," Colonel Dewey ordered in a hard tone.

"Agreed," offered Major Vorr. "It will be another two hours at least before the shuttle can land. We should use that time to find the culprit that triggered the alarm. Each of us should review the recordings leading up to the alarm and try to find even the smallest of items that could have triggered this."

"Very good, Major. Make it happen, people. We'll meet again when the shuttle lands. Let's hope we have something by then. Rotate the fighters every hour. Keep them flying until we figure this out," ordered Colonel Dewey before her image faded. When she was gone, the others vanished one by one. Major Huntsmann once again found herself on her command deck alone with her people.

"Bring up the tapes," she ordered out loud and moved closer to the screen to witness everything that had happened. "I want to see everything from five minutes before the alarm until the fighters launched."

*****

Sergeant Russ and Lieutenant Lee were seated in their shuttle. They had the forts on their screen but were still an hour away from having visual. They were unaware that the forts had gone to condition red and that all fighters had been scrambled from the hangars. To the two of them, it was just another ordinary flight. Small talk had been made when they departed, and each had made an attempt at keeping it going. Several times, the shuttle fell silent as each searched for another subject to discuss. They were now in the middle of who each thought would make the best Earth vice president. Each knew the importance of President Hoss selecting a senator that was a friend of the Service. The wrong person in that position could spell the end of everything, and they both took this very seriously.

"Out of all the senators, the logical pick is Senator Torra Tomenagua of Japan," Lieutenant Lee was saying. "He has the most experience in the Senate. The people of Japan love him, and President Hoss has met with him several times in the past. The two have a history together, and Tomenagua believes the war is still being fought."

"That's nice, but I prefer to see Senator Miguel DiFranco of Spain. He believes in the forts and that the war isn't over. He may not have the same connection to President Hoss, but the two aren't exactly strangers either. Yes, he's new to the Senate, but other senators have come out in support of him. That alone carries a lot of weight," Sergeant Russ countered.

"DiFranco isn't even a true Spaniard. His family only moved to Spain eight years ago. He made a name for himself in business and local politics before running for the Senate. He's green," protested Lieutenant Lee. "You take Tomenagua, now he's been around. He's experienced. He can get things done and more than one senator has come out in support of him. President Hoss would do good to pick him."

"Please! Tomenagua is getting old. He's older than Cologne was when he was picked. DiFranco is young. The youth of Earth will love him. He's a poster boy," Sergeant Russ said with a laugh. She was still laughing when the call came in.

"Gamma Squadron to shuttle. Gamma Squadron to shuttle. Come in, shuttle."

They could barely hear it. They were still some distance to the forts and hadn't been expecting any kind of communication for some time. The two of them stopped discussing the matter of who was best for the position, and briefly turned to face each other. Confusion was on both faces. Fighters had never met them before, and for the fighters to be this far out from the forts was not a good sign. They both snapped to attention and eyed the space in front of them, trying to pick the fighters out. Lieutenant Lee was the first, and he pointed them out to Sergeant Russ.

"There," was all he said.

"Shuttle to Gamma Squadron. We have a visual on you but just barely," Sergeant Russ said aloud.

"Shuttle, Gamma Squadron actual. You are ordered to increase speed to max and follow us to Fort Grant," came the order.

"Gamma Squadron actual, please explain yourself," the sergeant requested.

"Shuttle, all will be explained by Major Huntsmann. You are ordered to fire up your engines to max and follow us. That is a direct order."

Sergeant Russ and Lieutenant Lee faced each other with questioning looks on their faces. Questions ran through their heads. They weren't sure if the orders were legit or if something had happened to Major Huntsmann, and her name was just a ruse to get at them. The tension mounted. Both checked to make sure their sidearms were accessible.

"Let me speak to them. I used to be one of them. They'll know me. They'll talk to me easier than they'll talk to you," Lieutenant Lee said.

Sergeant Russ shrugged her shoulders and motioned with her right hand to the comm link. She sat quietly as the lieutenant cleared his throat and puffed his chest out. He tried to picture himself in the cockpit of the fighter and imagine he was giving orders to his pilots.

"Gamma Squadron, this is Lieutenant Jason Lee. Please explain your order. Who sent you and why? We've never needed an escort before."

"All will be explained by Major Huntsmann when we reach Fort Grant. She is still in charge. She sent us under the orders of Colonel Dewey. NOW FIRE UP THOSE ENGINES AND FOLLOW US!" the fighter pilot ordered. His temper had been pushed to the limit, and he was getting anxious to return home. "We haven't any more time to sit out here and discuss the matter. Move your butts!"

"Shuttle to Gamma Squadron, we are moving our butts. Engines at max and following your lead," Sergeant Russ said.

Sergeant Russ and Lieutenant Lee sat in silence as the shuttle lurched forward beneath them. Neither wanted to be the first to speak. Both feared the worst. Their previous conversation had been forgotten. They watched as the fighters flew past them, then watched again as they flew by once more and took up the lead. They both knew the procedures: two in front, two behind, two above, two below, two on the right, and two on the left. The other eight were scattered about, keeping an eye on their scanners for any signs of trouble. Their uneasiness was getting worse. Just the sight of the fighters this close was unnerving. Not knowing why the fighters were here was even worse. Each reached for sidearms at the same time, which lay close by, and checked to make sure they were loaded. Each then stood and strapped them on, then reseated themselves. The sidearms made sitting a little uncomfortable, but they felt better wearing them. These were their people, they knew that, but what they feared was that Devlin Shaw had made another move, and more heads had rolled, and now he wanted the information they were carrying. They were prepared to protect it at all costs.

*****

Two hours later, Commander Viscully escorted Sergeant Russ and Lieutenant Lee onto the command deck of Fort Grant. They still had not been briefed as to what had occurred, but from the actions of the squadron and the Service members about the fort, they knew it had been unnerving for all. On the command deck, they looked about at the actions of the crew. Service members were still moving at an accelerated pace, and orders were still being barked out. Major Huntsmann was still at the screen studying Saturn and communicating with the other fort majors and Colonel Dewey. Looking at the images from the other forts, they got the impression that whatever had happened had shook each fort into major defensive action. People were rushing about, and orders were being barked out on every fort in the sector. No one was sitting and doing nothing.

"Major Huntsmann and Colonel Dewey wish to speak with the two of you, ASAP," Commander Viscully said, showing them the way forward. The two snapped back into reality and started toward the major.

"You have to be kidding me!" came the raised voice of Major Vorr. She sounded more than a little agitated.

"That small of an occurrence started all of this?" questioned Major Wright.

"What happened to it once we responded?" asked Colonel Dewey in a restrained voice.

The three newcomers approached the meeting and stopped a short distance away until Major Huntsmann could motion them forward. The senior officers were engaged in a troubling conversation, and no one wanted to interrupt them until the proper time. Questions were being asked, and answers were being demanded. It almost sounded like an argument, but everyone knew otherwise. Everyone was staring at Saturn.

"That small movement in sector K3 is the only thing we see out of the ordinary. It was only there for a second or two, but we think it's what set the alarms sounding. After that second or two, it went back to wherever it came from. That's why our fighters couldn't find it and why our scanners couldn't pick anything up. I think they were just checking to see how we would respond," Major Blishman explained.

"Okay, people. We know they're still out there now. We also know how fast we can respond, and we *have* to do better. What I want is two squadrons from each fort to remain on constant patrol. Relieve them every ninety minutes. I want each fort to keep their defensive grid activated and pointed at that spot. We will remain on condition yellow until further notice. I'll report to Earth Force Command later today. Any questions?" Colonel Dewey ordered firmly. She now had her evidence that the Quill were still out there and still a threat. Her reservations about Major Blishman were slipping away, but she still didn't trust him totally. He was still late for meetings once in a while, and his excuses weren't holding a lot of water. But for today, he had earned his money.

The images faded, and Major Huntsmann again found herself alone on her command deck. She waited a minute before waving the three forward. She wasn't sure what to say to them. She trusted them with her life, but times were still dangerous and getting worse by the minute. She hated to blindly trust people.

"As you can see, we've had an incident here," she said softly. "The Quill are back, if they ever left. Space is now even more dangerous. What do you have to report, Sergeant?"

"We've heard rumors of two more battleships being moved away from this sector. We're not sure which two. Also that orders will be coming down that the battleships are to take orders only from senior command, not the fort majors. Not sure when that order will come down, but it doesn't sound good. Fort Harrington is reporting their CAG, and flight deck commander have been reassigned to the Mars colony. New Service members will replace them soon," Sergeant Russ reported.

"Not good," mumbled Major Huntsmann. "Too many things happening, and now this thing today with the Quill. Not good at all."

"Sir," started Lieutenant Lee quickly, "we've also heard that Lincoln Jacobson has gone missing. He's the strongman for Devlin Shaw who threatened the sergeant here a few months back. He wasn't exactly happy with her then, and it is my opinion that he may come looking for her again."

"I remember this Jacobson guy. You and he didn't exactly see eye to eye over more than a few things. It may not be safe out there for you."

"With all due respect, sir, space is never safe. The addition of one more thing to worry about is all this is. Out here, he's in my court. With the lieutenant here by my side, I think that takes a lot of pressure off of me, don't you?" Sergeant Russ explained in a more-than-cheerful voice. She didn't scare too easily, and remembering her last meeting with Mr. Jacobson only strengthened her resolve to stay on the line.

"You place a lot of trust in me, Sergeant," Lieutenant Lee said, looking at the sergeant and smiling slightly.

"I agree, Lieutenant," Major Huntsmann said. "If you think you're safer on a shuttle with the lieutenant by your side, then carry on, Sergeant, but I want the two of you to be extra careful out there from now on. The Quill have shown that they are back and have something new up their sleeve. Stay alert. If you need anything else, don't be afraid to ask."

"Thank you, sir. I'm sure I'll be fine," Sergeant Russ said, smiling at Lieutenant Lee in a sly way. The two saluted their commanding officer, then turned and walked off the command deck. They were returning to their shuttle so they could make their way to Fort Pershing and a meeting with Major Blishman. Neither one fully trusted the major, but after the events of this morning, their respect for him was growing.

9

Karl Cregg was sitting shirtless on a large rock near the ocean. The morning sun was beating down on him. His back was already showing signs of sunburn. His once neatly trimmed hair now down below his ears. A full beard and mustache adorned his face. Looking up to the sun, he spun himself slightly and let the sun hit his chest. His muscles twitched slightly as he once again made himself comfortable. His head turned slowly as he gazed out over his island, taking everything in. It had been home for him these past few months. He knew it would all end soon; he just wasn't sure when. It had taken him longer than he had anticipated to get accustomed to being alone, but now that he was, he enjoyed every second of every day. He had built himself a small two-room house that overlooked the ocean. Most nights he spent inside, but all days were spent outside in the fresh air. It cleared his head, and he found it easier to think. To plan.

Standing up, he began to walk along the thing that passed for a beach. It was rocky and uneven. More than once, he slipped and almost fell into the ocean. Getting his feet underneath him again, he continued on his way. He had done this twice a day every day since coming here. It was part of his daily exercise routine. Some days he would pick up a large stone and see how far he could carry it. When he had first thought of doing this, he could only carry it a few steps; now he was able to carry it halfway around the island. When he made it to the spot where he had to put the stone down, he began to run. He ran the rest of the way around the small island at top speed. Carefully he placed each step so as not to stumble. From one stone to another, he ran, sometimes almost jumping. It made him feel young again. It freshened him and cleared his head even more.

Every day he would end his run at the old cabin that had been here since before his arrival. It had come with the island, but he had found it much too small for any real use as a home. Instead, he had built the house that overlooked the ocean and turned this one into a sort of war room. Inside was a small desk with all his papers tossed about. A four-foot-by-six-foot sheet of wood rested on some logs in the far corner, and on it was a drawing of the solar system. Every planet and moon, plus the forts, were noted. Each battleship was listed along with its station. As far out as Saturn, he had noted as Earth territory; after Saturn, he listed as Quill. Each day he would enter the small cabin and read reports that had found their way to his island. Then he would make the necessary changes to the board. After that he would sit behind the desk and study the solar system and jot down anything that he believed would be of help one day. This could take anywhere from one to more than eight hours. He was thorough. He needed everything to be perfect, or the whole thing could come crashing down and end humanity.

Today was no different. He ended his run and entered the cabin. Touching the small device on the side of the desk his messages appeared on the board. He read them each, missing nothing. Then he moved some pieces on the board and stepped back to check it all out. A questioning look came over his face. He took another step backward and looked at it again. He checked with the message to be sure he had gotten it right. Then he studied the board even harder. It made no sense to him. He had to be missing something. Something small. So small it had gotten past him. Yet he couldn't find it.

"Two more battleships and three squadrons of fighters," he mumbled to himself. "From one side of space to the other. Away from the danger. Why?"

He walked around the cabin, keeping his eye on the board. His right hand came up to his chin, and he began to rub it softly as if something had gotten into his beard and was bothering him. His mind raced to understand what was happening out there. He couldn't make any sense out of the moves. Ending his walk, he went back to the board and looked it over again.

"It makes no sense," he said softly. "To take all this equipment and move it away from the upcoming battle makes no sense unless somebody wants us to lose big-time."

Turning from the board and moving over to the desk, he touched another button, and the messages disappeared. Another button and an electronic net went up over the island that could only be penetrated by the correct code, and that code was known only to him and to a handful of select trusted people. No more than five people knew the code besides him, and they were all loyal and trusted friends. Tomorrow, at a random time, he would be back in the cabin to check his messages again and make the necessary changes to his board. If he needed, he would send a message himself to one of those people, but today he would remain silent and think about what he had seen on the board.

Exiting the cabin, he began his walk back to his home. A trip around the small lake would end with him taking a short swim to clear his mind and body. The water was heated by underground steam that kept the temperature constant, be it summer or winter. After the swim, he would sit on the front porch of the cabin and watch the sun sink low in the sky. When it was nighttime, he would enter the cabin and prepare a small supper. Then it would be time to rest. Tomorrow, well before sunup, he would be at it again. Karl Cregg wasn't a man for sleeping in. He wasn't even a man who believed in a lot of sleep. Five or six hours a night, and he felt more rested than those that got eight or more hours.

*****

Kevin Base stood near the ship and peered out over the island. Jordan Schmidt was making her way toward the forest at the far end of the island, while Amber Jameson was headed toward the small lake opposite the forest. Behind the lake, she could see a small cave that she hoped would show some signs of where Karl Cregg was. Each of them, at different times, would call out in their loudest voice the name of Karl Cregg and wait for an answer that never came. They were more than a little confused. Karl had stated very clearly that he was going to be working on his tan, yet here, in the southern Pacific, with temperatures hitting the midnineties and the sun shining relentlessly, there was no sign of the man to be found.

"Karl!" yelled Jordan as she neared the forest. It wasn't a huge forest, only a few acres, and she could hear the ocean crashing on the beach on the far side, yet there was no Karl. She began to pick her way carefully through the trees, stopping every few feet to check for signs of life. The only life she saw was wildlife. "Karl!" she yelled louder, then stopped to wait for an answer. Shaking her head slowly, she continued on her way.

At the lake, Amber stopped and yelled Karl's name. She adjusted her head to hear his reply no matter how small, but none came. She looked in the lake and was amazed at the clearness of the water. She failed to spot any fish but thought they may be down the bottom due to the high temperature. Spinning around, she called once again for Karl and waited for his response. Then she slowly made her way to the pristine beach and found the water, once again, to be flawless. It lapped at her boots, and she bent down to stick her hand in it and splash some water on her face. She looked around both up and down the beach. She studied the sand for some time before returning to where Kevin stood.

"No signs of life anywhere," she told him in an angry voice. "There aren't even any footsteps on the sand. Karl was never here. He fooled us. He's sunning himself somewhere else."

"I thought for sure when he said he was going to tan himself, he would be here. He only bought two islands, and this is the southernmost. This is the place you would come to work on your tan. Not the other one. That one is too far north," Kevin explained in a shaky voice. He was sure this was the place. This was where they were going to find Karl. Now he was sure he had made a mistake. He only hoped it wasn't too big of one. "I'm sorry, Amber."

"Where's the other one, Kevin? How far is it from here?" she asked, motioning for Jordan to come over to their spot as quickly as possible. She watched as the retired general made her way through the small forest and came running up at full speed.

"What is it?" questioned Jordan. She wasn't out of breath entirely, but she was close. The sand on the island had proven to be difficult to run through.

"Kevin here made a mistake. Karl isn't around here. He's somewhere else," Amber explained quickly.

"North," Kevin said suddenly. "It's north of here."

"How far north?" Jordan asked harshly.

"Alaska. He purchased an island off the coast of Alaska. It's the only other place he could be as far as I know."

"Alaska!" the two women said in unison.

"Yeah. He wanted it to take time in case someone came looking for him. If they found this island, and he wasn't here, it would take them more than a little time to get to the other island. He's in Alaska," Kevin explained quickly.

"How long till we can get to Alaska?" Jordan asked Amber.

"A day at full throttle. This boat isn't exactly built for speed. A speedboat could do it in ten hours. This will take us overnight," Amber said, jumping aboard the small boat and heading toward the boathouse. "I'm going. How about the rest of you?" she yelled, noticing their slowness to climb aboard.

"Coming!" yelled Kevin, scrambling aboard.

"Move it out!" Jordan called as she jumped aboard and made her way to Amber's side.

Within seconds, the small boat was heading out into the ocean and turning north. A minute later, she was cruising at top speed and making waves in back of her. Five minutes later, and the small island had already disappeared from sight, and only the blueness of the ocean could be seen in all directions. The three passengers were huddled in the boathouse, trying to stay dry as the boat plowed its way through the water.

"I hope your boat holds together, Kevin," Amber said as she steered the vessel in the direction of the next island. Silently she knew it would, but she needed to vent some anger for this mistake that had been made.

"You built it, Amber," he replied, studying the water ahead.

"Yeah, but you bought it," she countered.

"Can we go any faster?" wondered Jordan aloud.

"This is it. Only the specialized speedboats go any faster. If we try to be like one of them, it'll fall apart long before we reach Alaska," Amber informed her. "She's solid, but at those speeds, even the best-built ships will fail."

*****

Karl Cregg's eyes shot open. He had heard it. It was a small sound. It almost fit in with the island. Almost. He had heard it. He slowly moved his eyes around the cabin, searching for the source even as he lay motionless. It was hard to make anything out in the darkness, but that didn't stop him. It was his home, and he wasn't alone anymore. He lay perfectly still, trying not to breathe too loud. He waited to see if he could hear the sound again and get a fix as to where they were. He was almost positive it was one person. Almost.

There it was again. Soft. Gentle. Someone trying to sneak around the place outside and doing a fine job of it. They were professional. Trained in the art of surveillance. Trained to be extra quiet, but not knowing the layout of this place, they had become slightly careless. Karl turned his head to try to catch a glimpse or see a shadow, anything that could help determine who and how many. He thought he saw a shadow, but the moon failed to give off enough light at this time of the year. Slowly, quietly, he slid out of bed. He was determined to get his quarry before it got him.

He softly made his way over to the wall opposite the bed and waited. He had the door in sight and could easily cover the few feet from where he stood. He stood still. Not even blinking. His breath was short and shallow. His fists opened and closed continuously. He was awake now. Fully awake and aware of what was about to happen. He had an idea of who they were, but he wasn't 100 percent, and he wasn't sure how many. He had to be sure before taking the appropriate steps. Before he had to kill them to keep this place a secret, to keep more from coming. He still needed time to figure it all out. Yesterday's messages still didn't make sense to him, but they would have to wait until this new threat was taken care of. So he waited. Quietly.

Slowly the door opened. Only enough for the person to enter, then it closed again. Very little moonlight came in with him. It wouldn't have been enough to wake him if he was asleep. He watched as the stranger moved closer to the bed. He waited for him to make the first move. Then he saw it. The weapon of choice. A cloth. A small piece of material that was stuffed inside a small container. So small it would go unnoticed if searched. Once the cloth was out of the container, he could smell the odor of it. A chemical compound that if inhaled long enough, and at close-enough range, would kill.

Karl watched as the man made his way toward the bed. It was only a ten-foot walk, but he was extra careful to be extremely quiet. It took almost thirty seconds. Then the man moved the blanket and made to put the cloth on the spot where Karl's face should have been. It wasn't, and he wasn't prepared for that. Karl bolted quickly toward the bed and shoved the man into the wall. His fist came up and connected with the man's face, sending him again into the wall. The cloth dropped, and Karl quickly moved it with his foot, then punched again. His assailant went down in a clump. He failed to move.

Karl grabbed the cloth, then found the container and put it back inside, sealing it up tight. He then turned his attention toward the intruder and found him still unconscious. Lighting a lamp on the table, he shone the light onto the face of his newfound "friend." There was no surprise there. His assailant was a young man with a full beard. A small triangular tattoo on his right cheek indicated who had sent him. He was one of a select group who was assigned to keep an eye on individuals the Service felt were unfaithful. Trackers. Paid to follow and watch. Paid to eliminate if necessary. Someone had found it necessary to eliminate Karl. The man began to move slightly, and Karl pulled a chair up close to talk to the man. He needed information. This man would be the fastest way to get what he needed.

"Your boss isn't going to be so happy about this," he said as he kept the man in his field of vision and watched him closely. "You failed your mission. I'm still alive."

"They have already sent another. You won't leave this island, Mr. Cregg. I hope you are happy here," the man said in a low tone, rubbing his jaw.

"Who sent you?" Karl asked, leaning in closer but knowing enough to keep his distance.

"Let's just say he is not a fan of you. You've caused him a lot of grief recently."

"Well, when I leave, you're coming with me, and we'll see what Earth Command has to say about this attempt on my life. I still have quite a few friends there, and they'll be interested to see who sent you. A mind probe could leave you worse off than dead," Karl said, leaning back in his chair and smiling at his opponent.

"I'm afraid I won't be leaving with you, Mr. Cregg. See, I knew there was chance I would fail, so I prepared for it. My death will come shortly, and there is nothing you can do to stop it. All the proper steps have been taken, and soon all that will be left will be this body which you can take care of any way you want. Just remember, others are on their way. They know where you are now. You can't hide anymore," the man said.

Karl sat there and watched as the man put his head on the ground and formed a smile on his face. He closed his eyes one last time and took a deep breath. His mouth moved slightly for a second as if saying a prayer. Then his chest heaved up, and he let out a deep groan.

Karl sat there for a minute, looking at him. The smile on the man's face annoyed him more than anything else, but he didn't have time to take care of that. Others would be here. They were already on their way. He had no idea of how far or close they were. It could be minutes, or it could be days. No longer than a week at the most, he figured, but he was more worried about the minutes. He had things to do. He had to pack, and fast. He had to try to get off of this island and make it to another in as short a time as possible. There were thousands of islands nearby. He would have to find one with people and try to blend in. Hide in plain sight. First, he had to gather everything together and leave no sign for them to follow. He knew them. They were relentless. They wouldn't stop until he stopped breathing.

Karl stood up and started moving quickly around the cabin gathering up his few personal possessions. He hadn't brought that much with him because of his fears of just such an encounter. He knew the Trackers. Had heard stories about them for years. He knew how deadly they were. He knew he would have to make a quick escape at some point and avoid them, so he had come here with minimal belongings. Within seconds, the cabin was empty except for the dead man. Next, he ran to the older cabin and began clearing that out. It would take longer but not much more. Then he had to signal for his boat. He had left that with some passing natives. They would have taken care of it. A small fire on the beach would signal that he was ready to leave. They would deliver it to him within a few minutes. Then something caught his ear.

*****

Kevin was piloting the boat. The sun was already over the horizon. The day was starting out sunny and a bit on the chilly side. They were already in Alaskan waters. From here, he knew it wouldn't be long before they would reach their destination. He looked in back of himself and saw that Amber and Jordan were still sound asleep. They had nodded off just after one in the morning. Yesterday had been a long day. They were angry with him for only a short time, but the sting of it had lasted until they had fallen asleep. He vowed that he would make it right by getting them to their destination long before noon. They would meet with Karl and leave his island before supper. Turning his attention back to the water, he allowed a small smile to cross his face. They were close, and he knew it. Once again, he could be the hero that he always wished he could be.

"Rise and shine, ladies!" he yelled over his shoulder. He didn't have to turn to know that they were moving. He could hear them moaning and straining to come awake. He knew they would be stretching and trying to bring themselves out of their slumber.

"How close?" inquired Jordan, coming over to take a place at his side.

"Real close now. Another five minutes and we'll be there," he replied with pride.

"What time is it?" asked Amber, joining them and rubbing the sleep from her eyes.

"I would guess about seven," Jordan informed her.

"I slept in. Back home, I would have been at work by five. I must be getting soft," Amber said with a chuckle. She placed her hand on Kevin's back and ran it in circles. "Are you feeling better about things today?"

"Yeah. Yeah, I'm okay. Thanks. It was just so stupid of me. I knew he had two islands, and he had told me that would make it that much harder for people to find him. I should have known that once he said he would be working on his tan that he planned to go to Alaska," Kevin said. He was still slightly disgusted with himself, but he refused to let it show. He wanted them to trust him again. Wanted them to feel that they could count on him. "There it is," he said loudly, pointing just off to his right.

"Doesn't look like much from here," mumbled Jordan as she strained to get a better view.

"It wasn't much. That's what appealed to Karl," Kevin informed her.

"Karl never mentioned anything about buying an island so he could get away from everything. He was always a city boy at heart. He enjoyed being around people. He never had trouble fitting in," Amber told them as she watched the island come into better view.

"Maybe that's why he bought it," Jordan said, turning to face her. "In case anyone came looking for him, they would never think about looking anywhere but in the cities. Out here, alone, that's just not Karl."

Kevin steered the boat close to the island, then cut the engines. They drifted the last couple hundred feet. Their momentum taking them to the one spot that he had found that looked safe enough for a landing. Climbing on deck, they tied the ropes to some large stones so the boat wouldn't drift away. They stepped from the boat to the rocks and looked around. There was no sign of life. It was quiet. It seemed all of nature was staying away from this island for some reason. Jordan motioned Kevin to go in one direction and Amber to go in another. Then she started towards the newer of the two cabins that they could see.

"Karl," Kevin called as he made his way down the stony beach. His head turned to his left, then to his right as he went. He kept Amber and Jordan in sight just in case something happened. He knew they could take care of themselves, but he felt better this way. "Karl," he called again.

"Karl!" yelled Amber as she made her way toward the small lake. She could see the ocean to her right and Jordan to her left. She could hear Kevin calling out. Turning her head to look around, she wondered where everything was. She couldn't see a single living thing on the island. "Karl!" she yelled even louder.

"Karl," Jordan said in a loud voice as she neared the cabin. The door was open, and she could see a few things inside. She could make out a hill of some sorts in the cabin near what appeared to be a bed. She came to a stop and tried to make out exactly what it was, but she was still too far away. "Karl," she said more softly than she wanted. Tentatively she stepped closer. She now could make out the "hill." It was a man, but she couldn't make out his face. "KARL!" she yelled louder than she meant to as she moved quickly toward the door.

The others heard her yell and turned to see what she had found. They saw her near the cabin door. Then the sound of her voice settled in, and they, in turn, turned and ran toward the cabin. Their worst thoughts filled their heads. They were too late. Kevin silently cursed himself for having made that mistake yesterday and costing them so much badly needed time. Amber had her future flash before her eyes as she sprinted. No longer did it include Karl Cregg. He was dead in the cabin, and she knew it.

"Don't go in there!" came a loud voice from behind them. It was near their boat. They stopped and spun to see who was with them. None of them had heard any sounds. Each of them was sure the island was deserted. They were sure they were the only living beings on the island. Now they were shocked to find that someone else was with them. Behind them. Someone had gotten behind them without making any noise. "We don't have any time. We have to get out of here quickly. The Trackers will be here shortly."

"Karl," they all said in unison. Each more surprised than the other to find their friend alive. Each not knowing who was inside, dead on the floor. They had sense enough to listen to him and ran to where he stood near their boat.

"You're alive," Amber said, throwing herself at him and kissing his cheek while hugging him. "I thought you were dead."

"What happened here?" Jordan wondered aloud.

"Tracker. Came at me early this morning. He thought I was asleep, and he tried to kill me. Someone high up wants me dead. I don't know who or why, but I did figure something out. I'll tell you while we're leaving here."

"Where to?" Kevin asked, climbing aboard the boat and heading to the wheelhouse.

"North," Karl informed him as he went aboard the boat behind Jordan and Amber. "My boat is just north of here, and it is much faster than this one. With any luck, we'll be back in warmer water before they get here."

The small boat's engines opened up, and the four of them found themselves rushing north through the cold water. Each of them was excited in their own way to be off the island, and found themselves glancing quickly behind to see it vanish from view. They each wondered how long it would be before the Trackers found the island and their fallen friend. They each wondered how long they would be free. How long before the Trackers found them? What would happen to them when the Trackers found them? It wasn't a matter of *if* the Trackers found them but when. Each knew the dangers. Each knew what could happen to them if events didn't change.

"What did you figure out, Karl?" Jordan said at last.

"It's a road. The fighters and the battleships being moved around out there. It forms a road. I just haven't figured out why. Why would someone make a road in space? Are they letting the Quill in, or are they getting ready to make their escape and leave Earth to her fate? Why would they do this?" Karl said as he looked around at his small band of friends. They had come looking for him, and he was thankful for that. Thankful for their timing. He knew he would be even more thankful to them when all of this was over, but for now, he had to put everything into figuring out why a road was constructed in space. Was it to let someone in or to let someone out? Let the alien enemy in or let the domestic enemy escape? Either way, he would have to find a way to close it.

"I uncovered some other information also, but that will have to wait for another time to discuss. We have to get out of here first as fast as possible, then we can talk about the other stuff. Speed is essential at the moment."

10

Colonel Dewey stood on the command deck of Fort Patton, staring at a magnified view of Saturn on the big screen. She watched it intently as the small object appeared in the lower left corner of the screen, showed itself for a brief second, then disappeared again. It replayed itself over and over again. Each time, she watched it more intently than the last time. Her eyes never moved off of the object. She stood there and stared at it as the images of her four majors stood behind her. They watched it again and again. Each one trying desperately to figure out what it was and what its mission was.

"You're telling me that this little object is responsible for all the alarms going off and for us launching everything we have? This tiny thing set each fort into motion. Every defense grid in this sector went on high alert simply because of this small thing rising up over Saturn, then settling back down. You're telling me this?" she demanded in a harsh tone. She turned and put her hands on her hips and looked hard at her majors.

"Colonel," Major Vorr said in a shaky voice. She had never known her colonel to be this agitated. "Not only did this thing set everything off, but in the short time it was visible, it scanned every fort in this sector. It knows our defenses."

"Nothing else moved out there, Colonel," stated Major Wright. "This tiny thing, whatever it is, is the only thing we could find out of place. For as brief a period of time as it was, this thing set off everything."

"Could it be a new type of Quill ship?" asked Major Huntsmann. "Some kind of ship we have never seen before. It has been a long time since we've seen them. Maybe this is where their technology took them. Smaller and faster."

"If it is some new kind of ship, we're in for a lot of trouble," offered Major Blishman. "In just three seconds, that thing scanned every fort in the sector and learned of our capabilities. We've got to assume it reported back to the Quill home world, and even as we speak, an armada is heading this way. We've got to make plans quickly and set up a new defensive posture to greet them."

"Okay. Okay," Colonel Dewey said, raising her hands up to settle her majors down. "Say it is a new ship, how do we defeat it? It's smaller than anything we have, and we haven't the foggiest idea of what it is capable of. For all we know, it could blow a fort apart with one shot. If it did alert the Quill home world, and an armada is headed this way, how do we hope to stop it? They will know everything about us and be ready for anything we do. Let me remind all of you that right now, this second, this sector is severely understaffed with people and equipment. Battleships and fighter squadrons have been moved out of here like there is no war going on. Whatever we do, we have to do it quickly. The fate of Earth could depend on what we do this minute."

"Colonel," began Major Blishman. "Might I suggest we each launch a squadron of fighters and keep them flying for as long as possible. Then when they are low on fuel, launch another squadron to replace them and bring them back aboard for refueling and to rest the pilots."

"We could get them to fly closer to Saturn than they ever have before," put in Major Huntsmann. "Let them go out in groups of five and head toward Saturn. See if whatever that thing is decides to show its face again."

"At the same time, they could be listening for any transmission of alien origin," said Major Wright. "Fly them as close as possible to Saturn and let them listen for anything."

"What do you suggest the pilots do if that thing shows up again?" questioned Major Vorr. "Should they take the shot or just turn tail and run?"

The command deck went silent for a second. Each one turned and looked toward the other for the answer. The fighters' guns could reach Saturn even from where they stood. Out there, in space, they would be closer and stood a better chance of hitting it. Each one ran it over in their head. Weighing the chances of a hit and kill against retaliation. If they didn't destroy it on the first hit, they risked retaliation on a scale that could be devastating. A war that had gone cold in recent years could suddenly heat up, and the killing could start all over again.

"Let's go with Major Blishman's idea. Launch one squadron each, and we'll see how that goes. If nothing happens, then the second squadron will launch when fuel is low and proceed like Major Huntsmann suggests. We'll fly closer to Saturn. See if this tiny thing suddenly shows its head again. *If* there is to be any firing, any shooting at all, I will make the call. Nobody is to fire at that thing unless the word comes from me. Am I clear on this?" Colonel Dewey demanded to know. Her voice had gotten higher as she reached the end of her order, and she was determined to get her meaning across.

"Perfectly clear, sir," responded Major Wright. "If any shooting is to be done on this particular object, you'll give the order."

"Correct. If our forces do come under attack, they are free to return fire," Colonel Dewey clarified. "If this thing shows up and does not fire, our people will not fire. If a shooting war is going to start again, I want it clear that the Quill started it."

"Perfectly clear, sir," Major Blishman said. "Our forces will only fire if fired on first. No war starts with us shooting first."

Colonel Dewey looked at her first line officers and gave a small grin. They understood, she knew it. Now she had to get them some real heavy equipment in case the Quill came back with an armada looking to finish what had started all those years earlier. The forts were powerful; they were the most advanced ever constructed, but maneuverability was not built into them. They were a sitting duck. She knew they needed something that could move and fire at the same time and have just as big a punch as the forts. She needed battleships, and she needed them yesterday.

"Once we're done here, I intend to call on Admiral Gordon Strayker. See if he can sneak a battleship or two back into this sector to help us out," Colonel Dewey informed the others. "One of those beasts should be enough to convince the Quill to rethink their objective."

"One of them should be able to hold them off until the fleet gets here," Major Vorr injected. "A battleship plus the forts and all our fighters should be able to do that."

"Then it's a plan, people. Let's put it in motion," the colonel said as she turned from her majors and moved closer to the big screen. Behind her, the images faded, and she was left on her command deck to her thoughts. She studied the screen some more, hoping to find something that might have been missed, but she knew that nothing was. Her people were thorough. Nothing got by them. She hoped the admiral could help but knew she might be grasping at straws and that Earth might be in its final days.

"What of Major Blishman?" questioned Lieutenant Merkel, walking up to her from behind and keeping his voice low. "Do you think you can trust him much further?"

"Not much of a choice right now. So far, he's done nothing to signal that he's against us. I have to trust him to stay that way," she responded softly.

"You know Admiral Strayker is going to say no. He's loyal to Earth Force. He hasn't once lifted his voice in opposition to the moves going on. He's saluted and said, 'Yes, sir,' while battleship after battleship gets moved out of this sector, and we are left defenseless," the lieutenant explained in a low but agitated voice. He could do little to hide his anger.

"I have to try," she said, turning to face him. Her anger was boiling, and she wasn't able to hold back. "They're out there. Right now. They know our capabilities. They know our defenses. I have to try to change the scenery just enough to catch them by surprise. One battleship should do that. If I can get my hands on two, all the better. But one thing I can't do is to sit here and do nothing. If the Quill attack, thousands more will die."

"It's my job, sir, to point out the obvious as well as the not so clear. All I was doing was my job," he said quietly.

"Sorry, Ethan," she said apologetically. "You are quite right."

"Understood, sir. Anything else?"

"When does Sergeant Russ and Lieutenant Lee land?" she asked in a louder voice.

"The sergeant and the lieutenant land in approximately ten minutes," he informed his superior. "Any orders for them?"

"Yes. Have them report to me here. I have a mission for them."

With that the lieutenant turned and left. Colonel Dewey returned to her studying of the surface of Saturn. She hoped she would find something but knew it would be difficult to find anything. She felt helpless. Moments like these, she missed General Schmidt. The two of them could discuss almost anything, and she would always leave those conversations feeling better than when she had entered into them. General Schmidt was gone now. She was tracking down Karl Cregg somewhere on Earth. She hadn't heard from the general in weeks and had no idea how things were going. She would have to do this alone, and silently, she hoped she was good enough. She called on all her past experiences to help. She had been through a lot in the Service and had seen plenty. Now she needed all her experiences to come together and give Earth a chance.

"Eve," she said aloud. "Admiral Gordon Strayker, please," was all she said. Eve would do her part. She would contact the admiral and let him know that Colonel Ruth Dewey wished to speak with him. All she could do now was wait and see if he would speak to her. She knew her chances were 50-50, but if she didn't try, she had no chance at all, and everything would be even worse.

*****

"What do you hear on the VP pick?" questioned Lieutenant Lee as he and Sergeant Russ sat in the shuttle and tried to pass time on the way to Fort Patton.

"I hear President Hoss has it down to a short list of five senators. His final pick is supposed to be sometime next week. I'm not exactly liking the final five," Sergeant Russ said. "I've heard of most of them, but none of them were on my wish list."

"Are there any that you don't have an objection to? Any that you could live with if they're picked?" he asked, turning his head to face her.

"I don't mind Senator Makumba of South Africa. I don't know all that much about him, but by looking at his record, he stands with President Hoss most of the time. He did object when the battleship *Churchill* was relocated, but that was the only time. Senator Lyedon of Canada is another okay pick. I don't know what it is about her that I like, but there is something there to like," she informed him.

"I'm kind of partial to Senator McVee of England. He's the strong-looking type," Lieutenant Lee said with a laugh. "He just looks like a vice president."

The two laughed together at that remark. Sergeant Russ had never given thought to just looks; she was more of an in-depth person. She checked the past voting record of the senators she liked. She wanted to know where they stood on this war. Did they object at any time to the removal of battleships and fighter squadrons from the battlefront? Looks just never entered her mind.

"Well, if you're going on looks, then you have to look at Senator Chase of Canada. He's a looker. Not too much upstairs, but his looks could win my heart over," she said laughingly.

"If you want brains, then how about Senator Chemsky of Poland? He graduated at the top of his class and has won the Nobel Prize in mathematics. Not much to look at, a bit on the heavy side, and thinning on top, but brains enough for two."

"Oh, I don't know. He's not too overweight, and I heard he can lift over one hundred pounds with one arm. I like men with a little meat on the bones," she informed him as she pointed out the window toward the lights of Fort Patton. They were almost to their destination and began getting ready for docking.

"Fort Patton, this is Lieutenant Lee in the shuttle. We have you on visual."

"Shuttle, this is Fort Patton. We have you on our screens, and you have a clear path to docking. Upon debarking the shuttle, you are to report to Colonel Dewey on the command deck. Docking bay is yours, welcome aboard," came the voice over the speakers.

Sergeant Russ and Lieutenant Lee faced each other and had questioning looks on their faces. Never during all these trips had they been informed that the CO of the fort would see them on the command deck itself. Usually it was in the CO's office. The delicate talks that took place were always best served out of earshot of the regular Service members. On the command deck was out of the ordinary, but if Colonel Dewey wanted to meet them on the command deck, then that is where they would meet her.

"Say again, Fort Patton. Where does Colonel Dewey wish to see us?" Lieutenant Lee radioed.

"Shuttle, Colonel Dewey will meet you both on the command deck per her orders," came the reply.

"Acknowledged, Fort Patton, we will meet with the colonel on her command deck per her orders. Thank you," Lieutenant Lee radioed. Then he turned back to Sergeant Russ and gave her a questioning look. "I've never heard of this happening. Even when I flew fighters, we never met the CO on the command deck. Something must have happened."

"Just a thought, maybe she's too busy to leave the deck, and it just makes more sense to her to meet us there. Could be something simple like a drill," she offered.

"Maybe, but I don't feel comfortable about it," he said. "Something isn't sitting right. Hopefully nothing is wrong, but I suggest we be ready for almost anything."

"We don't have a whole lot of time. We dock in a few minutes. What do you suggest?" she asked.

"Just be ready. Don't make this an ordinary stop. Be on the alert. Take nothing for granted. Be ready to fight our way out. Hope for the best, prepare for the worst. I have no proof that something is wrong, just a feeling," he said as the shuttle came into the shadow of Fort Patton, and they could see the docking bay.

As they entered the bay, they could see the fort was in the middle of something. Service members were scurrying about. Fighters were being readied for flight. Pilots were suited up and jumping into their ships. Maintenance crews were busy servicing both the fighters that were being readied for flight, plus the ones that were going to stay in their berths. Yellow lights were flashing on all walls, indicating a heightened alert but not a red alert. Red lights would mean the war had started up again, but the fact that fighters would launch once they landed was not a good sign. Now they understood why Colonel Dewey had ordered them to meet her on the command deck instead of her office. Something had happened, and she had her fort on alert and preparing for the worse.

Once they docked, and even before they could disembark the shuttle, they heard the sounds of engines coming to life and felt the ship shake as the fighters took off for their destination. When the door to the shuttle opened, they were greeted by an armed guard of two Service members. Other guards could be seen in the rear, near the door that led from the dock to the fort itself. They were heavily armed, and their eyes were constantly moving, checking every little thing.

"Follow us, please," the tall male member said in a deep voice.

"Colonel's order," said the second guard. A female of average height with short blond hair. Her hand rested squarely on her sidearm.

"Anything wrong?" questioned Lieutenant Lee, eyeing the female up and letting his eyes rest on her sidearm.

"Nothing to concern yourselves with. Colonel Dewey felt it prudent to have an armed guard escort you to the command deck. The fort is on yellow alert, and Service members are crowding the hallways. We'll get you there faster than if you tried to go it alone," the male guard informed them.

"This way," his companion said and motioned them to follow them.

As they walked through the halls of the fort, they began to understand the reason for the armed escort. Everyone who was anyone was headed in one direction or another at a hurried pace. Service members were wall to wall and yielded to almost no one. Once the armed escort was sighted, people flattened up against the walls until they passed, then the commotion commenced again. It seemed as if every Service member assigned to the fort was awake and moving someplace at the same time. It seemed amazing that no one got hurt. Yellow lights were flashing on every wall, and Eve was calling everyone to report to their assigned station.

Sergeant Russ and Lieutenant Lee tried to keep their vision straight ahead and follow in the footsteps of their escorts, but once in a while, they failed and something or someone caught their eye, and they fell out of step with their escorts and almost collided with a Service member who had done their best to move aside and allow them to pass. More than once, the escorts had to remind them to keep up and pay attention.

Once on the command deck, the escorts motioned toward Colonel Dewey, who was near the screen, then took a spot near the door and stood guard. Hands resting on their sidearms. Sergeant Russ and Lieutenant Lee continued on alone toward the colonel and observed the command deck personnel involved in their work and acting as if war had started up once again. Orders and counterorders were given, flight paths were changed, then changed again, communications with the other forts in the sector were monitored by no less than four members, yellow lights on all the walls signaled the situation. Colonel Dewey stood alone, Lieutenant Merkel close by, observing the screen and taking everything in. Nothing got by her. She caught sight of them out of the corner of her eye when they had walked onto the command deck, and she motioned them over to her after a second.

"Colonel, with all due respect, what is going on here?" questioned Lieutenant Lee in a somewhat calm voice.

"Eve, replay the recording again," she said and turned to face the screen. Walking forward, she stood near the spot where the object had made its presence known. She pointed to it. "Watch here," she said.

After a brief pause, the small object rose out of the corner of Saturn and sat just above the horizon. It did nothing else for three seconds, then it returned to its original location. Colonel Dewey turned and faced the other two. She took note of their expressions. They were as surprised as anyone else who had seen the video.

"The forts were put on yellow alert, and a squadron of fighters from each was launched. They will fly about, keeping a close eye on Saturn. When their fuel runs low, they will return home, and another squadron will launch which will fly closer to Saturn. Hopefully our little friend there will show itself once again, and we can get a clean shot at it."

"Do you know what it is yet?" asked Sergeant Russ, still looking at the screen.

"Not yet. I doubt we ever will. It did scan us, though. So we can be sure the Quill know everything there is to know about us," she answered calmly.

"Did it get a message off to the Quill home world?" asked the lieutenant.

"We're not sure. For all we know and suspect, a Quill armada is headed this way to finish the job they started all those years ago," she informed them.

"What does Earth know about that thing? Do they have any ideas?" asked the sergeant, pointing at the screen.

"We've sent them the video, but they haven't responded back yet. I'm afraid we're on our own here," she replied, studying their expressions. She saw what she expected to see—nervousness and terror. The thought of this war going hot again brought both nervousness and terror into everybody. If you didn't feel it now, then you were already dead.

"Anything we can do to help, sir?" asked Lieutenant Lee, looking at his unofficial CO with hope in his eyes. He had been retired by Devlin Shaw, but the colonel had brought him back from the dead once already; now he hoped for a second time. He longed to fly a fighter one more time and make a difference in this war.

"You volunteering, Lieutenant?" she asked with a smile on her face.

"Yes, sir. Whatever you need, I'm your man. The sergeant here is capable of carrying on her mission without my help. She is quite capable," he said with pride.

"It won't be in a fighter, just to let you know," she said, moving closer and putting an arm around his back and turning him around. "I need a shuttle pilot for a dangerous mission. Chances are you won't come back alive. You in?" she asked. She spun him one more time so that he faced her. The two stood face-to-face, eye to eye. She was serious about the mission, and he was just as serious about helping.

"I can fly a shuttle," Sergeant Russ spoke up. She stepped forward and stood next to the two. This was her chance to do something for the effort instead of just flying information missions from fort to fort. She needed something different, and in her mind, this was beneath the lieutenant's rank. He was, in the end, a fighter pilot. She flew shuttles. He would be needed elsewhere.

"Not this time, Lindsey. Sorry," the colonel said, looking at her. "I need you for something else. The lieutenant here is retired, as far as Earth Command is concerned. He's a civilian. You're still in the Service. He's expendable, and you're not. If I send you, there'll be a lot of questions and a lot of hell to pay if something were to happen to you. If I send Jason here, nobody will question it. He'll just be another civilian who stole a shuttle and went on a joyride. No one will care back home if he gets himself killed."

The three stood there in silence for a minute. No one on the command deck paid them any attention. They were in a world all their own. The noise of the deck fell behind them, and they had the feeling that they were the only ones left alive. Each looked to the other for support. Each looked to the other for the answer that all three of them knew was coming, yet none of them wanted to say it. Colonel Dewey looked to Lieutenant Lee, who returned her look before moving his eyes to Sergeant Russ. He noted a tear forming in the corner of her eye. He had grown close to her these past few weeks. Closer than either of them should have.

"Colonel, can we have a minute, please?" he asked without looking away from the sergeant.

"I understand," she replied and stepped away to give the two the space she knew they needed.

Sergeant Russ reached for the lieutenant's hand and gripped it tightly. The tear started to roll down her cheek, and her breath became ragged. She shook slightly. Lieutenant Lee returned her grip and reached out and gently touched her tear. He had plans for the two of them, if she was willing, when her Service days were over. He had run it through his head many times. It was getting harder and harder for him to picture his life without her in it. He hadn't meant for this to happen, but he wasn't sorry it did. Now it seemed he would have been better off if he had kept it purely professional.

"I'm sorry," he said softly. "I never meant to get this close to you. I should have kept my distance."

"You weren't the only one getting too close," she whispered. "I'm falling for you in every way, and I don't know how not to."

"Can you forgive me?" he asked, leaning in close.

"Nothing to forgive," she replied. "I was a willing partner even knowing the price that someday might have to be paid."

"I pictured the two of us retired, officially, sitting by some lake watching the sunset, holding hands. If I should somehow live through this, would you care to pick out the lake with me?" he asked, holding back the tears.

"I'll order the chairs. You have no taste in color," she told him while trying to smile.

The two came together and kissed, then gave each other a hug. Both trying their best to hold their emotions in. When they broke apart, Lieutenant Lee turned his attention toward the colonel and wiped a tear from his face. His efforts to hide his emotions had failed, as he knew they would. He held onto the sergeant's hand for a moment longer before finally releasing it. He had to put her behind him for now. He would need all his concentration if he was to come out of this alive.

"I'll fly the shuttle," was all he said.

"Good," Colonel Dewey said, approaching the two. "Seems the two of you have become more than friends, and I'm sorry for this. Lieutenant, your shuttle is being fueled now, so if you'll proceed to the flight deck by the time you get there, it'll be ready to fly, and the deck commander will fill you in on what to do. Sergeant, I have another mission for you, not as dangerous but nonetheless just as important. Come with me," she said, walking away with Sergeant Russ in tow.

Lieutenant Lee watched them walk away before turning and making his way toward the flight deck. As he hurried, he noticed various Service members still scampering about, oblivious to him and everyone else around them. They had their mission, and he had his. They wouldn't inquire about his mission, and he knew better than to ask about theirs. He struggled to get his emotions under control before he entered the flight deck. He had strong feelings for her and to know that he was going on what could be a one-way mission, and she was going on another mission to a destination he didn't know was making him sick. He struggled to get control. He was a Service member. An officer. He knew how he should be, and he fought to be that way. If he was to die today, he wanted her to be proud of him. He sucked it up and stood as tall as he could. He pulled in his stomach in and pushed out his chest as he entered the flight deck. Looking about, he saw the commander and made his way toward him. He pushed everything out his head and concentrated on what would be required of him.

11

Karl Cregg, Kevin Base, Jordan Schmidt, and Amber Jameson sat quietly in the small darkened room. They had been there for several hours now, yet they hadn't seen anyone for almost the same amount of time. At first, they had talked among themselves about anything and everything, but for the better part of two hours now, very little had been said. They were waiting for someone. Whom they didn't know. All they were told was that someone would come and take them to their next destination. Where exactly, and who exactly, they didn't know. It was all top secret, and everyone knew what that meant. They didn't exactly like it at the present time. Karl and Jordan accepted it. Amber understood it. Kevin never liked it. When the two words came up in conversation, he got agitated. He was more agitated now than he could remember ever being.

"Top secret," he muttered to himself. "Lot of bull if you ask me."

"You know how it has to be," Karl said in a low voice. "They have to protect both us and themselves. If word got out that we were here, everyone involved could find themselves in front of a firing squad. We would be hunted down by the Trackers, and no mercy would be shown. Whatever is going on is bigger than anything I've ever seen."

"I know. I just hate those two words. I'm not Service. I'm a civilian. We don't have those words. We have secrets. Not top secrets. We just have secrets. Eventually all of them come out, but in the Service, top secrets almost always stay that way. Hidden from prying ears and eyes. Long after the fact, they're still held as secrets that people, like me, can't know about because someone said we're not intelligent enough to handle them. Lot of bull," Kevin said in disgust.

"People like me most times aren't let in on top secret stuff either," said Jordan Schmidt, looking at him. "I was a general, and still they think I'm not capable of handling top secret information years after the danger has passed. If you think you're disgusted, try being in my shoes for a minute. Think of how I feel about top secret."

"I didn't know," Kevin informed her. "Why wouldn't they tell you? You were one of the top generals during the war. I figured you would be in every communication. Nothing would be hidden from you. Why would they hide things from people with your reputation?"

Jordan Schmidt stood up and moved over closer to him. Standing over him, she peered down at him and smiled. This was how she had felt at times when she was in uniform. Her looking down at her fellow Service members who served beneath her. It gave her a feeling of power. She could reach down and either push them down further or help them attain a higher rank. Most times, she would help.

"I fell out of favor a while back. I told the wrong people that this war wasn't over, and they passed it along to my superiors. It wasn't long after that that Devlin Shaw came into my life and forced retirement on me like he did to Karl. Now I'm on the outside doing the best I can. People on the inside that know me are taking a huge chance by helping me. They're putting their careers and, sometimes, their lives on the line. So when they tell me to wait, I wait. When they tell me they'll be back, I tend to trust them. If you remember, they said it could be a while before someone came to get us," she said while looking him up and down. She felt a little sorry for him. He hadn't asked for this. He was an outsider. He wasn't Service. She felt he didn't deserve this.

"You have to understand, Kevin," Karl said from across the floor. "Top secret is a way of life for us. Without it, things wouldn't turn out the way they are supposed to. Without top secret, this world would be a lot different. Some things have to remain a secret for the better of everyone. If some secrets got out, people would die, governments would be overthrown, chaos would rule. We need top secret. It helps people like Jordan and myself stay sane."

"Kevin, why don't you just sit down and try to have a little patience?' asked Amber. "Here, sit next to me. I won't bite. Promise," she said with a smile and little laugh. She looked toward Karl, and he nodded in agreement. She remembered back to a time, long ago, that he had said those words to her. Right now, she would feel a whole lot better sitting next to him with his hand on top of hers.

"Well, you know what it does for me?" Kevin asked Karl as he stood and looked at him and Jordan. He paid no attention to Amber's offer. "It makes me disgusted. It makes me feel like someone is trying their very best to hide something. It makes me feel angry," he said as he turned and bounced his fist off the wall. He stood there for a second or two, clutching his fist. His face trying to hide the pain.

"These walls are made of steel. They are not designed for someone like you to easily put their fist through," Karl informed him as he made his way closer. "Let me see."

Kevin turned and faced his old friend. He wanted to try to hide his feelings. Hide the pain. Hide the embarrassment, but he couldn't. Blood could be seen seeping through his fingers. Slowly he removed his good hand and held his hurt one up for Karl to see.

"Looks pretty bad from over here," commented Amber as she hurried over to the two men. She could see the blood dripping to the floor and forming small puddles.

"This is bad, Kevin," Karl said in a concerned voice. "Probably not one of the brightest things you've ever done. You need medical help immediately."

Karl tore his shirt off and quickly wrapped it around his friend's hand. Taking his belt, he wrapped it around Kevin's arm to try to stem the flow of blood. Jordan came over and took hold of Kevin's injured hand and raised it over his head.

"Try to keep it up high above the heart. The blood will not move as quickly that way. Don't use it. The less you use it, the better. Does it hurt a lot?" she asked, helping to hold his hand in the air.

"Depends on your definition of a lot. It hurts more now than before I hit the wall. Probably not as much as it will hurt in a short period of time," Kevin informed her. He felt foolish. He had let his anger get the best of him and did what he used to do as a youth. Back then the walls were a lot thinner. He hadn't expected them to be this hard. Looking around, he had made the assumption they were as flimsy as the ones back home. He was wrong.

"We'll have to get him some medical help," Amber told Karl. "No telling, though, how long it will be before that door opens and help comes in. If indeed it is help that opens the door."

"If the wrong person opens it, it won't matter how badly hurt Kevin is," Karl told her. "Why don't you sit down, Kevin. Save some of your energy. Don't need you fainting."

"Maybe we could take turns helping hold his hand up," Jordan suggested.

"Good idea," Karl agreed.

Jordan took her turn first since she was already doing it. Karl walked around the room, trying to figure out what was going on in the outside world. It had been just after sunup when they were escorted into the room and told to wait. It had been hours now, so he figured to himself it was close to, if not past, sunset. Change of shifts had already happened. So where were they? He had figured that once shifts had changed, someone would come and get them. Anticipated what he would say when they came at that time, but it was long past time, and the four were still here. The door still locked from the other side. Now his longtime friend was injured and needing help, and they still weren't coming. His anger began to get the best of him. He looked toward the others and didn't like what he saw.

"What are you thinking, Karl?" Amber asked as she moved over to stand next to him.

"Wondering where they are. They should have been here long ago if I have my time of day correct," he informed her. He looked her in the eyes and saw a touch of fear in them. She was worried also. He looked past her to his friend, who was sitting on the floor with his hand in the air. Kevin was getting worse by the minute.

"How are you feeling, Kevin?" he asked.

"Like the complete fool I am," Kevin informed him with eyes closed tightly. "Do you know what Angela is going to do to me when I get back home? Can you imagine her anger when she sees I've destroyed my hand? She has a temper, you know."

The other three laughed at this. To hear that Kevin was more concerned about what his wife would think of him than to wonder when medical help would get to him was on the funny side. Their laughter filled the room, and even Kevin joined in slightly. Then the pain kicked back in, and he winced. He tried to pull his hand down, but Jordan had a firm grip on it and stayed in an upright position. She patted him gently on the top of his head in an effort to comfort him.

"Try to sit still," Jordan told him gently. "They'll come soon. You'll see. They can't stay away forever."

"Easy for you to say," Kevin said harshly. "You're not the one with a destroyed hand. You're not the one whose wife is going to kill you once you get better."

"Do you have any idea how much longer we'll be here?" questioned Amber of Karl. "I don't mind being in here, but the place is becoming smaller by the second for me. Kevin needs help. People out there are going to die. We're supposed to be the good guys, and we're stuck inside this room with no way out. How much longer do you think?"

Karl looked at her and shook his head. His friend on the floor was becoming hallucinatory. Kevin was getting worse by the second, and it wasn't taking him long. The pain must be enormous, he thought. It had only happened a few minutes ago, and already he was losing it. Karl figured more damage must have been done than they could see. He slowly made his way toward the door. Something had to be done, and it had to be done sooner than later. As he neared the door, he could hear something. Then he saw the knob begin to turn. Light poured in as the door swung open, and a single figure stood on the other side.

"Mr. Cregg, are you okay?" the feminine voice asked. "Colonel Dewey sent me."

"Where has everybody been?" Karl demanded. His anger had grown to places he had never known existed in himself.

"Sorry, sir," she apologized. "I got caught in a small storm of fighters on my way here and ended up a few hours later than anticipated. I have your ride sitting on the launchpad. We have to leave now if we're going to be out of here before the next shift change."

"We have an injured member here," Jordan said in an elevated voice. "He needs attention *now*."

"I'm sorry, General, I don't have any medical personnel with me. All I have is the med kit on the shuttle. We can give him something for the pain, put him to sleep for the trip, but I'm afraid that's all we can do for him for now," she informed them, stepping into the room and seeing the injured man sitting there with his hand in the air.

Jordan Schmidt's face lit up when she saw the Service member who had come to aid them in their escape from this place. Her heart beat a little faster, and a gasp was let go from her mouth. Her eyes took in the sergeant, and a feeling of happiness came over her.

"Lindsey, is that you?" she asked.

"Yes, General. Colonel Dewey sent me. I am sorry I'm late," the sergeant said, moving over to her friend and saluting her.

The former general returned the salute as best she could while still holding Kevin's hand up over his head. She wanted to reach out and hug the sergeant but knew they had little time for formalities like that.

"Help us with Kevin," she instructed the sergeant. The two women took up positions on both sides of the injured man and helped him to his feet. Then they made their way slowly toward the door where Karl stood, making sure no one surprised them

"You're all alone, Sergeant?" he asked once they were out in the hall.

"Yes, sir. Colonel Dewey thought it best that way. Less chance of giving our position away," she informed him.

"We need medical. Did you pass an infirmary on your way down here?"

"Yes, sir. A small one. I'm not sure if it will have what we need for your friend here," she told him, struggling to make her way with Kevin leaning against her. "We must watch our time, though. Shift change will be happening soon, and if we don't get out of here before that, we'll never get out of here."

"We'll stop on the way out. Grab what we can," he told her as he led the way down the hall, prepared for anyone that might come out and attempt to stop them. He was aware of how bad things would be if they were caught, but they needed some medical supplies for Kevin.

"We don't have a lot of time, sir. Shift change is coming up, and we have to be gone by then, or they'll be on to us."

"I said we'll stop there and grab what we can. If that wasn't clear, Sergeant, I can make it clearer for you," he said in an angry voice.

"Perfectly clear, sir. Just trying to get you to grasp the tightness of our schedule," she said apologetically. "If I point it out to you, maybe you could go in, and the three of us can continue to the exit and meet you there. We have maybe twenty minutes before trouble comes looking for us."

"Agreed," Karl said as they continued down the hall and rounded a corner. He could make out the medical facilities sign on the door and motioned them to continue without him. He was in the room before they rounded the next corner, and he was grabbing everything he thought they would need to treat Kevin. A waste basket sat on the floor next to a desk. This he took and emptied onto the chair and began to fill with everything he had taken from the cabinets. His eyes roamed quickly over everything in the cabinets, and he reached out and took what he knew they needed. He knew what they needed most wouldn't be found here, but everything he took would have to do as a substitute. He wasn't in the room more than two minutes when he exited it and continued down the hall in search of his friends.

He found them at the exit to the facility like the sergeant had said. Looking past them, he saw the shuttle sitting there. He was surprised slightly that they had gotten this far without being detected. Surprised that the sergeant had landed the shuttle without being seen. He had helped write the regs on bases like this one, and no one was allowed to fly a shuttle or any other craft in without proper authorization. Where was everyone? The Service Police? Where were they right now? Why weren't they converging on her shuttle? Why wasn't the shuttle shot down when it was approaching?

"We have to hurry," the sergeant implored. "Time is short."

"Where is everyone?" questioned Karl as he made his way out of the building and across the field toward the shuttle.

"On their way as we speak. The night crew is with us. Once shift change happens, then you'll be dealing with Devlin Shaw's men," she told him as she almost dragged Kevin's body next to her with the help of Jordan Schmidt.

"Anybody coming to our aid once we're out of Earth's orbit?" wondered Amber.

"We'll be met by four fighters once we pass Mars. They'll get us to the forts safely. All the pilots are handpicked by Colonel Dewey," she told them as they entered the shuttle.

They set Kevin's unconscious body down on the floor and made him as comfortable as they could. Sergeant Russ quickly made her way to the pilot's chair with Jordan Schmidt close behind. She took her seat where Lieutenant Lee would have sat and strapped herself in. Switches were hit and doors closed. The engines rumbled to life, and the small shuttle began to rise. Karl Cregg sat on the floor next to his friend and held his good hand. Amber stood in back of them and held Kevin's bad hand up in the air. She watched as Karl rummaged through what he had taken and found some liquid painkiller. Releasing Kevin's hand, he grabbed a needle and partially filled it with the liquid and quickly jabbed it into his friend's bad arm. He watched the liquid flow into Kevin's arm, then threw the needle away and took hold of Kevin's good arm again. He hoped he had done enough. Hoped he had used enough of the liquid. Hoped they would make it to the forts before Kevin passed.

"How much time?" questioned Jordan as she turned her attention toward her old friend. She could tell how much Lindsey had changed. No longer was she the young corporal who wouldn't harm a fly and believed in what the Service stood for. Now, now she was different. Standing on her own two feet and prepared to fight for what she believed in.

"Not much," was all Sergeant Russ could say as she moved a lever on her console and the shuttle lurched forward.

"What happened, Lindsey? Why were you late?"

"I didn't respond to the Mars challenge fast enough. They scrambled fighters and stopped me between Mars and Earth. It took time for them to realize that I wasn't a spy. I didn't think…I came as fast as I could after that," the sergeant said as a tear formed in her eye. She had let her friend down. Something she never thought she would live to see. She let General Schmidt down. "Everybody is on alert now. All stations in the system. Not just the forts. Mars is on just as high alert status as the forts. All shipping is being stopped and questioned."

"No need for apologies, Lindsey. You did your best. You followed orders. You got us off of Earth in one piece. I'm proud of you," Jordan Schmidt told her longtime friend. She allowed a smile to come across her face as she reached over and took hold of the sergeant's hand.

"Who is he?" Sergeant Russ asked, nodding toward Kevin.

"His name is Kevin Base. Lifelong friend of Karl. He helped me find Karl," Jordan responded, turning her attention back to the forward windows and watching space go by. She had always liked the thought of being in space. Some of her earliest memories were that of studying space and learning what one had to do in order to survive the elements. Her career, unfortunately, hadn't afforded her the chance of working in the vacuum. This was one of her few trips into it, and she was determined to enjoy the ride, her only regret being the circumstances.

"What happened to him?"

"Smashed his hand against a wall in anger. Should have known they wouldn't be made of plaster. If we can get him to a medical facility fast enough, we should be able to save both him and his hand."

"My fault," Sergeant Russ said in a low voice. "I should have been there sooner. I let you down. I let Karl Cregg down. I let Colonel Dewey down. Now I let Kevin down. And the woman?"

"Amber Jameson. Shipbuilder. Another lifelong friend. She and Karl had something going on long ago, I'm not sure where they stand now. She also assisted in finding Karl's whereabouts" Jordan Schmidt looked quickly over at her friend. She was not to blame. No one was to blame. It happens in war. People get hurt. You can't change that.

No one was to blame for what happened to Kevin. She had to find a way to convince Lindsey of that.

"Ships!" Sergeant Russ suddenly shouted out. "Coming up from Earth. Five fighters headed our way."

"Can we outrun them?" yelled Karl from the rear compartment.

"I'll try," responded Sergeant Russ.

"How long till we're out of their range?" Karl asked as he entered the flight deck.

"Ten minutes. Maybe less," Jordan responded, turning all her attention to the console in front of her. This was her element now. One side against the other. A little war.

"I have a trick or two I can play," informed Sergeant Russ as she touched a spot on the console. A red light came on, and she smiled. "Let's see them follow us now," she said.

"What did you do?" asked Karl.

"Electronic pulse. It will blind their sensors for a few minutes and give us time to evade them. I'm going to switch course a little which should cause them to fly right by us without even seeing us," the sergeant said with a little bit of pride in her voice.

The small shuttle shifted slightly and moved to the portside. The move was so small that no one felt it. They waited silently to see what would happen. The sensor unit on the console showed the fighter gaining rapidly. It also showed them moving off to starboard. They waited a while longer. They could almost hear the sounds of the fighters' engines. It was a dull roar, and they had to strain slightly to hear it. The noise didn't last more than a few seconds. Then all was quiet again.

"By the time they realize that they passed us, we'll be on our way, and they will have to turn back for lack of fuel," Sergeant Russ informed them. "It will take a little time also for their sensor units to come back online."

"How long till Mars?" asked Karl, looking toward his friend on the floor.

"A few hours," Sergeant Russ informed him. She turned to face him and saw him looking at Kevin on the floor. "I'm sorry. It's all my fault."

"You didn't hit the wall, Sergeant," Karl told her. "He has a temper, and this time it got the better of him."

"But if I was on time, he wouldn't have hit the wall," she said.

"Maybe. Maybe he would have gotten so agitated that he would have hit the wall on this shuttle. If he had done that, then for sure his hand would be lost. He hit the wall. Not you. You got us out of there in time and avoided the fighters. If we had gotten caught, they would have put us on trial and shot us. Because of you, we're still here, and there is still hope for Earth," Karl told her. He placed a hand on her shoulder and squeezed it gently. "Nice work," he told her and then returned to his friend.

*****

President Wilbur Hoss was an elderly man in his midseventies. Standing six feet even, he had a small potbelly on him. A wrinkled face and snow-white hair made him stand out in a crowd. Now he was in front of a crowd that looked to him for his pick. He needed to name a replacement for Vice President Cologne from the senators that surrounded him. Two from each country on Earth. He had taken his time in going over all the files and questioning everyone that he thought would make a good VP. He reread the files and did second interviews and finally got it all down to a short list of five. These five sat in front of him now. They separated him from the rest of the Senate.

"The choice was not an easy one to make, to be sure," the president said as he looked out over the Senate. "It was hard, as it should be. I thought on it for days. Slept on it for nights. I lost a lot of sleep. I called on my advisers at all hours of the day and night. Sometimes waking both them and their families up in the middle of the night. I called meetings at two thirty in the morning to go over some of the files. When I finally got it down to a short list that I thought I could live with, I suddenly found myself going backward and adding names to it. My wife—God bless her—thought I was overthinking it, like I tend to do with a lot of things. But I told her I had to get this right. I had to find the right person in case something should happen to me. I had to find someone who shared my views on the planet and the solar system. Someone who could take over seamlessly and carry on without missing a step. Someone everyone would be proud to call Mr. President.

"So it is with great honor and pride that I announce today my pick to take over where Vice President Anthony Cologne suddenly left off. The person who will take up the reins and help lead this planet forward. The person—god forbid—that will take over if something should happen to me. The person that I most trust will lead this planet in my absence. I, today, announce that my pick for vice president of the planet is Senator Hedeckie Tanaka of the great country of Japan."

As President Hoss finished, the Senator from Japan rose to his feet and approached the stage where the president was standing. A roar of cheers rose up from the assembled senators, and each began to get to their feet. The middle-aged senator approached the older president, and the two shook hands and hugged each other. Then they turned and, with joined hands, faced the Senate, and each raised the other's hand over their heads. The cheers from the Senate rose to a fever pitch as they did a small turn so that all the senators could get a glimpse of them.

"Who the hell is Senator Tanaka?" asked Sergeant Russ as she touched the panel in front of her, and the image of the two men vanished and was replaced by the view of the darkness of space. She had heard the announcement might come as they were returning to Fort Pershing. She now turned to Jordan Schmidt and looked at her friend with a puzzled expression on her face. She had never heard of the senator, and he wasn't on Lieutenant Lee's radar as a pick either. Who was this man, and where did he stand on the war?

"Senator Tanaka is well known in his country and most of Asia. He's been in the Senate for the better part of a decade and a half. President Hoss has dealt with him numerous times in the past, and the two get along quite well. They prefer to keep it cordial, but they have talked numerous times, and it never made it outside of the presidential compound. He's a good man," Jordan told her.

Sergeant Russ shrugged her shoulders and turned back to the business at hand. They had passed the moon and would be coming up to the Martian patrol zone. She had no idea what to expect or what to do should the fighters stop them this time. She was afraid for the first time in a long time. She had been lucky the other day; she was by herself and had bluffed her way out of it. Now would be different. She was sure they would be stopped or, worse yet, forced to land and explain who everybody was and what they were doing in this part of space. She needed to concentrate on what was coming and figure out what to do about it.

"What's bothering you, Sergeant?" Jordan asked, noticing her friend had gone quiet and had a puzzled look on her face. She knew the issue of the vice president had been resolved, but she wasn't sure what was bothering Lindsey now.

"The Martian patrol, sir. They are bound to spot us, and I'm not sure how to talk my way out it this time. What do you think we should do?"

"When the patrol hails us, let me handle it," came the voice of Karl Cregg from the small cargo hold behind them. Soon he was standing in the doorway between the cargo hold and the flight deck. "Let me talk to them as soon as they call. I have it planned out. Took care of it a long time ago."

 # 12

"Shuttle to Fort Patton. Shuttle to Fort Patton. How do you read me? Over," called Lieutenant Lee. His voice was steady and strong. He was in the pilot seat of the shuttle on his way to what he considered certain death. In front of him was the planet Saturn. Still far away, yet it still took up most of his view screen.

"Fort Patton to shuttle. This is Fort Patton actual. I read you loud and clear. Over," came the voice of Colonel Dewey over the radio.

"Fort Patton, shuttle, how am I looking? Over," he questioned. He knew he was on course, but he needed to be sure. He needed someone telling him he was on course and headed toward the big ringed planet. He needed someone to give him a little comfort. He was more than a little nervous, but he had trouble picturing someone else flying this trip. He also needed a comforting voice. If he was to die today, he preferred that he was not alone, that someone was with him even if it was only on the radio.

"Shuttle, Fort Patton actual. You are on course, Lieutenant," Colonel Dewey informed him. She stood on the command deck of the fort and looked up at the wall screen to see his shuttle flying the exact course they had agreed on. She looked around the command deck and took note of everyone doing exactly what they were told to do. Everyone had a job. Everyone was working to give the lieutenant the best chance at coming home alive.

"Fort Patton, shuttle," came the lieutenant's voice again. He was sounding a bit more at ease, but the colonel could still hear a trace of nerves even in this short a transmission. "I'm adjusting course now toward the grid coordinates that you gave me. Sensors still show nothing. How do you read? Over."

"Shuttle, we read you on course and show no sign of earlier bogey," the colonel responded. She kept one eye on her console and the other on the wall screen. Her nerves were almost at the breaking point. She hated this part of the job. Sending a member out to do a mission that they had little chance of surviving never really sat good with her. She would much rather have someone in her office ripping them a new hole than doing this.

"How's he looking?" inquired Lieutenant Merkel, coming up to her and taking his place at her right hand.

"So far so good," she replied simply.

"Fighters are in the bays and ready to fly on your orders," he informed her quietly.

"The other forts?"

"All forts report ready. All birds will fly on your word and not before," he said, observing the screen in front of them. He could see the shuttle gradually change course. He looked to the wall screen of Saturn and glared at the spot he remembered the alien showing itself. He held his breath for a moment. His hands formed fists.

"Shuttle, still no sign of the bogey," she radioed. "All clear for next maneuver." She kept her eyes on the two screens in front of her. She watched as the shuttle slowly moved to starboard and slowed down. She waited. Holding her breath. Sweat began to trickle down her face. How she hated this.

"MOVEMENT!" came the call from the rear of the deck. "Bogey headed this way."

"From where?" she demanded.

"Behind us. Coming in slow and steady. Big," responded the male voice.

"Show me on the wall," she ordered, looking at Lieutenant Merkel for a reason as to why and how one of the Quill had gotten behind them and was coming in slow. The lieutenant looked just as confused as she felt.

On the big screen, the tactical vision of the forts in the sector and the shuttle appeared. The shuttle could be seen heading toward Saturn, the forts formed a solid defensive line, then they saw the ship coming toward them. It was big. Just three or four of them put together would be the size of one fort. It moved slow. Slower than a shuttle. She watched its course and tried to picture where it would hit them.

"Fort Washington," she said calmly. "That thing will pass close to Washington. Order Major Vorr to launch everything toward it. I want it intercepted and shot down."

"On it," Lieutenant Merkel said as he made his way quickly to the station that first reported the object. He would give the order from there, and within seconds, fighters would be flying out of Fort Washington's bays and heading toward the ship.

Colonel Dewey watched as the huge ship slowly made its way through space toward the forts. She tried to understand how this was happening. How had the Quill gotten in behind them and was now headed their way? How did none of the forts see them? How had Mars not seen them and notified forts? It made no sense to her. What really made little to no sense to her was why it was flying so slow. The Quill ships, even the monstrous ones, were faster than the fighters. Yet this thing was moving slower than a shuttle. It made no sense to her.

"Fighters on the way," called out Lieutenant Merkel from the reporting station. "Major Vorr reports she is ready to fire all weapons at the incoming bogey. She just needs your order to fire, Colonel."

"Acknowledged," replied the colonel. "Have her hold fire for now. Keep all weapons on alert. She is to fire only on my order. Refresh her on that, Lieutenant. My order only."

She knew the order was being passed on. She didn't have to hear the lieutenant confirm her order. He knew his job. He would do it without even telling her. She needed all of her attention right now focused on two fronts. She watched as the large ship came closer, then watched as the shuttle went through its maneuvers. She watched Saturn to see if it was taking the bait. Her mind went through all the things that could go wrong and all the things that were going right. The wrongs outweighed the rights at this point. She saw the fighters come into view. It would be a few minutes still before they were in range. She turned her attention back to the shuttle.

Lieutenant Lee made another turn. This time to port. He was heading ever closer to the ringed planet. She waited and watched. She wanted desperately to launch everything, but that would give their hand away. She needed to restrain herself. To hold back just a little longer. She would have the upper hand, she hoped. She would have the element of surprise on her side. The Quill would feel the full force of the fighters and the forts soon enough.

"There it is!" came the voice from behind her.

"Evasive!" she yelled into the radio and watched as the shuttle lurched and changed course once, and then twice, and then fired its boosters and tried to get out of range of whatever it was on the other side of Saturn.

The object rose up from Saturn and seemed to float above the planet. It was oblong in shape, much like an egg. The fatter half being higher above the planet than the skinny half. There were no discernible features. The colors of red, yellow, and orange seemed to have been splashed on to it. It didn't move once it reached its elevation. It more than dwarfed one nearby moon. Colonel Dewey stood and stared in disbelief.

"Lieutenant Lee, get your backside out of there," she shouted into the radio. She watched and waited for him to respond in some notion. The radio was silent. The shuttle just kept going in the same direction, making no attempt to evade the intruder. "Lee, get yourself out of there!" she yelled again, getting more agitated. Still the shuttle stayed on course.

"What's he doing out there?" questioned Lieutenant Merkel returning to his station. He also watched the monitor and couldn't believe what was happening. Orders had been given by the commanding officer, and still the shuttle stayed on course. No attempt was made to evade the intruder.

"Launch!" Colonel Dewey called firmly. "All forts launch. Protect that shuttle and shoot that thing down."

Lieutenant Merkel touched the console, and sirens sounded. The lighting turned to red. The fort came to even more life. Within seconds, they could hear and feel the roar of the engines as the fighters left their bays and headed out to assist the shuttle and shoot down the intruder that hovered over the planet's surface. They could hear the smaller motors of the defense grid coming to life and assumed the object was targeted by the computer. The only thing that remained was the order to shoot to be given. Colonel Dewey would do that when she was ready.

On the wall screen, the space around Saturn lit up with the engines of the fighters. They seemed to be everywhere. There was too many to count, and they flew in a pattern that appeared to be orchestrated chaos. One squadron turned its attention toward the shuttle, and the order could be heard over the radio for the shuttle pilot to follow the fighters. Another squadron headed straight toward the object and broke off at the last second without firing a shot. Still another came in from the portside and attempted to engage the object. Yet neither side fired. One side was attempting to get the other side to fire while the other side just sat there and made no move.

"Fighters coming up on the incoming vessel from our rear, Colonel," someone yelled from the rear of the command deck.

The colonel turned her attention from the confrontation in front of her to the one in the rear. It was bad enough the Quill were coming at her from the front, but somehow one of their larger vessels had gotten through and was now approaching from behind her. She needed to hear what was going on out there. She was deaf.

"Patch me through to the rear fighters now!" she yelled at the top of her lungs. Her voice was strong and firm, and no one dared to defy her.

"Vessel in visual," came the male voice over the radio. "This thing is huge. If we have to fire on it, I don't even want to think about what it could do to us if it returned fire."

"Lieutenant, how close do you plan on getting us?" questioned a young excited male voice.

"What happens if it fires first?" asked another.

"When do you think it will launch its fighters?"

"How heavily armed is this thing?"

"Pipe down. Keep the radio clear. No firing unless given the order by the colonel. All units continue to move in closer. Videos on. Record everything," came the female voice.

Colonel Dewey stared at the screen. She could feel for the young fighter pilots. She flew them once or twice early on. She knew the dangers and the fears of being a pilot. She had to let them get in closer. To see what this thing was. See what it was capable of. Could it take out a fort with one shot? The thought was almost more than she could take. She trembled slightly, but only for a second. She had to hold it together for the sake of her command. Her people were the ones out there fighting a two-pronged battle that she had never prepared them for. She had known it could happen—every command officer knows it could happen—but she had failed to plan for it. Now it was here, and she was playing it from the seat of her pants.

"I don't believe it," came the female voice over the radio.

"You're kidding me!"

"Why are they out here?"

"Can't be happening!"

The voices kept coming. Something was wrong. Something no one had ever thought would happen. The disbelief in their voices was evident. Whatever this thing was, no one had thought they would ever see it out here.

"Fort Washington fighter, this is Fort Patton actual. What's going on out there?" she demanded to know.

"Fort Patton actual, this is Lieutenant Christy Gold. You are not going to believe this, sir. I'm putting my video through to you now so you'll have a better understanding what this thing is. Seems we have a luxury liner out here on a cruise."

Colonel Dewey and Lieutenant Merkel watched together as the video came through, showing them a long luxury liner plowing gently through space. The ship was cigar-shaped, over half a mile long, and almost three quarters of a mile high. Windows lined the sides, and people could be seen moving about inside. The ship was red in color with yellow stripes going from front to rear. The two officers stared in disbelief. Space cruises had been halted when war broke out, and no one had given permission for them to start up again.

"Lieutenant Gold, escort that ship back to Mars and hold the captain there until this thing out here is over with. I'll speak to him or her then. Am I clear?" Colonel Dewey shouted in anger. This was all she needed at the present time or any time in the near future. Cruisers out here among the forts with a war getting hot only added to her agitation. She didn't need this kind of trouble.

"Acknowledged, Colonel. Escort the ship to Mars and hold captain for your questioning," the lieutenant repeated.

The video ended, and the command deck turned their attention back to the matter at hand. The object above Saturn had turned color and was now a shiny orange. It had also rotated more than ninety degrees on its axis and was moving toward the shuttle. Service members watched as the top opened slowly, peeling back, to reveal what everyone assumed was a weapon of some sort. It looked like a wide gun barrel. Then a round object was jettisoned out at incredible speed. In awe, they watched as it zipped past the shuttle. Then past the fighters without touching a single one. It went past the forts, and the vibrations from the incredible speed shook them like a small earthquake. Then it went past the fighters that were escorting the cruise liner. They watched in terror as the liner was hit.

They collided head-on. There was no explosion. It was as if two objects had just hit each other at high speed. The front one-third of the liner was obliterated. Debris went off in all directions. The rear two-thirds went backward at a speed exceeding that of its forward velocity. What was left of the liner took out two fighters. The ships and the crew that manned them were destroyed. The loss of life between the two collisions was considered to be enormous.

"All fighters, target that object and fire. Fire at will!" Colonel Dewey yelled out. She turned her attention from the liner to Saturn and watched as the fighters just sat there and did nothing.

"It's gone," one of the pilots reported. Disbelief in his voice.

"Nothing there to fire at, sir," came another. Her voice slow and staggered.

Looking to where the object was just moments before, the colonel failed to see anything. The pilots were right—it was gone. In a flash, it had disappeared. Faded back into the planet. There was nothing there to shoot at. She felt scared for the first time in a long time. Such awesome power and speed to go with it. Earth's chances had just taken a big hit. She stood there and looked at the scene in disbelief. It took her a moment more before she turned her attention back to the cruise liner that was floating helplessly in space.

"Lieutenant Gold, report," she said in a low but firm voice. She was trying desperately to gather her wits together and take control of the disaster, the way the Service had taught her years before.

"It's grim, sir," the lieutenant reported in a shaky voice. "The liner is all but destroyed. The front third or so is gone. There's a huge hole in what used to be the cabin area. The rear two-thirds is still intact. Looks like force fields came on automatically. That at least saved some of the passengers. We got wreckage and bodies floating all over the place out here. We're going to need help gathering everything and everyone up."

"I've got ships and people on the way, Colonel. We can clean this up for you," came the stern male voice. "We've been trained to handle disasters like this. We'll be there in less than half an hour."

"Who am I speaking to?" questioned Colonel Dewey as she looked about her command deck with a questioning look on her face. She was unaware of any ships being in this sector other than the fighters from the forts.

"This is Admiral Gordon Strayker. Sorry I didn't respond to your request sooner, but in my position, I have to be extra careful as to whom I speak to and when. My people will gather all this up, and I'll meet you on your command deck as soon as possible," he said in a flat voice with no emotion.

"Good to hear from you, Admiral," she said, suddenly feeling better about the situation. "I was beginning to worry that you had retired. How many ships are you bringing with you?"

"I have three cruisers and two destroyers with me. It isn't much, but it's all I could get past Earth Force without any questions being asked that I wasn't interested in answering," he said with a slight laugh.

"Glad to have them. Sounds like an entire fleet from where I'm sitting," the colonel responded with a broad smile on her face.

*****

THE QUILL CONSPIRACY

Admiral Gordon Strayker was a tall thin white-haired man in his early sixties, with a full white beard and mustache. When he strolled onto the command deck, everyone stopped what they were doing and came to immediate attention. Here was a Service member that demanded attention even when he simply walked into a room. He wore no awards or medals on his simple uniform, but his mannerism demanded respect. He looked around himself, found the person he was looking for, and headed in her direction. At the same time, he gave a small salute that signaled the crew to return to their duties.

"Admiral Strayker, sir," offered Colonel Dewey as she came to attention and saluted. She knew the regs as well as anyone. When a superior officer comes onto her command deck, she was required to salute and stand at attention and wait for a return salute before continuing.

"Lose the sir, Colonel," he said as he offered a salute and took a place next to the colonel. "It looked bad from where I sat, just how bad is it?"

"Bad, Admiral. We lost two fighters. Not sure how many were on the liner, but the first third of the ship is totally gone. I'm still receiving reports from both my fighters and your ships. Hard to say how many lives were lost," she said, looking at the admiral to gauge his feeling on the events.

"Any idea what that thing was that fired the shot?"

"No, Admiral. We noticed it awhile back and came up with the conclusion that it is of Quill design. We weren't sure until now just what its purpose was."

"Seems pretty clear to me that its purpose is to stop any large ships from straying too close to Saturn. Get too close, it shows up and shoots, then just as quickly disappears," the admiral said while looking at the wall screen and taking notes of where his ships were. He didn't need that thing showing up again and taking shots at his ships. That would only bring questions from Earth about his being out this far, and he didn't need that.

"We did have every intention of shooting it down before it fired, but things escalated quickly, and we didn't have the chance. Perhaps with your help, we'll be able to get another shot at it," Colonel Dewey suggested. She knew she needed help from the fleet, and the admiral was the only one she was sure of that was loyal to Earth Force and not to Devlin Shaw.

Admiral Strayker turned his attention from the screen back to the colonel. He eyed her up from toes to head. Studied her face and body language. In his brain, he ran her record over from the Academy to Fort Patton. He liked to know all he could about the Service officers who served in this sector. He felt it made him a better officer. He had respect for the colonel, but he had never talked to her in person.

"Right now, Colonel, the main objective is to get that cruise liner back to Mars and collect our dead. After that, I'll gladly sit down with you and your officers and see how three cruisers and two destroyers can help destroy that thing out there," he offered with a tone that didn't hint at a real chance of succeeding. "We don't have the firepower we need to take that thing out. From where I'm standing, we need at least four battleships, and they don't exist in this sector of space. Earth Force saw fit to move them elsewhere, and rather than argue with them and find myself in the same situation as General Schmidt, I chose to keep my mouth shut and live to fight another day."

The two officers stood facing each other and remained silent. Both knew the situation was basically hopeless. The Quill had outgunned Earth since the beginning of this war. It was just a matter of blind luck that they had stopped at Saturn and didn't see the need to continue on to Earth. Their ships were bigger, faster, and more powerful. Their weapons far outmatched those of Earth. At times, it seemed like the biggest most powerful Earth ships were like flies to the Quill. Insects that could be flicked out of the way or destroyed with the wave of a hand. Now they had this. A new kind of weapon that appeared to be able to take out a fort with a single shot without the Quill even being nearby.

This object just sat above Saturn and waited. Waited until something big got too close, then rose up and fired a single shot and tore one-third of a ship off and killed hundreds, if not thousands, of people. Then resettled back down and waited until another ship invaded its space and then did the same thing again. How could they fight this? They couldn't get close enough to use their weapons. If they tried to sneak around Saturn, there was no telling what they would find there waiting for them. It could be the entire Quill fleet was lined up there, waiting to launch an all-out offensive to eliminate Earth once and for all, or they could find more of these things sitting there. Help was needed, but Earth Force wasn't seeing the need for it. The war was over as far as they were concerned, and this cruise liner proved that beyond a shadow of a doubt.

As they stood in silence, a man appeared between them. He was only visible from the waist up and wore the bars of a captain. A young man in his late twenties, with blond hair and blue eyes. He looked first to the colonel, then shifted his position so he could view the admiral.

"Sorry to disturb you, Admiral," he said apologetically.

"Go ahead, Captain Stefanson."

"Thought you should know we've been picking up reports from the liner, and things are grimmer than we thought. That shot took out the entire crew. There is no one left over there that can fly that bird. Reports also indicate that more than three thousand passengers were lost. Power is on battery only. She's starting to drift," Captain Stefanson reported. His face had a concerned look on it, and his eyes kept drifting from the admiral to the screen that was in front of him onboard his ship. Behind him, other officers were giving orders out.

"Can you get some towlines on her, Captain?" the admiral asked in a raised voice as he stepped closer to the image of his subordinate.

"We think so, Admiral, but the ship is so big and injured bad enough that it would take at least two of our ships to get her back to Mars," he said before he was handed something by another Service member that made his face contort in anger and pain. "Sir, we may have to take most, if not all, of those people off the liner. Reports show she is losing power faster than originally thought, and she won't make it back to Mars."

Admiral Strayker and Colonel Dewey looked to each other. Both knew how bad the situation had just gotten. There were thousands of people still alive on this liner, and the transfer of them to a ship or a fort would have to be done in the vacuum of space. Each of the five ships out there, plus the five forts in the sector, carried the necessary equipment to move the people, but the operation would take days if not weeks. It would be a slow process, and with the Quill object sitting out there, the risk became even greater. One false move, one misunderstood action, could cause the object to rise up and open fire again, causing an even greater loss of life.

"Get some towlines her to stop the drifting," the admiral said. "Then have the other ships prepare the tunnels. Mount them up to the liner, have security standing by to maintain order and discipline. Get those people off that ship as quickly and safely as possible. Anybody—and I mean anybody—gets out of line, inform them that they will be the last one off of the ship and will spend the next two years in prison on Mars. If they persist, shoot them, then bring them to me without seeing a medic. I will explain their folly to them."

"Understood, Admiral," the captain said before his image faded, and the two officers were once again face-to-face.

"I'm sure it won't come to my people firing on anyone from the liner, but I have to get my meaning clear to those people. In order to get them off as quickly as possible, they *must* follow orders. No pushing, no shoving, and we must keep a watchful eye on our friend out there," Admiral Strayker claimed as he once again turned to face the wall screen.

13

Kevin Base still lay in the rear of the shuttle, unconscious. Amber Marie Jameson and Karl Cregg sat on the floor close by, keeping an eye on him. They had watched him twitch two or three times and heard him mumble once or twice but had failed to see him open his eyes since the shuttle took off. They worried for their friend. It shouldn't have happened, but it was one of those things that was out of anybody's control. It happened; now they had to move on. There was a small pool of blood on the floor from his wound. It was getting bigger by the minute, but it would still be some time before they made Mars, and Mars was the only place with a medical facility that would be able to treat his wound properly. If they had diverted to the moon base, he would possibly have lost his hand altogether. At least on Mars, he stood a good chance of keeping it. His functions would be reduced, that they were sure of, but his hand would still be intact.

"Karl," began Amber Jameson in a low voice. She didn't want the flight crew of Sergeant Russ and Jordan Schmidt to hear her. "What's really going on? Why are we sneaking around like thieves in the night?"

Karl took a moment to think of his response. He wanted to tell her the whole story, but he wasn't sure if he should. He didn't know how she would respond. She was a friend, a lifelong friend, but even friends keep secrets from each other, and he wanted badly to keep this whole thing a secret from her. To keep her as safe as possible until it was all over. He lifted his gaze and looked her in the eyes and knew he couldn't do that. There was something in her eyes that told him she needed to know and needed to know everything now. He began to think that if he held back, kept his secret longer, he would lose her, and that he couldn't do. He needed her. He wanted her to be in his life. He began to speak slowly and tell her everything.

For her part, Amber sat there silently and listened to every word. She never took her eyes off of his and paid close attention. She held her emotions in check, even when she wanted to reach out and punch something to let her anger be known. She felt sorry for both him and Jordan when he told her of how they were retired by the Service after serving for so long. She understood now the need for the two places he had bought. She also gained new respect for both him and Jordan. She knew the war was still going on and that the two of them would play a vital role once more in the defense of Earth. She also knew that she, Amber Marie Jameson, was now involved in that war more than she had ever thought she would be. She never harbored an idea of being in the Service; it didn't fit in with her personality, but she knew she was in it now, and she knew she would help Karl and Jordan out as much as possible.

"What do we do now?" she asked when he finished speaking.

"Now we let you and Kevin off on Mars, and the sergeant and Jordan and myself continue on to the forts to confront the Quill. You and Kevin will be safe on Mars," he said as he looked at her and smiled. "I need to know that you are safe."

"No way!" she said in a loud voice. "I'm in this thing now, and I intend to stay in it. I don't intend to sit back and watch from the sidelines. I'm in it, Karl, and you have to accept it."

"Amber, I need to know that your safe," he pleaded. "I need to know that you are safe," he repeated slowly.

"How much safer can I be than standing at your side? I sat home for years and did nothing but worry for *your* safety. Now you want me to do that again. No WAY! I'm coming with you this time. I'm a big girl now, and I can take care of myself. If I'm at your side, I'll be perfectly safe," she said in an angry tone. She had held back for years; now she was beginning to let go. She wanted to tell him more, to scream at him and hit him. She wanted him to know how she felt, but she found herself holding back. Afraid to go too far and lose him.

"You don't understand—" he began.

"Don't tell me what I understand and don't understand," she interrupted. "I understand that for years, I watched you walk out my door and go back to this war. For years, I cried every night when I didn't hear from you. For years, I wondered if you were dead or alive. Now that I'm in your world, up to my pretty little neck, you want me to go back to where I was because you feel I'll be 'safer' there. Well, my friend, I got news for you—forget it. I'm here and I'm staying. If anything should happen to me, then the only person anyone can blame is me. And that I can live with."

"I don't know if I can live with it," he said softly.

"Well, you're going to have to," she said, smiling. Her voice had suddenly come down from the near yell she was doing to a whisper that could be barely heard.

On the flight deck, Jordan Schmidt and Sergeant Russ couldn't help but overhear the shouting match that had been going on. They sat there, silently, listening to the two of them in the rear yelling at each other. Both understood the reasons Karl and Amber were defending; both understood the arguments being made. The two of them knew it had to be played out this way. There was no other way for this little play to end.

Karl and Amber were in love with each other, had been since childhood. She was tired of waiting for him, and he knew he was at risk of losing her, but now was not the time to make his move. He was a strategist, and he knew timing was everything. The time to move was not now, but he wasn't sure when. The damn war was getting in the way of everything again, and he needed her to be somewhere else for a little while longer. The only problem with that was that she wasn't having it anymore. She was ready for him, and he was just going to have to like it.

"Is it always like this?" wondered Sergeant Russ out loud.

"They've been like this for as long as I've known Karl," responded Jordan. "He doesn't like having her someplace unsafe, and she doesn't like it when he leaves her for months, and sometimes years, at a time. They're made for each other, they're perfect for each other, but neither one will give in to the other."

"You think this time might end differently?" asked Sergeant Russ.

"I truly hope so. I hate to think that I might have to take him on and force him to make a decision he doesn't want to make. Not that I can't take him. I just don't want to think that I might have to," Jordan let out.

Sergeant Russ looked at her questioningly. She wasn't sure what she had just heard. She ran it over in her head, but it still came out the same way. She shook her head to get the words to make sense, but it didn't help. If she had heard Jordan right, then the argument in the back of the shuttle was nothing compared to the fight that could be looming ahead between Karl and Jordan.

"Correct me if I'm wrong," she said in a low voice. "But did you just say that you're going to kick his butt if he doesn't make a move on her soon?"

"Yeah," was all Jordan said in response.

The two women looked at each other in silence. Then they started to smile at the same time. Then their smiles turned into laughter. Jordan was making it plain that Karl had better get his act in gear before she took him on and forced him to take up with Amber. The very thought made the two of them laugh out loud and uncontrollably. At one time, Karl was Jordan's superior; at another time, Jordan had professed her love for Karl. Now she was willing to fight him to get him to get in gear with Amber. The more the two thought about all the angles, the louder they laughed. They laughed so loud they almost missed the challenge.

"Mars security to shuttle, this is your final warning. Please identify yourself," came the voice over the radio.

"Shuttle to Mars security," responded Sergeant Russ as she tried to compose herself. "Sorry about that, we had a small problem onboard that demanded our attention. I'm Sergeant Lindsey Russ. I have four passengers, one of whom is in need of medical attention."

"Shuttle, state the nature of your medical need," came the harsh male voice.

"We have an unconscious passenger who had a mishap that could cause him to almost lose his hand," she stated, trying to avoid telling them just how he came to be in this situation.

"Shuttle, what is your destination?"

"After we leave here, we are continuing on to the forts," she informed them.

"Negative, shuttle," came the voice. Jordan and the sergeant looked at each other in disbelief. Never had a medical emergency been denied landing permission. "Shuttle, you are to turn around now and head back to Earth. This is your only warning."

"Shuttle to Mars security, to whom am I speaking?" came the male voice from the rear of the shuttle.

"This is Corporal Beth Windsmeir. To whom am I speaking?"

"This is Karl Cregg. Is Major Timothy Kasdom still the senior officer there?"

"Major Kasdom is still in charge. Once again, I must insist that you return to Earth. Do not attempt to go any further," she said in a harsher voice than before.

"Negative, Corporal. Put the major on the line," Karl said in an even harsher tone.

"The major has turned in for the night. I'm afraid—"

"Then wake him!" he yelled.

There was a moment of silence, and everybody on the shuttle wondered if the corporal was waking the major or just playing. They looked to one another, and each took turns shrugging their shoulders. Karl Cregg, though, simply stood his ground and clenched his fists. His breathing was heavy. His face had turned a dark shade of red. His anger had hit its boiling point, and he couldn't contain it anymore. He was tired, and the corporal just happened to be in the wrong place at the wrong time. Karl stood there and waited impatiently.

"Shuttle, this is Major Timothy Kasdom. To whom am I speaking, and why am I being disturbed?" came the angry deep voice over the radio. It made everyone in the shuttle sit up straight and take notice.

"Hi, Tim. This is Karl," Karl informed him in an even, smooth tone.

"Prove it," the major demanded, not being taken in by a possible impostor.

"For one thing, your parents weren't too happy with you going into the Service when your little sister wasn't even in high school yet. They needed your help at home, and you ran off and joined the Service. They didn't speak to you until you graduated, and even then, it was only via video. The first time you spoke to them in person after graduation was when your sister graduated from college. That happened in General Jordan Schmidt's office with myself and the general present."

The information was met with another minute of silence. Karl made his way to the flight deck and took up a position behind Jordan. She looked up at him with a questioning look on her face. She failed to remember the incident. For his part, Karl looked down at her and winked. A smile came across his face. He rested a hand on her back and turned his attention to the outside of the shuttle and watched as the fighters came speeding in. Silently he hoped the major remembered.

"That you, Karl?" came the voice over the radio.

"You know it is, Tim," Karl said with a broad smile on his face. He watched the fighters still coming in at them. They were getting closer.

"Shuttle, you are clear to land. The fighters will show you the way," the major informed them. "Come in and be welcome, Karl and company."

They all watched as the fighters got closer, then peeled off and took up positions on either side of the shuttle and acted as an escort to Mars. There was a collective sigh of relief, and smiles soon formed on their faces. Perhaps, each thought, their fortunes were beginning to turn. Up to this point, they hadn't had much to smile about, but now, being welcomed on Mars, they were beginning to feel better. The only down part anyone could think of was that Mars was still under control of Earth Force, and a major loyal to Devlin Shaw was in charge.

"Jordan," Karl said softly. "Can you give Amber and myself a hand in getting Kevin ready. We have to be really careful with that hand. One wrong move, and it won't matter what they do, he'll lose it."

"Sure, Karl," Jordan replied and rose from her seat to take up a place next to their fallen comrade.

Carefully she took hold of his injured arm and moved it so it was laying on his chest. Kevin gave out a low moan, then settled back down into his induced sleep. Sweat had formed on his brow and was forming small puddles on the deck. His mouth moved and took the shape of someone who was in intense pain. He never attempted to open his eyes, but everyone could tell that he was close to it. They just hoped he would remain asleep until they landed. Karl informed them that they should take a place on either side of his legs and that he would take the neck and shoulders. Once they landed, they would wait for the medics, then lift Kevin up and place him on the table.

The momentum of the shuttle suddenly slowed, and they realized they were in Mars. It seemed only a matter of minutes, but in reality, it had been nearly half an hour. They had been so careful in moving Kevin into position that they had lost track of time. The shuttle changed direction and began to descend to the red planet. They could hear the thrusters firing and feel the momentum begin to slow. Looking out the front viewer, they could see the Martian soil being blown in all directions. It wouldn't be long now, and they would be on the surface, and the medics would be entering to take Kevin to their sick bay. Hopefully they could do something for him and save that hand. Unconsciously each of them looked at that hand at different times and took note of how bad it looked and said a silent prayer for his recovery.

They touched down and waited for permission to open the hatch. Once done, the medics scrambled in with the floating bed and rushed over to where Kevin lay. They took his vitals and made grim faces. Karl, Amber, and Jordan took up their positions and lifted him off the deck and gently placed him on the bed and watched as they rushed him off the shuttle and across the landing pad. Soon he was out of sight, and the four of them were left on the shuttle alone.

"Come on out, Karl," the voice called. He was out of sight and made no attempt to come into view of the four remaining people.

The four remaining passengers slowly made their way to the hatch where they stopped and looked around. The hangar was full of armed Service members, who had their weapons trained on the shuttle. There were two rows of them; the front row was down on one knee, while the rear row was standing. They were attired in what could only be called riot gear. They wore helmets and heavy-duty vests designed to absorb the power of any shot. The hum of their weapons could be heard and shook the three to their core. This was not the reception they had expected. Karl let out a low curse and stepped forward, slowly raising his arms.

"Where are you, Tim?" he called out.

"Over here, old friend," came the reply from Karl's right.

Turning his head slowly, Karl looked over and saw the major standing in front of his people. He was dressed in his dress uniform and had the best shine to his boots that Karl had ever seen. The look on his face indicated he wasn't exactly happy to see the four of them. He shook his head slowly and took a step forward. He looked at the deck, then to the ceiling, finally to Karl and his people.

"You shouldn't have come here, Karl," he said flatly. "You were told to go back to Earth. Why didn't you listen?"

"Had an injured man onboard. The nearest help was here," Karl said slowly, taking a step out of the shuttle and turning to face the major.

"Poor excuse, Karl. He could still lose that hand here. We might not be able to help him. Now I'm stuck with him and the four of you. What do you expect me to do about that?"

"I was hoping you could get us to the forts faster than the shuttle. I was also hoping you could save that man's hand. One more thing, I was hoping for a happier reception than the one you're giving us," Karl said, stepping off the shuttle and onto the deck of the landing bay. He placed one hand on each hip and looked his friend in the eye to try to figure him out. He had thought they had an agreement; now he wasn't so sure, but he wanted to give the major the benefit of the doubt.

Amber, Jordan, and Lindsey stepped through the shuttle hatch and took up a position on the deck in back of Karl. They cautiously looked around at the weapons pointed at them. Each of them said what they thought would be their final prayer. The war was now over for them and not in a way they had figured it would end. They had come so far, hoped for so much, and now it would all end on the landing deck of Mars. They stepped forward and stood next to Karl.

If they were to die, then they wanted to be next to the man who had meant so much to each of them.

"You three can step away. This is between Karl and me. You have no stake in this," Major Kasdom said, pointing at the three women.

"We'll stay, if you don't mind," Jordan Schmidt offered as she stepped even closer to Karl. She watched as the other two women took their lead from her and did the same.

"You, Sergeant, are ordered to stand down and move off to the side. You have no business here," the major said, eyeing the sergeant up.

"Can't do that, sir. My allegiance is to the Service, and any order I feel is illegal I will not obey. I stand now with Mr. Cregg, and if I'm to die, I will die by his side," Sergeant Russ called out in a loud firm voice.

"I know where you stand, General Schmidt, but you," he said, pointing at Amber Jameson. "I don't know you. Don't think we've ever met. Who are you so I know what to put on the records?"

"My name is Amber Marie Jameson. I own Jameson Naval Construction. I'm a lifelong friend of Karl Cregg, and I've grown tired of this nonsense. If you're going to kill us, do it now so we don't have to listen to your nonsense any longer. Can't stand long-winded people. If you're going to do it, do it now so the universe can get on with its business," she said in a firm and loud voice. She had found herself taking more than a few steps forward and was now well in front of Karl Cregg.

Major Kasdom suddenly let out a loud laugh. He doubled over and put both hands on his stomach. He laughed long and hard, and when he finished, he stood upright again, and his face was red from the laughter. He pointed at Amber and stared into her face for a few seconds, trying to get his words to form correctly. Amber Jameson stood there and stared back. She wasn't sure if she had done the right thing. Her legs began to tremble slightly. She wanted to step backward but figured it would confirm her fear, so she stood her ground and tried her best to stand tall.

"I like you," the major said out loud. "I haven't laughed like that in a long time. Karl, you must really introduce me to your friend here, and if you're not careful, I'll steal her from you," he said, stepping forward and reaching out a hand for Amber to take hold of.

"I'm not too sure I like you," she said, refusing to take hold of his hand.

"It's okay, Amber," Karl said from behind her. "He's really not that bad a guy, but he does have a lot of explaining to do."

"Had to do it, Karl," Major Kasdom explained. "When we got your message, I was being watched. I had to make it look like I was going to kill all of you once you landed. It was the only way to get rid of the eyes."

"Earth Force?" questioned Jordan Schmidt, stepping forward to shake the hand that Amber Jameson refused.

"General, good to see you again," Major Kasdom said, shaking her hand. "Yes, Earth Force. I was in conference with several senior members. Once they heard who was calling, they got agitated beyond belief, so I explained that I would take care of you. That put them at ease, and they left me to do the job. For the sake of my command crew, I called the platoon here to greet you in full military gear," he said, waving a hand around at the armed members, who were still standing in their initial poses.

"Platoon, dismissed," came the call from somewhere off to the side.

The uniformed Service members came to attention, then saluted the four individuals that had come off the shuttle and filed out of the area. The sound of their boots was almost deafening. When they were gone, the area was almost completely silent. The four who came off of the shuttle and the major stood looking at one another. Amber still refused to shake the major's hand; Karl still stood his ground, not venturing any nearer to Major Kasdom.

"I had to do it, Karl. You know that," he said apologetically.

"I'm sure you did. I'm just not sure I like what just took place. I don't like to have weapons pointed at me and my life threatened," Karl told him.

"You don't know what's going on," Major Kasdom started. "Earth Force is everywhere these days. They check in on me several times a day, without warning. When your call came in, I was in a meeting with them. They wouldn't let me take your call at first. They demanded the message be sent that you go back to Earth. They're waiting for you there as we speak. You don't have a lot of time to get from here to the forts. Even when you get to the forts, you won't be safe. They have Trackers all over the system. They'll find you."

"We have to get to the forts," explained Jordan. "I know people there. We'll be safe, and we can figure out who is behind all this. We can expose them."

"I already know who is behind this," Karl said in an even tone, not taking his eyes off of Major Kasdom. "How long is the trip from here to the forts?" he asked the major.

"Even by Service ship, it'll take several hours. Fighters are faster, but they don't have the range. You might as well forget about the shuttle," Major Kasdom informed them. "I do have a ship here that will get you there, but like I said, it will be several hours. I trust the crew. Handpicked them myself."

"Famous last words," mocked Amber, still staring at him.

"What about Kevin?" inquired Sergeant Russ.

"My people will do their best. If the hand can be saved, they'll make it happen. But he won't be in any condition to travel for several days. I can keep his presence a secret for a short time."

"You're taking a big chance, Tim," Karl told him, finally stepping closer to him.

"No bigger than the one you're taking," the major countered. "I am sorry for the reception, though. Like I said, I had no choice. They won't be expecting to find you out here for several hours now. You have a head start on them, but their ships are faster. The Trackers will be on you like flies on dead meat. I can't help you out there," he said, pointing to the stars.

"I know. I do appreciate the head start. Wish there was time to sit and talk. Catch up on some things. Maybe next time," Karl said, reaching for his hand.

"Maybe next time, we'll meet at your friend's place and share a couple of drinks," Major Kasdom said, signaling to Amber. "I still would like to get to know her better."

"She's taken, I'm afraid," Karl said, nudging Amber gently.

"Too bad. A woman with that kind of fire in her would be good for me. I do hope the lucky man knows just how lucky he truly is," the major said, once again offering his hand to Amber in the hopes that she would finally agree to be friends.

Slowly, hesitantly, Amber brought her hand up and took hold of the major's hand. She gripped it as tight as she could and pulled him closer to herself. She looked him in the eyes and tried to give as mean a look to her face as she could. Her blood began to boil, and she could feel herself losing control.

"I hope never to see you again," she whispered. "I think he's beginning to understand how lucky he is. He does have an island the two of us can go together on after all of this and share a drink or two. Talk about the good old times."

"I would like that," the major said, releasing his grip on her hand. "The cruiser *Houston* is at your disposal. It'll get you to the forts fast enough to evade the Trackers, even in their new ships."

"Major, message coming in from the admiral, sir," called the female voice over the speakers.

"Put it through, Corporal," he said aloud without turning away from Amber.

Soon the image of Admiral Strayker was standing on the deck near to them. In back of him, they could see Colonel Dewey giving orders and Service members scrambling about. On the wall monitor, they could see the remains of a large ship with several Service ships floating nearby. Wreckage could be seen floating freely in space. It appeared as if the war had gone hot.

"Major, there's been an incident with the Quill. Put Mars on alert status and scramble all the ships you can to the forts in this sector. Put your medical unit on standby. They might have to receive several thousand injured civilians. Scramble all your fighters and have them in the air twenty-four hours a day. This war might have just heated up again," the admiral said as he tried to communicate with Major Kasdom and Colonel Dewey at the same time.

"Yes, Admiral," replied the major in a more serious tone than anyone had heard from him so far. "May I ask about the incident, sir?"

"Cruise liner. Seems someone thought it would be a good idea to operate a cruise liner out here, and the Quill shot at it with a new weapon so powerful it took one-third of the ship apart and severely damaged the other two-thirds. Three of my ship are doing rescue operations now, and the other two are trying to secure what's left of the liner. I need whatever you can spare so we can get this done as quickly and safely as possible."

"They're on their way as we speak, sir. Karl Cregg and his people will be aboard the cruiser *Houston*. They were on their way to your position when they made an emergency stop here."

The admiral looked at Karl and his people. A small smile came to his lips. His face lit up just a bit. He also recognized Jordan Schmidt. The thought of these two individuals on their way to the forts lifted his spirits immensely. If anyone could plan a counterattack and have it be successful, these two were the ones to do it.

"Good to see you again, Mr. Cregg. Been too long. See you in person in a few hours. Good to have you aboard. General Schmidt, it will be an honor to work alongside you once again," the admiral said before his image faded, and it was just the five of them again on the deck.

"This is goodbye again, Karl. You know your way to the launch bay from here. I have to get to the command deck as fast as possible. War waits for no one, you know. See you on your island when this is over. Looking forward to that drink, Ms. Jameson," he said as he waved goodbye and sprinted from the bay.

"This way," Karl informed the others, and they set off in a different direction in search of the ship they would take to the forts.

The goodbye was bittersweet for all of them. They were leaving behind Kevin without even knowing how badly he had injured himself. Also staying behind was Major Kasdom. In the final few minutes, they had come to believe that they could trust him. He had given them a head start against the Trackers. The Trackers. They would stop at nothing to get their hands on them, especially on Karl. The war. It had started up again with a new and terrible weapon on the side of the Quill. Knowing they still had allies made them feel just a little bit better about everything. Events were looking up, if only slightly, since their arrival on Mars, and now they were leaving the red planet. They had barely arrived, and they had to leave. The base seemed so peaceful, and a feeling of safety was settling in, but leaving was for the better. Their safety was in going forward to the forts, even though the Quill had raised their head again, and the war had become hot. The forts meant safety, if only from their own kind.

14

Lieutenant Lee stood in Colonel Dewey's office with the colonel and Admiral Strayker. The two senior officers were seated behind the desk, and the lieutenant was standing opposite them explaining what had happened out there by Saturn. He was getting redder in the face by the minute. His anger was getting the best of him. He had reached his breaking point. What had happened out there, combined with the destruction of the cruise liner, had taken its toll. He was tired, hungry, worried about Sergeant Russ, and more than a little agitated. From his point of view, they weren't listening to him.

"I never saw it, sir," he explained for the tenth time. "I was looking for it, but it never showed itself to me. I was following the route that had been laid out when I heard over the radio to take evasive action. I followed the route laid out in the EA and hit the boosters on the shuttle and got my ass out of there as fast as I could. The next thing I knew, there was this huge asteroid flying past and headed toward the forts. It went past them and exploded onto something I had never even seen coming. That is all I know. I swear."

"Lieutenant, that explosion was a cruise liner losing its front one-third," the admiral informed him. "More than five thousand people are presumed dead. We're still trying to get a firm number. The only person out there with a front-row seat on that thing coming up over Saturn was you. The fighters were too far back, and the forts' cameras barely caught sight of it. You are the only one to see it up close and personal."

"Lieutenant Lee, you have to understand, your shuttle was closest to that thing. You had to have seen something. Anything," the colonel began. "All we want to know is what you saw. What you heard. Your route took you up close and personal to Saturn. That thing popped up right in front of you. You couldn't have missed it. It's impossible to believe that you saw nothing. You had a front-row seat to it."

"Sir, I didn't see a thing. I was looking right at Saturn, then I heard a voice telling me to take evasive action, and I moved my back side out of there. The only thing I saw was that boulder flashing past me and hurtling through space. I had no idea where it came from. I had no idea where it was heading. All I knew was I was glad I wasn't in its path. I feel sorry for those poor souls on the liner, but I'm glad it wasn't me nor the Service members onboard the forts and the ships we have out there," he explained.

"That warning came from me," the colonel told him. "Glad to know you heard me. Now tell me what exactly you saw. What did you think? How do you explain the fact that your camera was recording perfectly until that thing popped its head up and fired, then your equipment malfunctioned, and we got nothing from that point on until the boulder crashed into the cruiser? Explain that. Did you turn your camera off for some reason?"

"I saw nothing. How many times do I have to tell you that? I saw *nothing*! I didn't touch my camera. As far as I know, that thing recorded the whole trip. This is the first I'm hearing that something went wrong. If it stopped, I don't know why. It should have kept on working. Check with the techs and see what they have to say about a malfunction," the lieutenant said, getting more agitated by the second. His anger was rising up to the point where he was ready to turn and walk out and never come back. He had nothing to come back to; he had been retired by Devlin Shaw. He was only here on the request of Colonel Dewey, and she was beginning to get on his nerves. He was a civilian in military garb. He didn't answer to them; he answered to himself.

"Settle down, son," said Admiral Strayker softly. "No one here is accusing you of anything. We have questions, and you are supposed to have the answers. Something happened out there today, and we need to get to the bottom of it. The cruise liner is tragic, but we need to know what that thing was—how does it operate, where does it come from, and where does it go? You are the only one who could have seen it, so it makes perfect sense for us to turn to you for answers. Just tell us what you saw. Tell us what you know. Speculate on things, if need be, but we need to know what it is we're up against."

Lieutenant Lee took a deep breath and closed his eyes for a second. When he exhaled, he opened his eyes and took the two of them in. He studied them hard for a second. He wanted to reach across the desk and punch the two in the face, but that would only create more trouble and more questions, and he really didn't want to answer any more questions. He was answering enough already. More would lead to a longer stay in the colonel's office, and he was ready to leave there. He bowed his head and took another breath. When he raised it again, he started his tale from the beginning, just as he had been doing.

He explained to them how he had flown the shuttle out of the fort. How he input the agreed-upon course into the flight computer. He told of sitting back and trying to relax for the next few minutes while the shuttle got closer and closer to its goal. He heard the computer alert him to Saturn proximity. He told them of his next step in getting ready to make a flyby. Told of saying his final prayers and goodbyes to loved ones and friends, both old and new. How he suddenly heard the evasive action alert over the radio. How he took that action just in time to see what he thought was an asteroid zooming past and heading toward the forts. Lastly he told them, again, of seeing the asteroid missing the fighters and the forts and colliding with the cruise liner. When he was done telling his story again, he stood there silently and let his head drop down to hide his eyes. He didn't want them to see his emotions on his face.

Colonel Dewey and Admiral Strayker sat there in silence and took it all in. When the lieutenant had finished his tale, they looked at him for a minute, as if they were trying to figure out if he was lying or not. Then they turned to each other. It was a tale that was hard to believe. A front-row seat to the incident, and he saw nothing. Silently they wondered if he was either lying or if he had blacked out. He was a fighter pilot, though retired, so blacking out didn't seem possible. Colonel Dewey had vetted him thoroughly, so lying didn't seem to fit either. Admiral Strayker had a third idea. He leaned over and whispered in Colonel Dewey's ear. It was far-fetched, but he felt it did fit the facts.

"A new Quill weapon could be at play here, Colonel," he said softly with his right hand blocking his mouth. "They could have used something to wipe his short-term memory clear. Make it look like he blacked out when in fact he saw something."

"Could be," Colonel Dewey whispered back. "Do we have any way of verifying this option?"

"No. It's just a thought that happens to fit. He's a fighter pilot, blacking out doesn't fit. You vouched for him, so lying doesn't fit. A memory wipe does fit. We're not sure what kind of weapons the Quill possess. This could turn out to be one of them, and if it is, it could be a dangerous one."

"I agree," she whispered while looking at the lieutenant. "Do we risk keeping him active? Do we send him back to the shuttle to try again, or do we stand him down?"

"I think we're done with trying to lure that thing out into the open. We've seen the damage it can do, and I prefer not to see it again. What we need is more firepower, and we're going to need every pilot we got, including the lieutenant here. We send him back out to fight again and keep an extra eye on him," the admiral said before sitting upright again and taking the lieutenant in. He looked him up and down once, then informed him of his plan, leaving out the part where they keep an eye on him.

"Then you believe me when I say that I saw nothing?" Lieutenant Lee inquired.

"To a point," Colonel Dewey replied. "It is possible that you saw something, but the Quill wiped your short-term memory. We can't be sure, but we are prepared to put you back on the line in a fighter. Hopefully the effects of their wipe are short term and have no side effects. You are dismissed, Lieutenant. Report to the launch bay for further orders."

"Thank you, sirs," he said and threw a salute, then turned and left them.

The two sat there for a moment after he left. Neither felt great about what had just happened. Both had reservations about putting him in a fighter again. Both agreed that extra precautions would have to be taken with him. For now, though, he was an experienced body, and they needed as many of them as they could get their hands on.

"What about the extra firepower?" asked Colonel Dewey after a few minutes.

"I am going to ask Major Kasdom to send whatever he can out here. Hopefully it will be enough," Admiral Strayker informed her.

"If not?"

"Then we won't have to worry about Lieutenant Lee or anything else."

"Lieutenant Merkel," called out Colonel Dewey. "How are the rescue efforts proceeding? How much longer do we need?"

"Slowly, Colonel," came the voice of Lieutenant Merkel over the speakers. "We've managed to remove more or less than a thousand people from the liner, and we're being told there were as many as twelve thousand onboard, not counting the crew. Most of the exit areas have been heavily damaged. We're having to cut through the hull. Recovery has reported more than a thousand souls have been recovered. Sensors show no indication of our friend out there making another move."

"Thank you, Lieutenant. Carry on," she called out.

"Eve, please connect me to Major Timothy Kasdom on Mars," Admiral Strayker called out.

The two waited for some time before the image of the major appeared before them. Admiral Strayker explained to the major the severity of the situation and that he needed every ship that Mars had to both defend the forts and assist in the recovery. He managed to hold his joy in check when he saw the figures of both Karl Cregg and Jordan Schmidt standing with the major. His feelings of despair suddenly vanished, and hope came into his eyes. When he finished with the major, he dismissed him and watched as the image of the major faded, and the two were left alone again in the room. They felt somewhat better about their situation, but the fact that Earth Force was sending ships to meet Karl Cregg and escort him back to Earth was unsettling. They needed Karl here to help them fight the Quill. They both knew they stood a better chance with Karl than without him. The war was still going on; it wasn't over, and Karl Cregg was the best person anyone could think of to formulate a plan of attack. The fact that General Schmidt was with him was all the better for them. They felt better, but there was still the matter of Lieutenant Lee. Was it a new Quill weapon, and if so, how long did the effects of that weapon last? Could they count on Lieutenant Lee in a battle?

*****

Captain Jason Stefanson was a middle-aged graying man who towered over the rest of the crew. He now stood near the tunnel that had been erected from his ship to the liner and was monitoring the progress of removing passengers from the crippled liner. He watched as one after another of the passengers moved past him. Slowly he shook his head in the negative. His face was set in a frown. He was flanked by security guards armed with the latest weapons. They were there as a precaution. Captain Stefanson knew, or at least hoped, no one would get so far out of line that it became necessary to hurt them and then have them dragged to see the admiral. The problem he faced now that was making him grim was the slowness of the operation. The passengers were coming off the liner but slower than he had originally thought they should.

"It's going slow, Captain," a young corporal informed him as he left the tunnel. "They're lined up on the liner okay, but the hole we had to cut through the hull really slows things down. It's too small."

"If we stop the evacuation to open the hole up, it'll take longer. To open that hole enough for two to pass would take another five hours, and we just don't have that kind of time," the captain explained.

"Going like this, it's going to take at least four days, sir," the corporal protested. "Can't we do anything to speed the process?"

"Already working on that idea," Captain Stefanson explained as he watched a passenger go past with his head bandaged. Again he shook his head, then turned his attention for a brief second to the floor. "I have engineering working on another tunnel further up the hull. We're going to use explosives to open up a bigger hole. That should ease the pressure here."

"Sir, explosives could blow that hull apart. She's barely holding together now," protested the corporal in a raised voice.

"A small controlled blast should do the job. I'm having another tunnel flown in from the forts to be used in that location. That will give us seven total. Combined with the other ships, we'll have twenty-five tunnels operational. We should be able to get everyone off within thirty-four hours," said the captain in a matter-of-fact voice. He looked toward the corporal to make sure he was getting his message across. Speed was imperative.

"What if the hull gives, sir? What then?"

"My decision, Corporal. We need that hole, or the whole mission is in jeopardy. I need you to go back onboard and make sure that no passengers are in that area. I hope to have the hole blown in two hours. You have that much time to clear whoever is there. Take whoever you think you may need to do that. Am I clear?" the captain said, staring down the corporal.

"Crystal clear, sir," the corporal told him. "I'll grab a few people on the liner, and we'll head in that direction. We should have it checked out within the hour. I'll report back when we're done," he said as he saluted and turned and re-entered the liner. He wasn't happy with the decision, but he had been trained to follow orders, and he had just been given one. He was proud of himself for having argued the point, even though he had known from the beginning he was going to lose.

After the corporal left, Captain Stefanson stood there watching more passengers coming through the tunnel. Silently he cursed the initial efforts that his crew had done in opening holes in the hull of the liner. They had done their best at the time, but their best was beginning to look woeful. The holes on several of the openings were way too small. For one person to fit through was proving to be a chore of almost impossible proportions. One had to bend down, lift one leg and place it through to the other side, then force their heads through without serious injury, then try to lift and bring their other leg through. For the young, it was almost a game, but for the elderly, it was nearly impossible without assistance. Three of the openings were of the correct size, but even those were proving to provide their own problems. True, they were unloading faster at those points, but still the operation was moving slower than the captain liked, and he knew the admiral would be infuriated. He said a prayer that the explosive would prove much better than the cutting.

He watched as a middle-aged woman with two small children came out of the tunnel and lost her footing. She tumbled to the ground and opened up some wounds that she had received in the initial attack. Blood slowly flowed from her left arm and spilled onto the deck. He quickly bent down and assisted her to her feet and assured her children that she would be taken care of and would make a full recovery before they returned to Earth. He pointed the way to the infirmary and watched as she walked away, trying to wrap both children into her good arm.

"Damn war," he said under his breath. "Make sure she gets to the doctor and is taken care of as quickly as possible," he ordered one of the security guards who hastily followed the woman down the hall. "This day is going to go on forever," he said out loud to the other guard. He didn't expect an answer or comment but felt it necessary to say what he had said.

"Are you the man in charge here?" came the female voice from the tunnel. She was young, maybe in her early twenties, and fancily dressed. Her face was made up with heavy makeup, and her hair didn't move as she rushed out of the tunnel toward the captain.

"Captain Stefanson, and you are?" he asked, turning to face her.

"Allison Lisa Morrisonn, with two *n*s. I want to lodge a protest over the handling of this event. Whoever is in charge—that would be you—should be thrown out of the Service and replaced with someone more competent. This whole thing is embarrassing," she said, coming to a stop right in front of the captain. She looked up into his face and tried her best to scare him.

"Ms. Morrisonn, I assure you we are doing the best we can under these circumstances. Your cooperation would make the whole thing go more smoothly, so I suggest you move along and allow the others to keep moving."

She eyed him up and down and took a deep breath. Pushing her chest out, she readied herself for her next assault on him. She didn't take kindly to him dismissing her so quickly. She was used to people dropping what they were in the middle of and doing her bidding. The fact that he barely acknowledged her presence infuriated her.

"Do you know who I am? Do you know who my family is? The damages we can bring to you and the Service? Now I suggest you do something to make this thing better and more civil for the rest of us," she screamed into his face.

"Ms. Morrisonn, I really don't care who your family is nor do I care what they can do. Right now, my duty is to empty that ship as fast as I can, and you are standing in the way of that chore. Now move along before I have security move you," he said, looking down at her.

"Captain, my family and I are not used to being talked to that way. We can make life miserable for you and yours. My luggage was left back there, along with everything else I brought on this trip. I expect you to send someone back for everything I own. I expect you to make a private room available to me. I expect to be treated in the way I am accustomed to. When we get to the forts, I expect a ship to be ready to take me back to Earth so I can be reunited with my family," she said, doing her best to get into his face.

"If you don't move your backside out of the way in the next five seconds, you will have your own cell to live in along with a ship to take you back to Mars, where you will be held in detention until this whole thing is over, and then prosecuted to the fullest extent of the law for hindering a rescue mission in space. In case you're not aware of the penalty for that, it is fifteen years in the Mars penal system with no chance of early release. Now *move along*," he said, lowering his head so that he was eye to eye with the young woman.

"You don't have to get huffy," she said, stepping away from him and moving down the hall. When she was ten feet away from him, she turned and looked back. "Captain, my parents will be made aware of how awful you treated me, and they won't be happy. You'll be lucky to get a job scrubbing decks on a garbage ship after this," she called, then turned and continued down the hall.

"Corporal," he said, looking toward the tunnel and watching the people slowly walk out, some hurt, some not. "Get in touch with your superior and tell her to keep an eye on that woman. If she gives anybody—and I mean anybody—trouble, she has my permission to lock her up and throw away the key. If that woman so much as sneezes the wrong way, I want her to spend the rest of her time here behind bars. Am I clear?"

"Perfectly clear, sir," the corporal responded before stepping away for a second and contacting his superior officer. After he relayed the message, he returned to his place and smiled at the captain.

"What did she say?" Captain Stefanson asked.

"She wanted to know if she could do that with the rest of the passengers. Some of them are getting a little testy. Trying to push themselves around and demanding to be taken back to Earth immediately," the corporal informed him.

"You tell her whatever makes her life easier, she has my permission to do it," Captain Stefanson said before walking away. He laughed out loud as he stepped down the hall, and the corporal relayed his message.

*****

Admiral Strayker and Colonel Dewey were standing on the command deck of Fort Patton while keeping an eye on their new friend behind Saturn and awaiting the arrival of Karl Cregg and his people. Karl would be landing at any minute, while their friend hadn't made a move since it attacked the cruise liner that was now crippled in space. The Service fleet was removing the passengers as quickly as possible, but circumstances were preventing that. Both knew that Captain Stefanson was working on an idea which could quicken the exodus, but neither was sure when this plan would be put into place.

"Explosion on the liner!" came the call from the rear of the deck.

"How bad?" questioned the admiral.

"Small. Barely noticeable but definitely there," came the response.

"Captain Stefanson said he wouldn't be doing anything huge," the admiral said to Colonel Dewey. "Could be he decided to blow a hole in another wall to speed things up."

"Any movement from our friend out there?" called out Colonel Dewey.

"Nothing, sir," came the response from the rear.

"Eve, get me Captain Stefanson," ordered Admiral Strayker as he stepped forward to study the wall screen more intently. His eyes were focused on that one corner of Saturn that the object had risen form earlier. Silently he prayed that the object hadn't detected the explosion.

"You wanted to see me, Admiral?" came the voice from behind the admiral.

Turning, the admiral noticed Captain Stefanson's image next to Colonel Dewcy. The captain had that look that indicated he was having some kind of problem onboard his ship. Behind him could be seen his command crew scrambling to solve a problem. Orders were being barked out, and security guards stood near the doorway to the command deck.

"Everything okay over there, Jason?" Admiral Strayker asked.

"Just some passengers demanding to be taken to Earth immediately. Security is rounding them up now and locking them up. They'll be let loose in due time, Admiral," he responded.

"Need any extra help?" wondered Colonel Dewey out loud.

"Not at this time, sir. Thank you for the offer," he answered.

"Jason, we just monitored a small explosion on the liner. Is this related to your efforts to quicken the operation?" asked the admiral, stepping back toward Colonel Dewey.

"Yes, sir. We blew a hole in the hull big enough to allow almost two people to pass through at the same time. We're setting up another tunnel and are directing the passengers to it at this time. We figure this will cut the time from a few days to almost a day and a half. We could be done here by tomorrow, sir," Captain Stefanson said, flashing a small smile.

"What about the other rescue ships? Have you alerted them to this operation?" wondered the admiral.

"We kept them in the loop the whole time, sir. We have passed this on to them. You can expect a few more explosions in the upcoming hours. Nothing huge. Our calculations for emptying the cruiser are based on the others doing the same thing," the captain explained.

"Good work, Captain," said the admiral with a sound of pride in his voice. "Carry on. Keep me appraised of the situation, and don't hesitate to ask for additional help, including with security."

"Thank you, sir. I'll be speaking to you again soon," the captain said as his image faded, and the admiral and colonel were left standing there.

"A day and a half with that thing out there looking over our shoulders is still a long time," Colonel Dewey whispered to the admiral.

"I know," he responded slowly. "Nothing more we can do. Right now, a day and a half is better than four or five days. We just have to keep an eye on that thing and hope we can empty that ship faster than anticipated and get it out of here before our friend out there decides he's seen enough and starts taking shots at us."

15

"Karl Cregg is now onboard," the female voice informed them. She wasn't in the room; her voice had come over the speakers. It was a soothing voice, yet it held a quality of authority in it. The four men who were in the room sat up and took notice when they heard her voice. Each was middle-aged, muscular, and, if stood up, was over six feet. After that, they differed vastly, yet each had one thing in common: they were Trackers. The best of the best. They were each assigned the task of bringing Karl Cregg back home to Earth, along with whoever got in their way, or kill him wherever he stood. None of them cared how the job got done, but each was determined make sure it got done.

"Where is he now?" asked one.

"What room has he been assigned to?" questioned another.

"How many bodyguards?" another wanted to know.

"What kind of sidearm is he carrying?" asked the last.

"Easy, boys," came the voice again in a flirty manner. "All in due time. We have to let him get settled in some before we make our move. He's not going anywhere in the near future. He's here for the foreseeable future. He has to reconnect with Colonel Dewey and Admiral Strayker. Then he has to tour the flight deck. Then get briefed on the rescue mission. Thanks to the Quill, he'll be here even longer than originally thought. When the time is right, we'll make our move. Nobody does anything before that. You are to make like passengers from the liner and blend in with them. I'll keep you informed as to when and where we make our move."

"Are we each going to take a shot at him or is only one going to do the job?" one of them wanted to know.

"We operate as a unit. We'll do everything together. The four of you are lifelong friends who were out taking a cruise. There was no particular reason for the cruise other than to tell tall tales of your childhood. No one moves against Cregg on his own. Am I clear, gentlemen?" she asked in a harsh tone. She was in charge, and there was no arguing that fact.

"Clear," the one called out. He looked around at his friends, and each of them shook their head in agreement.

"Good. Now you are to leave this room and go down the hall to your left. At the first junction, turn right and proceed to the next junction. There you will find a Service member who'll take care of your every need. Tell him Olivia sent you. He'll understand and set you up with new quarters. Wait there until I get in touch. No one leaves that room for any reason. I hope I made my meaning clear. Remember, Trackers seldom hunt with just one team. Other teams are here for the same mission, and if one of you disobeys, it would be really unfortunate for the team to have to be removed from the field," she finished saying.

The four men sat there for a minute to take her meaning in. Then they rose and left the room. As they walked down the hall, they imitated the wounded that were walking alongside them. Men, women, and children that had been brought aboard from the wounded liner, that were still able to walk about, though slower than normal. They did their best to fit in, to blend in so no one could tell they hadn't come from the liner. They followed her orders exactly and came across a young private. He was guarding the junction, making sure nobody got lost and entered a restricted zone. He saw them approaching and knew instantly who they were and why they were here. He ignored all others who were in the hall and turned his complete attention to the oncoming men. He smiled broadly at them as they approached.

"Olivia sent us," one of them said, reaching out a hand.

"How is she doing today?" the private inquired as he shook the one man's hand.

"She sounds in good spirits," one of the others said. "She told us you could assist us. We're new here."

"Olivia is always ready to help those in need," he told them as he motioned down the hall. "Follow these people here. About half a mile down, you'll see room number 702. That room has been assigned to the four of you. Please stay there. Don't roam about. This fort is huge, and it is easy to get lost in it. Someone will come and escort you to the mess hall when it's dinnertime. Please enjoy your stay here," he said as he motioned for the men to continue down the hall.

The four men stumbled down the hall slightly, faking injuries for the sake of fitting in. One leaned against his companion and walked with a limp. Another folded his arm across his stomach and partially closed his left eye. The four of them blended in and avoided the occasional security guard. Every now and then, they would bump into another passenger who was nursing injuries, and they would be sure to put a hand in a small pool of blood and then wipe it on their own clothing. By the time they stood in front of their assigned room, their clothes were more than half covered in someone else's blood, and no one paid them any attention. Slowly they stumbled into their room, the door closing automatically behind them. Then the charade ended, and they began to act normal again.

The room was sparsely furnished: a small desk against the far wall, two bunk beds, one on each wall, and a small chair. The wall by the desk held two small windows from which they could look out into the darkness of space. They didn't afford a view of the other forts in this sector, but they could see the fighters patrolling the area and the crippled liner that was still being unloaded. A door led to a modest bathroom with a shower.

"Not much to look at," one of them commented.

"Remember, you're on a military base. Comfort is secondary," his one companion explained to him as he climbed into one of the top bunks. "We should get some rest, could be the last time we have a chance to do so."

"I'm still not sold on this idea of taking Cregg on a military fort in space," one of the others told his companions. "Could end up bad for all of us."

"This is where he fled to, so this is where we'll have to take him. If we do it right, do what we're told, don't improvise, everything will be fine," explained the man who had climbed into the top bunk. He lay on his back, his eyes closed.

"I'll do my part. I just hope whoever is pulling the ropes decides to do their part," the last man said as he climbed into the bottom bunk and lay back and closed his eyes. "I don't need any surprises. Don't need the one in charge suddenly changing their mind and leaving us as collateral damage. Got a lot to live for yet."

"You worry too much," came the feminine voice, seemingly out of nowhere. "I have everything taken care of. All you have to do is your job. Do what you're told, when you're told, and don't think for yourselves too much, and everything will go down as we planned."

The four men shot up in bed and looked around themselves, searching for the owner of the voice, but she was nowhere to be found. They were in the room all by themselves, and she was somewhere else. They were even more nervous than before. If they could be in one room, and she in another, knowing what they were talking about, then they had best be on their best behavior and make sure they didn't screw up. Too much was riding on this mission, and now there was an unknown person watching and listening to their every move and word. There was no room left for free thinking.

"Just who are you, lady?" the one in the top bunk blurted out.

"Never you mind. Just remember this—I know everything you do and say. If I think, for one second, that you are about to go rogue, I will contact another Tracker team, and you will not make it off this fort alive. None of you," she told them in a harsh tone. "I run this outfit, not any one of you. If you want your reward, you will do as I tell you."

"What if something should go wrong?" questioned one of the others.

"Nothing will go wrong as long as you do what you're told, when you're told. Now get some rest. Dinner will be served 1700 hours. They will come and escort you to the mess hall. Act like you did when you entered the fort, and there should be no problem. I will contact you again when I see that you have returned to your room."

The voice faded and was gone. The four men sat in their bunks, looking more confused than when they first arrived. She was pulling the strings, and they had no choice but to go along with her. It didn't sit well with the man in the top bunk. He was used to being in charge. He never liked being told what to do, even when he was a boy. Now he just lay back and gave a huff. He pounded the wall with his left hand, and it echoed throughout the room. A small dent was left where his hand had met the wall. He gave it a quick look and grunted at it.

"Settle down and get some rest," he told the others in his best authoritarian voice.

*****

Karl Cregg, Jordan Schmidt, Amber Jameson, and Sergeant Lindsey Russ walked out onto the command deck searching for Admiral Strayker and Colonel Dewey. It didn't take them long to locate them and head in their direction. They were standing near the large screen overseeing the rescue operation while, at the same time, keeping an eye on their newfound friend behind Saturn. They could hear orders being given, countered, and more orders given as they approached. Looking to the screen, they could see the situation out there wasn't good. The liner still was drifting, even though four ships had towlines and tunnels attached. Bodies could still be seen floating in space. A small explosion took place aboard the liner that made all the ships involved with the rescue lurch slightly.

"Admiral Strayker, good to see you again," Karl said as he walked hurriedly up to the admiral and colonel. "Colonel Dewey, always nice to see you," he said as he shook the hands of both of them.

"Karl, nice to have you onboard at last," the admiral said in a loud voice.

"Karl, good to see you," the colonel explained. "General Schmidt, it's been a long time, sir."

"Jordan, please. I was retired, remember?" Jordan Schmidt said, reaching for the colonel's hand.

As the two women shook hands, the colonel's eye took in the other people in Karl Cregg's party. The sergeant stood out more than Amber Jameson, who stood close to Karl for comfort. She wasn't used to the military protocol. She preferred to stay in the background and get to know people better before stepping to the front. That was what she had done as a child to get Karl Cregg's attention. It had always served her best.

"I'm Amber Jameson, a friend of Karl," she suddenly said and stepped forward, reaching out for a hand to shake. The admiral was the first to shake her hand and nod his head in acknowledging that she was there and that she was a friend of Karl Cregg. He had no idea of how close the two of them really were.

"A pleasure in such horrific times," he told her, flashing a small smile.

"Thank you, Admiral," she said and slowly slipped back to Karl's side.

"Ms. Jameson here is responsible for building some of the most advanced ships in the fleet," Karl informed them. "She is the owner of Jameson Naval Construction. You'll see that name on many of our ships. You have her to thank for our past success against the Quill, and our successes yet to come, and yes, we will be victorious."

"I've heard of you," Colonel Dewey told her as she turned her attention to the woman who was now trying hard to get as close as possible to Karl. "Karl has mentioned you a couple of times. Best shipbuilder on the planet. Learned it all from your father, then improved it. We might be able to use a person of your knowledge."

"I used to fly your father's ships when I was younger," Admiral Strayker told her. "Easy as anything to fly. Handled like a bird. Best thing to ever happen to the fleet. Nice to have you aboard."

"Thank you. Both of you," Amber said, suddenly holding her head higher with pride. "Glad to be able to help."

"Now that the niceties are over, we can get down to business," Karl said with a measure of authority. "What's the whole story on this thing out there? Where did it come from? What do we know it can do? What makes it move?"

"We don't know much, Karl," Colonel Dewey began. "We tried to draw it out into the open, but it ignored us and fired on the liner. By the time we got it into our sights, it had settled back down near Saturn, and we don't have a clear sight range to fire on it."

"I got several ships headed here from Mars, but they won't be here for several hours yet. Right now, we're using fighters to protect the liner while we unload the passengers. That also will take more time than we have," Admiral Strayker informed Karl.

"Who authorized the liner to come out here? This area has been off-limits since the war began. Why would anyone give a cruise liner permission to fly out this way?" wondered Jordan Schmidt out loud.

"Good question for another time," Karl informed her. "Right now, we have to figure a way to unload that thing faster while, at the same time, not antagonizing our friend out there."

"What if we distract it somehow?" asked Sergeant Russ. "Divert its attention from the liner to something else."

"You got anything in mind?" inquired Colonel Dewey. "We tried a shuttle. It just ignored it and went after the liner."

"Distracting it is only one part of the problem. Once we have its attention drawn away, how do we speed up the unloading? For that, we're going to need more ships," Admiral Strayker said while shaking his head.

"How soon will your ships be here?" asked Karl.

"Like I said, several more hours," the admiral told him. "Even with those ships, it could take another day to unload that hulk."

"Maybe, but they might solve all our problems at once," Karl said as he stepped away from the others and approached the wall screen. "If we divert its attention from the liner, then send the additional ships off in the opposite direction, have all guns on the ships locked onto it, all weapons from the forts aimed at it, all fighter squadrons standing by, we just might be able to take it out."

"But what do we have that is big enough to make a distraction?" asked Amber Jameson to no one in particular. She stood just behind Karl and moved slightly out of his shadow after asking her question.

"The *Zhukov* will be behind the other ships coming from Mars. They were being resupplied, so they left an hour or so later. She's big enough to get that thing's attention. But like I said, she will be later than the others," Admiral Strayker said almost apologetically.

"The *Zhukov* is much bigger than the regular ships, isn't she? Built later in the war. Supposed to be the next generation of ships,"

Amber said aloud. Her company had had a small part in her construction. "She was much too big for just one company. If I remember correctly, she needed more than twenty companies to build her."

"You're quite right, Ms. Jameson," Admiral Strayker told her. "She came into service in what was the final year of open conflict. Right after she made her maiden trip to the forts in this sector, the Quill suddenly stopped fighting. Some said it was because the Quill had never seen a ship of her size. Others said it was just a coincidence. Either way, no other ship in her class was ever completed. She's like a white elephant."

"Just the thing we need," Karl said, almost in a whisper. He studied the screen hard. Looking from the forts to Saturn, and back again. His right hand came up to his face and rubbed his chin absentmindedly. His eyes darted back and forth. He never blinked. His mind raced with the options that were in front of him. He knew the question but wasn't quite sure of the answer. He needed time, not too much. He needed rest, if only for a short time.

"The ships won't be here for some time, Karl, would you and your people like to rest for a period? Maybe get something to eat and drink?" wondered Colonel Dewey.

"That would be good," Jordan Schmidt said quickly. "We haven't had much to eat or drink in a while, and rest was basically nonexistent the past few days. I'm sure we would all appreciate that."

"I know I would," Sergeant Russ told them. "Been a long past few days. I could use some shut-eye."

"Lieutenant Merkel," Colonel Dewey called out. "Would you please show our guests to their quarters? We'll alert you when the ships are close. There's a mess hall right around the corner from your quarters. You will have to forgive us for putting the four of you in the same quarters. Rooms are quite scarce at the moment, as you can all imagine."

"Not a problem," Sergeant Russ said as she looked at the others. Everyone seemed to be in agreement on the need for rest, food, and that the quarters would be acceptable.

"Indeed," muttered Karl as he continued to look at the screen. He acted as if he hadn't even heard any part of the conversation that had just taken place. His mind was elsewhere, and he didn't have time for current affairs. He was busy studying the screen and making mental notes of where everything was.

*****

"Wake up, people," the female voice called over the speakers. "Karl Cregg and his band are on the move to their quarters. Our time is near."

The four men stirred and slowly opened their eyes. It felt as if they had just gone to sleep and had slept a matter of minutes, when in reality it had been over an hour. Each man sat up and rubbed his eyes and stretched out his arms. They looked about, reacquainting themselves with their surroundings. There wasn't much in the room, but each needed to know where everything was. Habit. If something had been moved, something small, they needed to know. Intruders were not looked upon kindly in their line of work. Everything appeared to be where they had left it. Slowly they got out of their bunks and made their way to the door.

"They're going to be housed four decks down on the other side of the fort. The elevator is out the door and to the left. Remember to act as if you are wounded and lost. Service members will assist if you need help. Fortunately there is a mess hall near Cregg's quarters. You are looking for P-Deck, hall M, room seven hundred. If a Service member asks you, all you are looking for is the mess hall on P-Deck." And the speaker went dead.

"Not much to go on," one of them said.

"I've gone on less and brought my person in. She was young and feisty. Nearly broke both my arms in the process," another one offered.

"All we need to do is get to the elevator and go to P-Deck. From there it'll be a piece of cake," a third one offered.

"You forget where we are," the one who had acted as their leader earlier told them. "Service members on forts are a different breed. Hardier. Tougher. They have to be to be on the front line. To be out here, away from friends and family, nothing around for millions of miles, you have to be tougher than anyone else."

"Doesn't matter how tough they are, eventually they all slip up. They make a mistake, and that's when we hit them," the first one out the door told them.

"Just a matter of how long we have to wait for that mistake to be made," the leader said.

The four men proceeded down the hall, passing several people who all looked like they had just come from the crippled liner. The smell of smoke and blood filled the air, and they felt their stomachs becoming queasy. Service members lined the hall and pointed out rooms to some of the survivors. They watched with careful eyes and saw some of the injured leave the hall and enter what they considered quarters. Catching a quick glimpse into one of the rooms, they noted that the inside looked to be the same as their own. One of the Service members put a hand up and stopped the four.

"How badly injured?" they were asked.

"Minor injuries, we're told," the leader told him.

"You got quarters yet?" he asked.

"Back down the hall. The four of us are friends and were put into one room together. We're headed to a mess hall on P-Deck. We hear the food is pretty good there."

"I don't know about it being pretty good," the Service member said with a laugh. "It will fill you up, though, as long as you can hold it down. Just go down this hall to the elevator, and when you get off, follow the signs," he said, pointing down the hall.

"Thank you, sir," the leader said and headed his people in the direction he was told to go. Each of them acknowledged the Service member and told him thanks.

When they reached the elevator, it only took a second for it to arrive, and they were the only ones on it. Instantly they voided themselves of their fake injuries and acted normal. They scanned the elevator, checking for signs of being watched but found none. They silently counted the seconds it took for them to reach their designated level. Once the door opened, they again put on their injured faces and looked for both the sign showing the way to the mess hall and the room where they would find Karl Cregg and his people. They encountered more of the injured, along with more Service members. The hall was near capacity, and the going was slower than when they were on their own deck; it made searching about harder than they expected.

"We're in hall M," one of them whispered.

"All we need is room seven hundred," another responded.

"Keep it down," the leader cautioned. "We get caught now, and she'll make sure we never see Mother Earth again."

"We must be getting close," another one said. "I can smell the chow now. Hope it's something decent."

"Man said it would fill you up," one of the others told him.

"There," said the leader, nodding his head in the general direction. "Seven hundred. Near the mess hall like she told us. We'll go in, get something to eat, find a table off to the side, and make our final plans. By tonight, Cregg and his people will be history, and we'll be on our way back home."

"Works for me," one of them said as they entered the mess hall.

The mess hall was a sea of humanity, most of them injured. The place was filled from side to side, and more of them came in after the four men. The sounds of moaning filled the place, along with people shouting to be heard. Metal trays banged off of the tables. In the distance, silverware could be heard hitting the trays and the floor. The place was filled, and it was loud. If they were to complete their plans, they would have to shout to be heard. They took only a few steps into the hall, then turned and left.

"Too loud in there," the leader said. "I've got a headache already, and we were only in there a few seconds."

"So do I," one of his colleagues told him.

"Where to now, boss?" another inquired.

"Back to our room. We'll make our final preparation there and come back down here later. Not to worry, we'll still be seeing home soon. This is just a minor setback."

16

Jordan Schmidt was seated at the table with the others when she saw the four men enter the mess hall. There was something in their mannerisms that caught her eye, and she turned her attention to them and continued to watch their every move. She wasn't quite sure what it was about them; they appeared to be like all of the other passengers that the fort had recently taken on. They had blood on themselves, they limped, they seemed disoriented, but somehow, they didn't fit in. They were out of place. She tried to keep both eyes on the four and listen to the conversation going on at her table, but she found it harder than she remembered. She left the conversation and turned all her attention toward the four men. She watched them stand there, stare around the hall, talk for a second or two, then turn and leave. She found it unnerving. She knew the place was crowded, but tables were still open. Then it hit her. Her training kicked in, and she knew what was wrong.

"Tackers!" she said in an elevated voice.

"Where?" demanded Colonel Dewey, spinning around in her chair so she could see the doorway.

"They just left. They were here for only a minute, then left and went down the hall. There's four of them," Jordan informed everyone hastily.

"Which way?" questioned Admiral Strayker, getting to his feet.

"Straight ahead. Toward the elevators," Jordan said as she rose and started toward the door.

"Eve," shouted Colonel Dewey. "Four men just left the mess hall, my location, follow them and inform me of where they go. Alert Lieutenant Merkel of their destination and have him meet me there." Then she moved toward the door with the others.

They stood at the door and stared down the hall in the direction of the nearest elevator, but only the wounded from the cruise liner could be seen, and they were traveling in groups of two or three. No grouping of four men could be seen. Service members were on both sides of the hall and took note of the command brass and approached them.

"Trouble, sir?" one asked.

"We witnessed four men leaving here and heading toward the elevator, did you see them?" inquired Colonel Dewey, who was still straining to see down the hall, past the injured.

"Yes, sir. They headed off in that direction, but they appeared to be wounded passengers from the cruise liner. None of us thought anything different about them.

"Thank you, Private," she said, dismissing him. "Go back to your post. We'll handle this."

"Yes, sir," the private responded before returning to his post and signaling the others to do the same.

The six people stood near the door of the mess hall, staring out at the injured that were both walking their way and retreating up the hall. They strained to see through the mass of people but couldn't find the object of their search. The four men seemed to have vanished into the masses. They knew the four were trouble, that they would have to find them before they found the object of their mission. It was almost clear who the four were after. They would have to find them before the four men could complete their mission.

"Admiral," began Karl Cregg as he continued to stare down the hall. "You take the colonel and the sergeant and head down that side of the hall, and I'll take Amber and Jordan and head down this side. We'll meet by the elevators. Be careful. If they are Trackers, then they'll stop at nothing to complete their mission, which is to kill both myself and anyone who is with me at the time. Even the passengers from the liner are expendable as far as they are concerned."

"You be careful yourself," the admiral responded. "If they are after you, then you won't be safe on this fort. We can't afford to lose you now. Not this late in the game. If they know you're here, and they sent Trackers after you, then they're scared and feel time is running out to finish their plan. We need you and everyone else here alive for the finale."

"Understood," Karl said as he and his friends started up the hall.

They didn't have an easy time of it, as the crowd of people didn't understand what they were trying to do and refused to move out of the way. People had to be shoved hard so that they had a clear path toward the elevators, and all the while, they had to keep their eyes open for the four Trackers. They could smell the smoke and blood on the injured and felt sorry for them a little, but there was a war on, and everyone knew enough to stay away from the forts, yet someone back home had given the okay for the liner to travel into restricted space. Sympathy for these people was there, but not as much as would have been given if this had happened back home. Karl and Jordan didn't think too much about these people, but Amber did, and silently she cursed them for being ignorant enough to think that space travel at this time was safe. She knew better, why didn't they? Who was it that claimed space was safe to travel in again?

They had gone less than fifty feet when they heard the noise. It wasn't particularly loud, but it was unique, and everyone knew instantly what had caused it. The injured from the liner began to scream and run at the same time. Karl and his people fell to the floor, pulled their sidearms, and looked about as best they could for the source.

"Everyone, down!" yelled Colonel Dewey from across the hall, but the civilians didn't pay her any attention and kept on running and yelling.

"Down, everyone!" yelled Admiral Strayker even louder from his position on the floor.

A second shot rang out, and someone fell, bleeding from the back. The screams from the liner's injured got louder, and a stampede happened. People did their best to get out of the hall and didn't care who got hurt in the process. Another shot occurred, and a blackened spot appeared on the wall above where Admiral Strayker and Colonel Dewey were lying.

"Near the end of the hall," called Karl Cregg. He was lying flat on the floor but had a clear view of the hallway's ending. He couldn't tell who was doing the shooting, but he could tell where it was coming from.

"Eve!" yelled Colonel Dewey from her position on the floor. She was trying to locate the shooter but was having no luck. "Dampening field!"

It only took a second, but it seemed to take minutes. Then a soft hum could be heard, and the gunfire ceased. People still scrambled to get out of the line of fire. Several people were sprawled out on the floor, crying in agony. Three people could be seen motionless, blood forming small pools. Karl looked in the direction of the shooter and saw the man shaking his gun, then throwing it down on the deck and scampering up a side hallway. He glanced across the floor and noticed the admiral and colonel getting to their feet. Sergeant Russ rolled to the nearest injured civilian and started to administer first aid. Looking about, he failed to see any injured in his vicinity, and he quickly got to his feet and ran to the side hallway where he had witnessed the shooter escaping into. He stopped at the intersection of the two hallways and cautiously peered into the corridor. After failing to see what he was looking for, he returned to the others and assisted with the wounded.

"Medics needed, P-Deck, hall M, near the mess hall!" called out Colonel Dewey. She was on her knees, tending to a young man who was no more than twenty, who was on his back, holding his stomach, trying to stop the bleeding. "You're going to be okay. Listen to me, you are going to be okay. Medics are on their way."

"I need help over here!" screamed Jordan Schmidt. She was on her knees near a young woman who was holding a toddler in her arms. The mother's face was etched in pain, and the child was crying. Blood was forming on the floor, and the puddle it was forming was getting bigger by the second.

Karl Cregg and Sergeant Russ rushed over to her side. Both reached for the toddler at the same time, with the sergeant winning the small argument. It was then that they both noticed the wound on the mother and let out a small gasp. Blood was pouring from her chest. A hole about three inches in diameter was there, just to the right of the heart. She was fading fast, and Jordan Schmidt was doing her best to keep the mother awake and stop the flow of blood; she was losing both battles.

"Where are the medics?" she screamed at the top of her lungs. "I need help here, fast!"

"They're on their way," called Colonel Dewey from across the hall.

"Hang in there," said Karl to the woman in a soothing voice as he knelt down by her side. "Help is on the way."

He looked the woman in the eyes and gave her a small smile. Taking hold of one of her hands, he gently squeezed it and tried his best to reassure her that everything was going to end with her being reunited with her baby back on Earth. He watched as she looked toward her baby, then back toward the Service member who was trying to help her. She managed to form a grin, then nodded her head slightly, before closing her eyes and taking a deep breath and letting it out slowly.

"No!" screamed Jordan Schmidt. "You hold on. They're almost here. You stay with me!" she demanded.

"She's gone," Karl told her in a soft voice. "There was just too much damage. Even if the medics had gotten here sooner, there was just too much damage. She's gone," he said as he rose to his feet, reached down a hand for her to take hold of and get to hers.

"The medics are here, Karl," Sergeant Russ said in a low voice. She was still holding the crying toddler, and tears were forming in her eyes. She hated this place now. Hated what had just taken place. She hated the existence of the Trackers. Looking about herself, all she could see was blood and death.

"You okay, Sergeant?" came a voice from her right side.

She came back to reality long enough to see Admiral Strayker standing there, holding out a hand for her to hold. Blood covered the front of his uniform, and he was doing his best to hold back the tears. For all the war he had seen, he still wasn't able to hold the tears when it came to innocent blood.

"Are you okay?" he asked again.

"I will be, hopefully," she responded as she pulled the toddler closer to herself.

"Hang on to that thought. Never let it go," he told her as he pushed gently past her and made his way over to Karl Cregg and Jordan Schmidt. "Did you see where he went?" he questioned Karl.

"Up the side hallway. I lost him in the crowds," Karl informed him as he turned and looked back toward the hall. "Hopefully Eve is following him."

"The medics have this. We should head back to the command deck and follow things from there," Admiral Strayker told him. "Eve can fill us in on the casualties here and the whereabouts of our friend, plus the Trackers."

"Agreed," Karl said and started toward the elevators. He looked around himself and shook his head at all of the destruction and loss of life. To him, it made no sense. Why would someone fire on him in a hallway full of injured civilians from the crippled liner? There were too many witnesses. There was too big a chance that people would either get injured or killed. There were too many Service members here that could have responded to the shooting. Plus, the fact you're on a fort in the middle of space, where would you go once the killing was done? You couldn't just leave. It all made no sense at the present time. He needed more time to figure it all out, but time was something he didn't have a lot of.

"Karl, what do you make of all this?" questioned Colonel Dewey as the two of them started toward the elevators. "Why would someone do this?"

"It was done to get to me. They want me dead," he told her in a calm voice.

"I thought that was what the Trackers were for," said Amber from behind them.

"It is. Where there is one Tracker gang, there is bound to be more," Karl informed her.

"More?" she questioned in a slightly raised voice. "How many more?"

"As many as it takes," Colonel Dewey told her without ever turning to look at her. Her mind was already racing with what to do once they were on the command deck.

"So your life is in constant danger until they kill you. How safe are we then?" Amber wondered aloud. "Should we get you some extra bodyguards while you're here?"

"Once they see that I'm surrounded by extra security, they'll go into hiding, and we'll never find them. No extra security. Eve is all the security I'll need." He told her as they reached the elevators.

As they were loading into the elevator, the alarm began to sound. The lighting turned to a reddish color. Orders came over the speakers, but they failed to hear them once the door closed, and the elevator began to move. They quickly looked to one another, then Colonel Dewey spoke.

"Lieutenant Merkel, report," she called out.

A moment later, the lieutenant appeared with them. His face was red, his eyes open and not blinking. Behind him, people were rushing about and calling out orders.

"It's happening, sir. That thing out there has rose up from Saturn and is targeting the forts. All forts in this sector are launching everything they have and putting themselves on condition red. That thing will be ready to fire in less than a minute. You had better get up here as fast as you can," he informed her in a hurried voice. When he finished speaking, he turned his head toward the screen and watched as the object continued to rise up from the planet's surface. He turned and barked out orders to the command deck crew. "When it's in range, I want everything we have firing!" he yelled.

His image faded, and they were alone to wonder what was happening and how bad it was going to get.

"When it rains..." the admiral mumbled.

"How much longer?" questioned Sergeant Russ.

"Soon," was the only response she got.

The ride was no more than thirty seconds, yet to everyone involved, it seemed an eternity. They wanted to help, to do something, but were unable to do anything. Each of them took the time to say what they thought would be a final prayer, then they whispered their goodbyes to friends and loved ones who were not present. Each of them felt this was going to be the final battle with the Quill, and with that new weapon out there, they thought their chances slim to none in coming out alive. When the door opened, and they stepped onto the command deck. They got their first view of just how bad matters really were, and it only deepened their feeling of dread.

The object was on the screen, and it had more than doubled in size. Its opening was pointed at the forts. It was clear of the planet's atmosphere and still rising. It was just a matter of time before the thing fired. Everyone remembered the amount of damage done to the cruise liner, but now this thing was bigger, and it was aimed at the forts. What kind of damage it could do now was anybody's guess, and no one really wanted to know.

"Report!" Colonel Dewey yelled as she walked onto the deck.

"Estimates put that thing in firing position in less than twenty seconds," Lieutenant Merkel informed her. "The ships the admiral has ordered here are still a few minutes away. All forts report armed and ready. We have over two thousand fighters out there, all of who report armed and ready."

"Are all airtight doors closed and locked?" asked the colonel as she stepped up beside her first officer.

"All airtight doors closed and secure. All nonessential personnel secured," Lieutenant Merkel informed her. His eyes were glued to the screen, and he paid no attention to the newcomers.

They stood on the command deck and stared out at the object, waiting for it to fire, while the rest of the command deck crew rushed about doing their jobs. Orders were being yelled out, followed by counterorders. People were running from one desk to another. The overhead speakers were carrying orders from the other forts to their fighters and from fighter to fighter. Everyone tried to keep one ear on the orders from the forts and the orders from the fighters. Everyone kept their vision locked on the object in space. The red lights that illuminated the command deck gave off the impression of the bloodbath that was soon to come.

"Estimated time to fire is five seconds," the lieutenant said loudly.

"Brace yourselves!" yelled Karl.

"Shields at full!" someone yelled from the rear of the deck.

They watched and silently counted down. When they reached zero, they grabbed onto anything they could for support and waited. It took another three seconds, but then it happened. The mouth of the object opened wider and slightly retracted before a round object was expelled and hurled toward the forts. Though they were still thousands of miles away from it, it took only seconds for the object to collide with Fort Pershing.

As soon as contact was made, the fighters and the other forts opened up with everything they had, and space lit up as if the sun had moved from its position and relocated to Saturn. The fired shots from the fighters didn't move as quickly as the object fired from near the planet's surface, giving the object hovering above the planet plenty of time to fire a second shot. It was hurled toward the forts but then shifted and went toward a group of fighters that were stationed above Fort Bradley. The fighters had no warning nor time to move, and in an instant, more than seventy of them were destroyed. The first volley from the fighters and the forts found their target now and slammed into the hovering object. The thing flinched slightly before releasing another round.

The round came in fast and made contact with Fort Washington. The fort seemed to shake and roll slightly. Flames poured out of the hole that was now in its side. Karl and his people stared in disbelief. They had come to think of the forts as indestructible; now they were witnessing what might prove to be the end of Earth. They had nothing that could stand up to this weapon, and a feeling of sudden helplessness was filling them.

The three remaining forts were firing along with the fighters, but their shots were merely bouncing off the object and going into space. Then the sky lit up like never before. Huge lightning bolts came from behind the forts and made their way through space toward Saturn. There were four bolts in all, and they turned the darkness into day, causing the Service members on the command deck to shield their eyes. Some let out gasps before closing their eyes as tightly as possible, while others screamed and turned away, fearing the worst. It took more than a minute, but the bolts hit their target and silenced it for a moment. Then the object came to life again. This time even deadlier than before.

The first shot went out and flew past the forts in the blink of an eye. Those on the command deck instinctively ducked and turned their heads to try to see where the shot went. A second shot flew out of the object and slammed into the side of Fort Grant. It lit up space even brighter than the shots that had come from behind the forts. Karl Cregg watched on the screen as the fort rocked back and forth, and fire leapt from its interior. His mind was racing, trying to find an answer to this horrible new weapon.

"The cruiser *Saint Bernard* is hit!" someone yelled from behind.

All eyes turned toward the screen in time to see the cruiser turn and return fire with all its guns. Behind the *Saint Bernard*, they could see three other cruisers firing at will. They never stayed in one place too long, they kept moving and firing. They seemed to change course at will. A shot would be let out, and the huge ship would turn and move in a different direction, then let out another shot.

"Keep them moving!" Karl yelled to the admiral. "Don't let them stop. Take them high, above the forts. Fan them out as far as they can go. Have them fire with everything they have and tell them to aim for that part of the object that appears to be the barrel. Maybe if we hit it enough times, we can damage it."

"You got it," the admiral replied and went about relaying the message to the ships. Silently he hoped the battleships weren't far behind and could add their enormous firepower to the fight.

"Battleship *Churchill* coming into range, sir," a voice called out. "She wants to know if there is any specific place you would like her to be."

"Have the *Churchill* and any other battleships that show up go below the forts and target that gun barrel!" Karl yelled out as he stepped toward the screen to get a better look at the battle. He stopped just steps short of the screen and studied it hard. His eyes ran the whole length of it, and never once did he blink. His right hand came up to his chin and absentmindedly started to rub it. His mouth opened slightly but only for a second. Closing it, he took a small step forward. A grin came to his face. "Have the fighters fly past the object and come up in back of it. Have them hold their fire until I say so," he said aloud.

The orders were being relayed when video came in from Fort Patton. It showed a ghastly sight. The damage to the command deck was extensive. Smoke seemed to pour from every corner. Bodies could be seen lying in grotesque poses. Fires still burned even after the suppressors had supposedly finished their jobs. Major Valera Huntsmann was seated on a workstation holding her right arm with her left; blood flowed down her face from an open wound above her eyes.

"Colonel, it's bad over here. That thing hit us hard. Shifted us twelve degrees on our axis. Early reports have over 1,500 either dead or missing. We are still able to fire, though," she said in a shaky voice. She moved her head slightly in an attempt to wipe the blood from her face onto her uniform.

"The battleships are here, Major. They can fight for you. Your people might be better served by remaining silent for now. Let that thing think you're dead. Then when Karl gives the word, open up with everything you have and hit that gun barrel. For now, though, see to the wounded. Take care of them. I'll let you know when to fire," Colonel Dewey said in a low voice. The sight of the damage bothered her more than she liked. She and Major Huntsmann had become friends, and to see her friend hurt this bad, and know she couldn't do anything about it, bothered her.

"Battleships *Potemkin*, *Kennedy*, and *Franklin* coming into range, sir. I've advised them to follow the *Churchill*'s lead," someone called out. His voice brought everyone back to reality, and the horrors they had seen from Fort Grant soon faded.

"I think we're getting the upper hand," the admiral said optimistically. "It doesn't seem to be firing as fast now. I think if we hit it with everything at the same time, we can disable it."

"That's my plan, Admiral. That's why I sent the fighters behind it. They can fire from back there while we let everything go from in front," Karl told the admiral. He still stood near the screen, studying it still.

"As long as nothing fires from behind that thing at the fighters," Colonel Dewey said. She hated to be the bearer of bad news, but she had an obligation to keep things in perspective.

"Yeah. As long as nothing is behind it," Karl said in a voice he could only hear.

17

From her vantage point of the cockpit of a fighter, Lieutenant Annabelle Bishop followed the battle. She saw the object fire on the forts, inflicting what looked to her to be extensive damage. Then she noted the arrival of the cruisers and followed their efforts to inflict the same amount of damage on the object, and their failure to do so. She witnessed the arrival of the battleships and noted the small success of their efforts. Now she was leading half of the fighters to the other side of Saturn in what she hoped would be a decisive strike against the intruder, made by the fighters, the forts, the cruisers, and the battleships. She looked out over the vastness of space and could barely see the other group of fighters following their leader, Lieutenant Jason Lee. She knew they would meet up on the far side of the planet, and she knew that the man she had replaced would end up being her commanding officer and lead all the fighters in the final attack. Gazing at her screen, she noted that parts of her group were straying off course.

"Let's try to keep it tight back there," she called over the radio. "Make sure everyone is flying full open. We don't need any stragglers out here. Fall behind, and you're on your own."

She noted that her words were taken to heart and saw the stragglers pull up to the group, and those that had strayed slightly off course were now moving to pull in tighter. A smile camel to her face, and for the first time in a while, the thought of final victory was allowed to filter into her brain. She just wasn't sure what final victory would look like. How would she fit into the future plans of the forts? Who would end up being her immediate superior? Where would she be stationed? She wanted to stay out here, with the forts, but that might not be possible. She may be stationed on Mars, and that would certainly be a disciplining move. She shivered and brought herself back to reality. The mission had to come first, everything else would take care of itself at a later date.

"There it is," she called out.

Her fighter had rounded the planet, and she could see the far side of the object. She watched in horror as it fired again. She couldn't see where the shot landed, but she instinctively knew that it had inflicted heavy damage on its target. Her determination to eliminate the threat increased. She looked around in an effort to locate the other fighters, but by now, they were too far away even for her screen to pick up. She found herself turning her attention to deep space. The Quill were out there, but she wasn't sure exactly where. She strained to peer into the darkness, to try to locate a light that would indicate the enemy was still out there, waiting. She turned her screen to scan out as far as possible. Nothing. She couldn't see anything, and her scans showed nothing out there. A thought entered her mind. A grin came to her face. Her spirit lifted. They were gone. They had left the solar system, leaving only this thing behind.

"Why?" she asked out loud.

Then the sky opened up. Streaks of light flashed across the vastness of space and crashed into the object floating above the ringed planet. They roughly brought her back to reality, and she flashed into action. The final attack on the object had begun. Her hands reached up and brought down the dark visor on her helmet to protect her eyes. She took control of the ship and angled it toward the planet, while she spoke loudly but evenly into the radio.

"All ships, attack!" she called.

She could see out of the corners of her eyes that the fighters under her control had done the same thing that she had done. Hundreds of small fighters broke their formation and were now headed toward the huge object. Their guns were firing constantly, and she watched as they hit their target. She pulled the trigger on her guns and kept it pulled as tight as she could. She looked out across space to where she had expected Lieutenant Lee and his fighters to appear and was met with flashes of light that joined up with the ones from her group on top of the object. Instantly she knew that both groups had survived the trip around the planet and were carrying out their mission. Turning back to the object, she noted other shots coming in from the Earth side. These, she assumed, were coming from the forts and the big ships. All shots were finding their target. The massive gun barrel was being pummeled and was beginning to show signs of damage.

It was small at first. The barrel would bend slightly, then straighten out again and threaten to let loose another shot. Seconds later, another shot would find its target and the barrel would bend again. It managed to let loose with a round, but Lieutenant Bishop couldn't afford to follow it with her eyes. She was single-mindedly set on hitting her target with each shot and felt she couldn't afford to change her focus at such a crucial time. They had this thing on the ropes, and she was determined to see it through to the end. She let out a scream as her fighter screamed in. Then her scream ended, and her eyes opened wider. Her mouth fell open.

She watched as the barrel let loose another round while under constant fire from the fleet and the forts. The shot went out from the barrel but stopped short of its intended target. It sat there, suspended in space. Then it seemed to explode, sending shrapnel in all direction. In horror, she watched as several fighters were hit in the first split second and exploded into fireballs. She watched as the fires were there one second, then gone the next. Another life had been lost in this senseless war. Then she felt something hit her ship. It changed her direction and sent her spinning out of control.

"Crap!" she screamed as she gripped the control arm harder and tried to regain control, but it was no use. She was spinning uncontrollably on her axis, and nothing she tried could regain control of the fighter. She watched as one second, the object was in front of her, and the next second, she could see Saturn. Over and over again this played out, and she felt herself getting sick. She was trained for spaceflight, but this was too much for her system to handle. She saw the object firing once more and thought how awful it would be for the ones who would feel the power of this new weapon.

*****

"Report!" yelled Colonel Dewey as she slowly got to her feet. Looking around, she marveled at how lucky they were to still be breathing.

The command deck was smashed. Sparks were flying from every corner of the deck. Small fires burned, threatening to spread. The lights, which were a steady red, were now flashing and giving the deck an eerie appearance. The alert siren was sounding, and it hurt her ears to the point that she had to cover them with her hands just to be able to think about what condition her fort was in. Service members were scattered across the deck itself. Some were unconscious, while others were moaning in pain. Smoke hung thick in the air.

"Are you all right, Colonel?" came a voice from behind Colonel Dewey.

She lowered her hands and turned to see who was speaking to her. She came face-to-face with Admiral Strayker. He had blood flowing from an open wound above his left eye. He held his right arm close to his side as if it had been damaged. He blinked quickly, trying to come to terms with what had happened and with what was before him.

"I'm okay," she said quietly. "How about yourself?"

"Right arm is broken in two places, open wound on my forehead, and I think I broke a rib or two. Otherwise I'm fine," he said in a labored breath.

"Report!" she called out again. She turned her attention to the rows of workstations and was amazed to see that more than half of her Command Crew was not at their stations. Fear took over, and she pushed past the admiral and made her way toward the stations.

Looking down the rows, she saw the wounded trying to move, their blood leaving puddles on the floor. Others simply lay there, making no effort to move but letting it be known that they were still alive. The rest were thrown about, and no sign of life could be found coming from them. At first, she made an attempt to count the dead, but she gave it up when the dead began to number more than the living.

"Working on a report, sir," someone called from the rear of the deck. Lieutenant Merkel had been in that area before the fort had been shaken violently by the object fired by their friend out there. Now he was getting to his feet, and blood was coming from his mouth. He spat some out onto the floor and moved his mouth slightly to make sure it was still working properly and not broken. A smile came to his face, and he forced himself fully erect and started to gather data from the rest of the fort.

"When you have it, Lieutenant," Colonel Dewey told him as she acknowledged his presence.

"How bad are we?" questioned Jordan Schmidt, getting to her feet. She appeared to be unharmed physically, just shaken up quite a bit.

"Working on it," Admiral Strayker told her as he extended a hand to assist her to her feet. "Might take a few minutes."

"Do we have a few minutes?" wondered Amber Jameson as she lay on her back and looked up at the three people standing over her.

"Not sure," commented Colonel Dewey as she moved closer and bent over to examine the woman who was making no attempt to get up. "How bad?" she asked.

"Both legs," Amber told her in a hushed voice. "I think they are broken below the knee. My back isn't feeling its best either. My head is foggy, and my vision is blurred. Otherwise I feel great," she said with a small laugh. "Never better."

"I'll call for medical," Sergeant Russ told the colonel as she made her way toward one of the stations while she held her right side. She had developed a severe limp, and she groaned with each step she took.

"Karl?" questioned Admiral Strayker as he looked about the area in which they were all standing before the fort was hit. He moved about slightly, his eyes searching for the one person that they still needed, but he was nowhere to be seen.

All eyes turned and began searching the area. They needed to find Karl Cregg and find him alive. Colonel Dewey stayed on the floor next to Amber Jameson, holding her hand and trying her best to reassure the woman that she was going to be fine. The others began to move the wreckage that was once the command deck in an effort to locate their missing comrade. Tables, computers, and wires were soon being piled in a corner. They worked in a circle going out from where they remembered the man standing. It was a grid search, and nothing was left just lying about. Everything was moved. Everyone who could walk participated. Everyone was aware of how important Karl Cregg was to this war.

"Report, sir," Lieutenant Merkel said as he made his way to the colonel's side. He knelt down and first looked at Amber Jameson, then turned his attention to his colonel. He felt sorry for the young woman on the floor, but his first duty was to Colonel Dewey. "Portside has a hole in it from J-Deck to P-Deck. It measures more than a hundred yards wide at its widest point. Power is out to more than 60 percent of the fort. Deck reports coming in number the dead at more than two thousand. The injured are still being counted. We can't take another shot like that."

"What about the other forts? Do we have communications with them?" she asked quietly.

"Working on it, sir. We hope to have it back up in the next few minutes. We do have internal communications."

"Medical?" she asked as she looked from Amber to the lieutenant.

"Overwhelmed, but the sergeant has managed to get a small team to come to the command deck. Without power, they will have to walk, and it could be some time before they get here."

"Tell them to do their best. Only thing they can do," Colonel Dewey told him as she turned her attention back to Amber Jameson. "Help is on the way. Hang in there."

"Don't see me going anywhere, Colonel," Amber responded with a smile.

"Got him!" came a voice from some forty feet away from where the colonel and Amber were situated.

The search group left their areas and headed over to where a young female corporal was moving some equipment around in an effort to get at whatever was lying behind it. She tossed some computer consoles and wires without regard as to where they were going to land. She grunted as she tried to shove some heavy benches that were refusing to be moved. It took the strength of three men to move each of the tables and reveal the limp body of Karl Cregg sprawled across the floor. Blood formed a puddle on the deck, and it was being soaked up by his shirt.

"He's alive. Just barely," called out the young corporal as she reached in with her one hand and felt for a pulse. Pulling her hand back, she noted the blood that now covered part of it. She glanced over at the colonel and Admiral Strayker and made sure they were aware of the situation.

"Find the bleeding and stop it as best you can," Admiral Strayker informed her. "Medics are on the way, but it could be some time before they arrive."

It took only minutes before the limp body of Karl Cregg could be uncovered, and cautiously several Service members picked him up and moved him to the big table that still stood in the middle of the command deck. Several of the men removed their uniform shirts and folded them together to make a sort of pillow for his head. As they lifted his head to put the makeshift pillow in place, blood trickled from his mouth, and he gasped for air. Quickly they removed the pillow and rested his head on the table. His breathing became more stable.

The front of Karl's shirt was heavily stained with blood, and more was coming into view underneath him. The young corporal who had found him grabbed hold of his shirt and began to rip it so as to reveal his muscled chest, which was now red from blood. With each breath Karl took, blood leaked out of his body and now pooled on the table.

"We have to seal him up," a young male corporal said.

"We need something to seal him with," the woman told him as she took the shirts and placed them against Karl's chest and held them there as tight as she could.

"Let's move, people," Admiral Strayker called out as he looked at the scene in front of him. "Find a needle and thread, and let's get this man sewn up. Then we'll concentrate on whatever else is going to have to be done to make this command deck operational again."

As the four young topless men took off in search of the needed medical equipment, the admiral looked at the young corporal and nodded approvingly. He took his gaze from her to Karl and then back again. He gave her a wink and then turned and went back to where Amber Jameson and Colonel Dewey were. He looked first at the colonel, who was still holding onto Amber's hand and trying to convince the young woman that everything was going to be fine, then he looked at Amber Jameson and took note of her contorted face. She was in pain, which he thought was a good thing. If she was feeling pain, then maybe her back injury wasn't too severe.

"Admiral," came the voice of Lieutenant Merkel, who had returned to the station at the rear of the command deck. "Message coming in from two levels down, sir. Reports of weapons being fired. Civilians from the liner being targeted."

"Any Service members in the general area, Lieutenant?' he hurriedly asked.

"None, sir."

"Who isn't doing something urgent right now?" the admiral shouted out loud.

"I can go, sir," stated Sergeant Russ, who was still holding her side slightly. She still had a limp, though it wasn't as noticeable now that she had had some time to rest. "I can check it out and report back."

"Grab an extra sidearm and be on your way, Sergeant. Be careful down there. We don't know much about what's happening or how damaged the fort is."

"I'll report in as soon as I can," she said as she saluted and headed off toward a back staircase that would take her to the lower levels of the fort.

"Garbled message coming in from Fort Pershing, Admiral," Lieutenant Merkel called out. "They want to know how bad we are and if they can do anything to assist."

"Relay our status to them and tell them we are making repairs," the admiral shouted back.

"They want to know how many people they should send over to assist in repairs and the injured," Lieutenant Merkel informed the admiral. His voice was hurried, and his pain could be heard.

"Tell them to stay put and to put all their efforts into destroying that thing out there. Once that is done, then they can send as much help as they deem necessary," Admiral Strayker informed the lieutenant. He was standing over Colonel Dewey, but he was slowly moving in the direction of the lieutenant. "I assume we now have ship-to-ship communications?"

"Barely, sir. I can just make out what Major Blishman is saying. There's a lot of static, and one out of every six words is lost. I'm doing my best to clear up the airwave, but it will take time, which I know we don't have a lot of."

"Do your best, Lieutenant. The sooner we have communications, the better off we'll be. Any word from the medics?" the admiral inquired as he paused halfway between Lieutenant Merkel and Colonel Dewey. He was doing his best to be in two places at the same time, but his brain was stuck on the table with Karl Cregg and the corporal.

"They report they should be here in roughly five minutes. They caught a break as some of the med staff was four levels below us. Problem is a lot of the fort between here and there is heavily damaged, and they are moving at a snail's pace," the lieutenant told the admiral. He hoped the fact that aid was closer at hand than originally reported would lift the spirits of all who were on the command deck.

"Well done, Lieutenant. Let me know the second they arrive. We have some badly wounded people up here, and I suspect we'll keep those medics busy for the remainder of the day," the admiral told him before turning around and walking back to Colonel Dewey to inform her of the good news.

*****

Two levels down, Sergeant Lindsey Russ was carefully picking her way through one of the heavily damaged corridors of the fort. She had one eye searching ahead for danger and the other trying to find any signs of life. She favored her injured leg but didn't let it slow her down. She held her sidearm in her left hand and carefully moved aside fallen debris with her right. Her ears were straining to hear any signs of life. One cautious step after another, she made her way down the damaged corridor. Every few steps, she would stop and strain her ears to find any signs of life, but she always received the same reply. Then she would resume her search.

Sparks would fly out from behind damaged equipment, and she would have to stop and shield her eyes. Pieces of the ceiling would threaten to fall on top of her, and she would be forced to push forward faster than caution would advise and watch from a safe distance as only small pieces would fall, leaving the much larger ones still holding on. Smoke could be seen in the distance, and she wondered silently if she would die from that or at the hands of the person with the weapon. One cautious step after another, she pushed forward, straining to hear any signs of life.

Turning a corner, she came into a corridor that was not as heavily damaged as the one she had left. Smoke hugged the ceiling, but there was no sign of a fire. The ceiling was still intact and not threatening to fall down on top of her. No sparks from broken equipment lit up the area. She felt grateful to be in a somewhat-safer environment. Looking down the hall, she took note of all the closed doors and wondered if her shooter was hiding behind one, just waiting for her to go by so he could shoot her in the back. Silently and carefully, she slowly made her way down the hall toward the next intersection. That's when he stepped out.

He was tall and muscular. His hair was ear-length and neatly combed. Dark glasses covered his eyes. He stood spread-legged and slowly brought his right arm up until it was straight out from his body. The gun he had in his hand was now aimed directly at the sergeant's head. Taking his left hand, he brought it up to his face and removed his glasses and put them in his shirt pocket. An evil grin came to his face.

"Remember me?" he asked in a deep tone with a slight laugh.

"Lincoln Jacobson," she whispered just loud enough for him to hear her.

"I'm flattered, Corporal. To think that you would remember me after all this time. Now why don't you just throw that weapon of yours off to the side. You're not going to need it anymore," he said menacingly.

Sergeant Russ continued to look him in the eye and hold onto her weapon as tightly as she could. She wanted to push him a little more. Find out if he was really intent on killing her swiftly or dragging the ordeal out. Her initial thought was that he would get more enjoyment out of her slow death than he would by shooting her between the eyes. She had kept her left arm only slightly raised as she had walked down the hall. She kept it in the same position now and gave a slight smile to show him that she wasn't afraid.

"I know what you're thinking, Corporal. You think that I would get more enjoyment out of killing you slowly rather than shooting you between the eyes. What you forget is that I can do a lot of damage to your person without killing you. I can have you on the floor begging for me to kill you without ever putting your life in real danger. Now why don't you just toss that gun, and we'll see where this goes." Lincoln Jacobson gave a loud laugh and continued to aim his weapon directly at the sergeant's face. His hand tightened on his weapon, and he inched it out from his body even more.

Sergeant Russ stood her ground and ran all her options through her head. She found she didn't have too many. He held most of the cards, and she was being raised. She either had to toss her only defense or risk possibly being shot multiple times without being killed. Thoughts ran through her head. She studied him, trying to figure out if he was being truthful with her. Slowly she lowered her arm and tossed her weapon far enough away that he wouldn't feel a need to send her after it and toss it a second time.

"That wasn't too hard, was it, Corporal?" he asked as he took a few slow steps in her direction.

"Sergeant," she corrected with a tempered tone. "I was promoted after our last encounter. I'm now a sergeant."

"The Service really doesn't know what it's doing. Promoting someone like you instead of just booting you out. Soon, though, they will have no choice. Your beloved Service won't exist much longer. Soon you'll be out on your butt along with all your friends."

The two stood less than twenty feet apart. Jacobson still held onto his weapon, but slowly he lowered his arm and allowed himself to relax slightly. A grin came to his face as he holstered his weapon and locked it into place. Reaching toward his midsection, he unbuckled his belt and allowed his holstered weapon to fall to the floor softly. His right boot kicked it off to the side where it slid under some debris. He clasped his hands in front of his chest and stretched, his knuckles cracking in the process. He spread his legs so that they were shoulder-length apart.

Sergeant Lindsey Russ steadied herself on her injured leg. She clenched her fists and put her best snarl on her face. Her training kicked in to high gear as she stepped to her right, searching for better footing. Her eyes never left her quarry's face. She felt her heart pounding in her chest, along with the sweat flowing down her face. She was confident she could take him if she was in peak health, but with an injured leg, she wasn't so sure. The one thing she was sure of was that she would give him a fight to remember. She took a step forward, and that's when he pounced.

Lincoln Jacobson took this step to lunge at her with everything he had. His fist encountered her stomach and sent her stumbling backward. She tried to brace herself with her hands, but they found debris, and she tumbled helplessly to the floor. Jacobson hurried over to her side and delivered a heavy kick to her ribs, which sent her rolling into a wall. She glimpsed him stepping toward her and sent her left leg out and swept him off his feet. He crashed to the floor and bounced his head hard. The sergeant got to her feet and tried to walk off her injury. She slowly circled her enemy, then jumped on his back and quickly landed three hard blows to the back of his head before he grabbed her left ankle and yanked it forward, causing her to lose her balance. Again she went down and bounced her head hard on the floor. Blood began to flow from an open wound on her head.

Sergeant Russ rolled in an effort to escape her enemy, but she was too close to the wall, and she rolled into it. Blood ran down her forehead and found its way into her eyes. She was temporarily blinded, and that was all the time Lincoln Jacobson needed to quickly get to his feet and locate her. He needed only two steps to reach her, and then he pulled her to her feet and slammed his fist into her midsection, which elicited a loud grunt from his quarry. Taking his other fist, he slammed it into the side of her face, sending her tumbling down the hall and falling to the floor. Blood began to flow from her mouth. She made a feeble attempt to get to her knees so she could stand, but Jacobson was there quickly and delivered an even harder kick to her stomach than before, and she was sent flying across the hall. She lay there helplessly and watched as he made his way toward her, laughing loudly with each step he took.

*****

"Reports coming in, sir," Lieutenant Merkel called out from his station at the rear of the command deck. "Fighters are all reporting that the object is either dead or near death. All our firepower is having a devastating effect on it. All ships are continuing to fire."

Colonel Dewey and Admiral Strayker were both taking in the damage reports which were trickling in. The injured had been tended to and removed from the command deck. They both quickly turned their attention to the large screen and took note of the battle before them. The object still floated above Saturn, but its color had faded to a dark gray. The gun barrel was leaning to one side and seemed to be ready to fall down totally. Rounds of ammunition still pounded it, yet it refused to surrender. At one point, it came back to life, if only for a second. They watched as the fighters would streak in and release their fury in volley after volley, all directed at the same point, and each one finding its target.

"Are we getting any life signs from the object?" Admiral Strayker inquired.

"None, sir. No life signs before, and the same now," responded Lieutenant Merkel.

"Tell the fighters to continue the battle. They are to be prepared to disengage shortly so they can be refueled and rearmed. We'll land them on a rotating basis," Colonel Dewey told him. She watched as the fighters rolled in, firing their weapons. She saw the shots coming in from the cruisers and the battleships. Every round found its target, and she silently hoped this whole thing would be over soon. She had injured people down below and a fort that desperately needed help.

"Report from below, sir," Lieutenant Merkel suddenly shouted out louder than he normally would have. His voice had a tone of urgency in it. His head jerked upward, and his mouth opened wide. "Service member severely injured. The injuries don't correspond with the shelling we took. Looks like she was attacked by another person and left for dead."

"Have medical respond immediately. Get security down there," the admiral ordered before Colonel Dewey had a chance to even open her mouth. "Find out who the injured is and how badly injured they are."

"Civilians indicate the injured is Sergeant Lindsey Russ," the lieutenant informed his commanding officers. "She's in pretty bad shape. Blood all over the place. They indicate that she may have several broken bones. Her breathing is shallow and labored. They'll stand guard over her until help arrives."

"Have medical respond immediately. Get security down there and have them search the area for whoever is responsible," Colonel Dewey ordered. She turned her attention to Admiral Strayker and indicated that she was more than a little concerned for the sergeant. She moved closer to him on shaky legs. "I have to go to her. General Schmidt entrusted her safety to me, and I take that trust very seriously," she whispered.

"What about your command? The rest of these people, plus the pilots out there, and the Service members and civilians on this fort are also your responsibility. What about them? Are they worth less than the sergeant?" he asked her in a lowered voice.

"No, sir. I take their lives just as seriously as that of the sergeant. But if the person I think is responsible for this is responsible, then I made him a vow a long time ago to avenge her, and I mean to take that vengeance out now," she confided in him. She stood shaking slightly and tried to look him in the eyes. She never had trouble doing that before, but she found it hard to do now. She had respect for him, and she knew he respected her, but she felt that respect being torn away from her. This was out of character for her, and she well knew the price of her actions.

"Would you like for me to relieve of your duties temporarily so that you can handle this?" he offered. He knew her reputation. Knew that if it wasn't extraordinarily important, she wouldn't do what she was about to do. She was looking for a way out, and he felt it important to give her one.

"Thank you, sir," she whispered after exhaling heavily.

"Eve," the admiral called loudly as he stepped away from the colonel. "Note that I am taking command of Fort Patton at this time. Colonel Dewey isn't feeling herself and has asked me to take over temporarily. Show me any video of Sergeant Russ's attack."

The command deck crew watched as a video began to play in the middle of the deck, a 3D version of what had occurred earlier. They watched Sergeant Russ toss her weapon off to the side, then her opponent did the same. They watched as the two struggled together and exchange heavy blows that would have taken any civilian down in a split second. They grimaced as the sergeant was slammed heavily against the wall and tumbled to the floor. Anger built to a boil as they saw her opponent stand over her and deliver several blows with his foot to her midsection. Stomachs turned as they saw him bring his booted foot down on her leg and break it in two.

"Enough, Eve," the admiral ordered, and the video disappeared. "Keep an eye on the sergeant and one on the colonel. Do a search for the person in the video and alert me as to his whereabouts. Lock the fort down. No one leaves without my knowledge. Recall all fighters and have them watch all docks for any departures. Any ship leaving without my permission is to be fired on. Am I clear, Eve?" the admiral ordered in an angry voice. He wasn't any different from the rest—this video had sickened him. He had experienced war and all its horrors, but this was different. This was personal.

"Understood, Admiral Strayker," the answer came over the speakers. "Her assailant has locked himself in docking bay 7, two levels above the attack. All outside doors are locked and password protected by me. Inside doors are also locked and coded. He's trapped. Fighters are closing and have been informed of the situation."

"Thank you, Eve," Admiral Strayker said aloud. Turning to Colonel Dewey, he looked at her and nodded his head. "He's all yours, Colonel."

Colonel Dewey nodded her acknowledgment and turned to make her way off the command deck. As she walked toward the rear of the deck, she noted the looks on the faces of those who were still able to carry out their duties. Each face was etched in anger directed toward the person who had done this deed. She noted their eyes and saw the hatred in them. She knew that each one would gladly go with her, but this was all hers. She was the one that had to do avenging. She had warned him months earlier, and he had chosen to ignore it. She didn't care if he thought she wasn't capable, or if it was said in jest; she only cared about her friend.

18

Amber Jameson lay on the bed in sick bay and stared at the ceiling. She still couldn't move any part of her body below her neck. The doctors had told her that it could be temporary, and that at some point, movement would return, but she wasn't sure. She tried to hold the tears in, but some of them escaped from her eyes and trickled down her cheeks. She wanted to be strong. There were others she knew of that were hurt more than she was. There were others that had lost friends and loved ones in the attack. She had heard the unofficial death count before being removed from the command deck. She grieved for them. At one point, she had even wished she was one of them. Now lying on her back, she tried to move her head and eyes so she could see if anyone else was in the room with her.

Raising her head slightly, she moved her eyes back and forth, taking in the surroundings. There was a bed to her right, but she wasn't able to see if anybody was occupying it. A chair was located at the foot of the bed, and she could see Jordan Schmidt seated in it. The former general was silently keeping a watch on whoever was lying in the bed. Her eyes moved to her left, and she could see another bed with a nurse hovering over whoever was lying in it. She was about to call out to the nurse when she heard her name being called from the other side of her bed. She blinked quickly and moved her eyes to see who was calling to her.

"Amber," Jordan Schmidt said again. She was out of her chair and moving over to the crippled woman. "You're awake. Thought you might sleep the rest of the day away. You could use the sleep, you know."

"How long have I been here?" Amber inquired as Jordan sat down on the side of the bed.

"Just over two hours. Doc says you're going to be okay. You just need some downtime to heal. Movement should come back in a few days," Jordan told her as she sat there and reached for her hand and squeezed it tight. She noted the lack of response on the woman and allowed her head to dip slightly.

"How's Karl?" Amber asked, hoping the answer would be better than her own prognosis.

"He woke up for a second or two, then went back out. Doc claims he'll be fine with rest."

"The fort?" asked Amber, starting to get her hopes up after hearing about Karl Cregg.

"Power is slowly coming back. We lost a lot of good people with that hit. Between the fighters and the big ships, we took out that object. The battle is over. We lost a lot of good people out there also," Jordan explained quietly. She didn't like the part about losing people. She believed they were all family. To lose even one of them was devastating.

"Where's Sergeant Russ?" Amber asked. She failed to see her traveling companion in the room, and Jordan had failed to mention her. She hadn't known her for that long a period of time, but she had come to think of her as family.

Jordan sat there, speechless for a minute. She squeezed Amber's hand even harder. She turned her head away from the shipbuilder and stared at the far wall. She could feel the tears coming to her eyes and rolling down her face. She tried to control her breathing but found it more difficult than she remembered. Pulling herself together, she turned back to Amber and took a deep breath.

"Sergeant Russ, Lindsey, was attacked a while ago and is in surgery. Medics think she may not make it. There is so much damage to her internal organs," she said in a ragged voice.

"Do they know who did it?" quickly asked Amber.

"Lincoln Jacobson. He's Devlin Shaw's right-hand man. The two had a run-in some months back, and it didn't seem to sit well with Jacobson. How he got on the fort isn't known, but he's trapped on one of the flight decks, and Colonel Dewey is on her way to get him," Jordan told her. The thought of what might happen to

Lincoln Jacobson brought her spirits up slightly. She was close to Sergeant Russ and wished it was herself that was going into battle with Jacobson, but she knew that closeness would be a weakness. Colonel Dewey was close to the sergeant, but not as close as she was. To the colonel, Lindsey Russ was a friend and a comrade; to Jordan, she was a sister.

Amber lay there on the bed and gently gave Jordan Schmidt's hand a squeeze. It wasn't much, but the former general felt it like a wall falling on top of her. Jordan Schmidt looked up with surprise on her face, and her face broke into a smile. She felt her heart skip a beat, and she put her other hand on top of Amber's and pulled it close to her face. Giving it a kiss, she bent down and planted another on Amber's forehead before releasing the woman's hand and putting both of hers under Amber and lifting her up gently in order to give her a bear hug.

"I felt that," she almost yelled at the top of her lungs. "I felt you squeeze my hand. You're moving, Amber."

"I didn't mean to do it," Amber told her with a laugh. "I wanted to save it until I could get out of this bed and walk across the floor. I wanted to wait until Karl is up and about. I'm sorry."

The two women hugged each other and laughed out loud. It all sounded so funny, yet here they were in sick bay, with Karl on the bed next to Amber, and another Service member on the other side of her. The knowledge of other Service members in surrounding rooms, fighting for their lives, failed to temper their joy. The only thing that mattered to the two women was that movement was returning to Amber Jameson.

The sirens brought them both back to reality. They were loud and long. The nurse who had been changing bandages on the patient in the next bed dropped what she was doing and rushed out into the hall. Jordan jumped up off the bed and rushed to the doorway and took a step into the hall and looked up and down to find the reason for the alarm. Amber lay on the bed and took several deep breaths, hoping it wasn't another Quill attack. A groan came from the bed next to her, and she moved her eyes in that direction in an attempt to find out what was happening there. Two things happening at once, and she was forced to lie there and just let them happen. She silently cursed the Quill for her paralysis.

"Are you all right over there?" she called out as she strained to see.

"Could you turn that alarm clock off, please," came the male voice.

"That's the alarm, and I can't turn it off," she replied.

"Can you at least put it on mute so I can get some sleep?" he asked.

"If I could move, I would come over there and slap you silly, if you thought that would help," she told him with a smile.

"You and what army?" he asked, suddenly starting to laugh.

"I'm a shipbuilder, remember. I don't need an army to slap around a strategist," she said harshly.

"God help you if I get out of this bed," he told her before breaking into a deep-throated laugh. "What did I miss, Amber? How long have I been out?"

"Couple hours, that's all. Can you please stand in front of me so I can see you? Always so difficult to deal with in the morning," she informed him.

"All you have to do is stand up if you want to see me. I'm kind of comfortable lying here."

"I'm paralyzed," she told him even more harshly. Her anger was rising up, and she was trying her best to keep it hidden.

Karl Cregg sat up quickly and turned to face the woman in the bed next to his. His laughter suddenly gone from him. Concern took over. He cared deeply for Amber Marie Jameson, and the thought of her being paralyzed was frightening. She was the woman he wanted to retire with to his tropical island when this war was over. They were supposed to walk the beach together at night, holding hands. She was supposed to walk down the aisle to marry him. All the thoughts he had about the two of them when this war ended suddenly came crashing down. He knew he would still do them with her, just not the way he had imagined.

"What happened?" he asked when he was on his feet next to her bed, holding her hand. "What did the doctor say?"

"Relax, Karl. I'm getting some movement back. Doc says I should make a full recovery. He just didn't say how long it would take," she told him as she looked up into his face and saw a tear start to form. "I'm going to be all right with time."

"You scared me, Amber. The thought of you being paralyzed for the rest of life scared me. I love you, you know. When this is all over, I plan on marrying you and spending the rest of my life with you on my island," he informed her as he pulled her hand up to his face and kissed it softly.

"You've said that before. On more than one occasion. Now I think you really mean it," she told him with a smile. "It's dead, you know. That thing out there is dead. We won."

"Then why the alarms? What's going on?" he wondered as he glanced toward the door and saw Jordan Schmidt re-enter the room.

"Pilot coming in. Badly hurt. She was struck by debris and lost control of her ship. She was almost out of oxygen when the recovery teams found her. Word has it she's pretty banged up," Jordan informed the two.

"Who is she? Do you know?" Karl asked quickly.

"Lieutenant Annabelle Bishop. She was leading one wing of the attack. Word has it that thing let go something that nobody had ever seen before, and pieces of shrapnel took out her fighter. She crashed into several other fighters that had suffered the same fate. Her oxygen reserve was down to less than 1 percent when they found her. She's lucky to still be alive," Jordan told them.

"She took over for Lieutenant Jason Lee a while ago, right?" said Karl.

"Correct. He was leading one of the other wings out there. He should be landing soon. Admiral Strayker has agreed to inform Lieutenant Lee of Sergeant Russ's condition," Jordan told him while stepping closer to the bed.

"Admiral Strayker is going to inform him? Why not Colonel Dewey? It's her post. She should be the one to inform him," protested Karl loudly. "And what happened to Sergeant Russ?"

"The colonel is down near one of the docks preparing to take care of Devlin Shaw's man, Lincoln Jacobson. He about beat the sergeant to death in one of the hallways. She's going in to return the favor," Jordan informed him.

"Lincoln Jacobson is here? On this fort?" blurted out Karl as he released Amber's hand and stepped closer to Jordan. "Do you know when he arrived?"

"No one is sure. He might have been on the cruise liner. No one knows for sure how many people came aboard from her," Jordan said.

"Was he accompanied by a young woman?" Karl quickly asked.

"Not sure. Like I said, nobody saw him come aboard. Why?" Jordan told him.

"She's the key. She's the key to this whole thing. She holds all the cards. She is why the Trackers are here. She knows I know who she is. She brought them in to take care of me," he told her. His voice remained level, but his heart was beating faster.

"Who is she?" asked Amber from her bed. The thought of Trackers coming after Karl still angered her. She had hoped that once the Quill was eliminated, the Trackers would be called off, but now it seemed they were here to stay.

"Allison Lisa Morrisonn. She is the sister of Lincoln Jacobson. She is the wife of Devlin Shaw. She took her grandmother's maiden name so that no one would recognize her. It took a lot of digging to find this all out," Karl informed them. He slowly started to pace the room and had the look of worry on his face. "Now Devlin Shaw is a childhood friend of one Charles Dawson Endover. It turns out that Mr. Endover is the primary owner of the firm that runs cruises out here into space. The firm is about to go belly-up because of the travel ban to see the outer planets. Devlin and Charles met up a few years ago at a college reunion and found a way to make each other richer. Devlin would find a way to open up the planets and forts to travel, and then Charles would name Devlin vice president of the company."

"But how does Allison fit into those plans?" wondered Amber from her bed.

"Turns out Allison Lisa Morrisonn has connections to a few people who were able to send Trackers out without official papers. Those Trackers are the ones that are here on the station. They have no ties to the Service or any other government agency," Karl filled them in.

"Mercenaries," Jordan whispered as she closed her eyes. She knew their kind. Selling their services for the highest dollar. There was no way to call them off once they were assigned to take someone out. They would only stop when their target was eliminated.

"Mercenaries," Karl repeated. "We have to find a way to get to them before they get to us."

"How?" asked Amber. "If they only stop when their target is dead, how do we stop them before they kill you?"

"I have a plan," Karl informed them with a grin coming to his face. "If we do it right, the whole thing should be over today. Tonight at the latest."

*****

Commander Vath Kung was waiting by the door to the flight deck. He had a grim look on his face as he watched Colonel Ruth Dewey make her way through the rubble. He tried to hold his anger in but was finding it more difficult by the second. He understood what the Service meant. He had respect for everyone who put the uniform on. To know that someone had savagely attacked a Service member and left her for dead turned his stomach. He had wanted to handle this himself, as did every other Service member, but the order had come from the command deck that the colonel would handle this herself, and he wasn't one to disobey an order. Now he stood watch over the flight deck to make sure that Lincoln Jacobson didn't attempt to re-enter the fort now that the fighters were circling like vultures out in space.

"He's inside, Colonel," he told her when she was within earshot. "There's no other way off the deck, and the fighters are outside. He's not going anywhere."

"Thank you, Commander," she said as she came to a stop in front of him. "What's the deck look like? Much damage?"

"We were in the middle of clearing it when he arrived. I have twenty-six people in sick bay with serious injuries from the Quill attack. We got everyone else out without much shooting. Once outside, I barricaded all the doors save for this one. I would like a crack at him, if it's okay with you," he said, pushing his chest out as far as he could.

"Thank you, Commander, but this is one that I'm going to handle myself. I made a promise a while back, and today I keep it," she told him in a firm voice. "Stay here. Make sure that if I fail, he doesn't get away."

"Yes, sir," he said as he pushed a panel on the wall near the door that brought the door alive.

The two watched the door swing open, and peered inside into the darkness of the flight deck. Each turned and looked at the other. No words were spoken; they weren't needed. Both knew what was about to happen, and both had the same ending in sight. The man hiding inside had to be killed. He couldn't be allowed to leave the flight deck and do any more harm to Service members. As far as they were concerned, he was a criminal on a military station.

Colonel Dewey cautiously took a step onto the flight deck and listened as the door was closed and sealed behind her. She took a deep breath and tried to get her eyes to adjust to the near-dark conditions. She turned her head from right to left, taking everything in. She tried not to miss even the smallest of things. She made an attempt to commit everything to memory, knowing she would need it in the fight to come. She took another step forward. She stopped and listened intently. She waited nearly a minute to see if Mr. Jacobson would move from his advantage point. No sound came to her. She took another step and repeated the process.

"What are you afraid of, Colonel?" came the question out of the darkness. "When we were back in General Schmidt's office, you sounded like a big hotshot. No fears. Giving orders and expecting everyone to follow them. So tell me, why are you afraid now?"

Colonel Dewey steadied herself and looked about herself, trying to find out where the voice came from. It had an echo to it, which made it harder to locate. She didn't want to respond yet. She would in time, but not right now. She wanted him to sweat a little. Become impatient and make mistakes that she could use to her advantage.

For now, silence was her ally. She took another step forward and followed it up with one to the right.

"Come now, Colonel," the voice said. "I can see you. I know where you are trying to go and what you are after. They're not there anymore. Once everyone vacated the deck, they were the first things I moved. You're all alone here. Your only weapon is that firearm you carry. What are you going to do when that runs out? Do you really think you can take me one-on-one? I have twice the strength you have. I know where you are, and you haven't a clue as to where I am. I can sit here all day and just watch you."

Colonel Dewey stood her ground and made no move. He was right. She had been headed toward the armory. To know that it was empty was a blow to her plan, but it didn't completely destroy her plan. She had been trained to make more than one plan at a time. She needed more than one now. She took another step to her right while still looking around for any signs of her prey. She wasn't sure who was hunting who, but she was confident of who was going to be the victor. She had no doubt. Another step, and she was within eyesight of the armory. She could see the open door. She wondered silently if he had taken everything or only those things that he could see immediately. One more step in the general direction.

She cringed as a shot rang out and watched as the wall next to the armory erupted with the impact of the shell. Sparks flew in every direction, and a small fire burned for a spit second. She instantly crouched low and flung herself forward toward a small pile of debris. Once there, she rolled to her left and traced in her head where the shot had come from. She was right—he was getting careless. He had fired before knowing exactly where she was headed. He had assumed her destination, and he was wrong. She pulled her weapon and aimed it into the darkness but held her fire. She hoped he would fire a second time, thus exposing his location. She didn't have to wait too long.

The shot rang out, and sparks and a small fire formed on the wall just past the armory. She didn't pay it any attention, instead focusing on the spot where it had come from. She gently pulled the trigger and watched as her shot flew into the darkness and found its mark. She let go a second one and allowed a smile to come to her face as she heard cursing.

"What's wrong?" she called out. "That couldn't have hurt so much. Big man like you, smarting from an itty-bitty gunshot."

"Lucky shot, Colonel," he yelled in reply. "It won't slow me down too much. You're still no match for me."

"You're getting sloppy, Lincoln," was all she said.

Looking about herself, she noted that the pile of debris she was behind stretched for roughly twenty feet to her right. Steadying herself, she began to crawl on her stomach toward the end of the pile. She made every attempt to remain silent and hidden. Surprise would be her friend. As she crawled, she listened for any sign that he was moving. She knew exactly where he was, but she had to be certain that he would still be there when she got to her destination. When she was less than ten feet from the end, she heard a noise and immediately stopped. Holding her breath, she listened even harder. There it was again. He was on the move. Another sound, and she knew he was headed toward where she had been only minutes before. He had no idea that she had moved. Surprise would truly be her friend.

She moved herself away from the pile and toward the wall, all the time keeping an eye on where she had started from. She needed to be able to see the spot where she had come from. The darkness would hide her most of the way, but once she was against the wall, she would be in what little light there was. There was no escaping that fact. It was a risk she was willing, and ready, to take. Another step from the distance. She knew he would be at the spot in another step or two at the most.

Picking up the pace, she made it to her designated spot in just a matter of seconds. Silently, she hoped he hadn't heard her movements. Lying on her back, she aimed her weapon as best she could while trying to keep the limited light from reflecting off of it. Another soft step, and she knew it would only be a matter of another one before she would see him. She said a silent prayer and prepared for the final conflict.

The top of Lincoln Jacobson's head appeared over the pile. Colonel Ruth Dewey steadied her arm and took careful aim. His chest came into view, and she slowly pulled the trigger. He took aim over the debris pile and was prepared to fire at his prey. Her weapon released its fury, and she watched as it found its target, and his weapon was knocked out of his hand, and he screamed in pain. Jumping up from her position, she sprinted over to where he stood holding his hand, and lashed out with her weapon hand against his face as hard as she could. Lincoln Jacobson was sent sprawling across the deck. It took only a few seconds for him to regain his bearings, and when he did, he shook his head violently to clear the cobwebs. Colonel Dewey stood there, waiting for his reply. She had put her weapon away and had her fists clenched, ready for hand-to-hand combat.

"Get up, you worthless piece of human flesh," she snarled.

"You broke my hand!" he screamed as he got to his feet.

"Be thankful that's all I broke," she replied. "I heard and saw what you did to Sergeant Russ. I warned you what would happen if you ever even attempted that."

"I only have one good hand. You're really going to fight me when I'm crippled like this?" he asked as he prepared himself as best he could for the fight.

"The sergeant had one bad leg. I didn't see where that made a difference to you. As far as I'm concerned, this will be an even fight. One-on-one."

Colonel Dewey stepped forward and found herself in a pool of light. The only spot on the deck that was totally lit up. To her, it seemed appropriate. It resembled a boxing ring, and she was prepared to fight the fight. She moved slowly to her left, keeping her eyes on Lincoln Jacobson. For his part, he took a step backward and tried to flex his right hand in order to try to get the pain to subside. His fingers barely moved. He snarled and cursed some more. Moving to his right, he flexed his good hand and brought it back to shoulder-height.

Colonel Dewey saw the danger quickly and let go with a leap to his midsection, sending him flying backward. He had never seen it coming. Crashing hard to the floor, he rolled over and found himself being pounded on the back of the head by the colonel. She landed one punch after another before he was able to roll over and topple her off. Getting to her feet, she gave him a hard kick to the chest that sent him rolling uncontrollably across the floor. Putting his good hand on the floor in an attempt to rise to his feet, he found himself receiving another kick, only this time to his good arm that broke the arm.

Lincoln Jacobson went down hard but flung out his one leg and managed to connect with Colonel Dewey's one leg and knock her to the floor, eliciting a groan of pain form the military leader. Rolling across the floor, she came up and shook her hair out of her eyes and looked for her enemy. He was gone. He wasn't where she had expected him to be. She was certain he was still in the room, just hiding in the darkness once again. Silently she cursed herself for being so careless as to get too close to him. She needed to finish this. She needed to check on her people. To see to their injuries. She looked around, trying to see into the darkness. She failed to see him. She listened to see if he would give himself away like he did before. There was no sound to be heard. Slowly she backed out of the light while pulling her weapon and making it ready to fire.

"Clumsy of you, Colonel," came the voice out of the darkness. "You had me until you broke my arm. Pain, though, is nothing new to me. I once fought a man who was twice my size and outweighed me by a hundred pounds, with two fingers on my left arm broken and my right arm almost cut off. I visit his grave now and then, and drink a toast to my victory."

Colonel Dewey sat in the darkness, listening to him brag. She had no doubt that he had done what he said, but his opponent then wasn't in the Service. She knew how to fight. She knew how to give her enemy false hope. She knew how to kill him slowly. She only needed the right time, and that time had come. She shifted her position and crawled forward toward where his voice had come from. She knew where he was now. He had gotten sloppy again. She was determined to make him pay dearly for that mistake.

Holstering her weapon, she began to crawl even slower than before. She held the pain in from her bruised leg. Every movement brought new pain to her leg, but she was determined to hold it in at all costs. He had done a great deal of damage to her with that single kick. She was determined to hold it in until this was over, then she would see the doctor about how bad it really was. For now, though, she crawled slowly toward the man who had done this damage to her and even more damage to a friend of hers.

"Come now, Colonel. You still don't believe you can take me. Do you?" he called out. "This is nothing. They could cut off both my arms, and I could still take you. Pain is only in the mind. Outside of that, it doesn't exist."

"You just go right on talking, big man," Colonel Dewey whispered to herself. "You'll lead me right to you."

"Why don't you just show yourself now. Save a little time and suffering. I promise I'll kill you quickly. I'll make it as painless as possible," he said out loud. "I'll even kill myself afterward so your friends out there won't get hurt," he finished saying. There was a long pause after that. "What do you say, Colonel?" he asked, as if hoping she would fall for his suicide promise.

"No deal," she told him softly as she swung her right arm out and slammed it into the back of his head.

It had caught him by surprise, and it sent him falling forward onto some piled debris. Quickly she jumped over the debris and landed squarely on his back, sending him even closer to the floor. She took to one knee and sent another blow onto the back of his head before getting off and sending a series of kicks into his side. She gave a thought to backing off so as to give him a fighting chance, but a second later, she returned to kicking him and then grabbing the back of his head by the hair and slamming his face into the deck. Blood now began to flow from his face, and he had given up all efforts of defending himself against the onslaught. He was a puppet now, and she was the puppeteer. She continued to drive his face into the deck, and when her arm grew tired, she would step back and deliver more kicks to his already-broken ribs. He had promised to kill her quickly, but she had made no such promise. She was more than content to see him die as slowly as possible and with as much pain as possible. Her onslaught continued, and she lost track of what she was doing and how many times she had hit him. She stopped only when her arm and leg grew tired, and the grunts stopped coming from his mouth.

Taking a step back, she looked down at what used to be a man. He resembled nothing of a human being now. He looked more like a pile of blood and bones. She tried to control her breathing. She brushed the hair from her face. Bending over, she placed a hand on each knee and took deep controlled breaths. Blood and sweat dripped from her face onto the deck.

"I warned you," was all she said.

19

Sergeant Lindsey Russ awoke in sick bay hooked up to a bunch of tubes and machines that were keeping her condition stable. Her last memory was of the Quill object launching an attack against Fort Patton. Looking around at the other beds, she was somewhat surprised to see most of them empty, and the ones that were occupied held people that didn't seem as injured as she was. She was glad to notice that power was still running through this area and that the shot hadn't been as bad as she was led to believe it would be.

"Good morning, Sergeant," someone said to her from her left side.

She made an attempt to move her head far enough to see who was there, but the pain was too much, and she closed her eyes and grimaced. She wanted to hold her head in her hands but found she couldn't move them that far. Opening her eyes, she saw a hand coming in from the left and falling on top of her own. It rubbed her hand softly, and the pain in her head seemed to disappear. She smiled slightly.

"Good morning yourself, Lieutenant," she said in a sheepish voice that she couldn't believe it came from her throat. She tried to turn her head far enough to see the man standing there, but the pain became too much for her. Then she tried to roll her eyes in his direction, but she failed at this also.

"Easy, Sergeant," he said in a soft voice. "You've been seriously injured. The swelling won't go down for at least another few days."

"The least you can do is to move in front of me so I can see your face," she told him.

"Better?" he asked as he positioned himself closer to the bed and nearer to her side.

Sergeant Lindsey Russ looked up at him and flashed the biggest smile she could. A tear began to form in the corner of her eye as she saw the smiling face of Lieutenant Jason Lee looking down on her. She had thought him dead or at least seriously injured to the point that he wouldn't remember her, yet here he was, in apparently great health, and remembering everything about her. Her tears began to flow freely, and she made no attempt to stop them.

"I thought you were dead," she managed to tell him as she began to cry.

"Not even close," he told her as he leaned in and kissed her cheek.

"I probably look terrible," she warned him.

"Never better."

"I'm in the hospital, tubes running everywhere, I can't move most of my body, machines everywhere helping me to live, and you think I never looked any better," she mocked him. "Do you need glasses to help you see what's right in front of your face?"

"What's right in front of my face is the woman I've come to know and love," he told her as he leaned in and kissed her face again.

"As you were," came the order from the doorway.

Lieutenant Lee stood up straight and turned to face the two newcomers. Both were in their dress uniforms with multiple medals on their chests. Admiral Gordon Strayker and Colonel Ruth Dewey walked side by side toward the bed, where Sergeant Russ lay and Lieutenant Lee stood next to. Both had smiles on their faces and an extra bounce in their step that hadn't been there for some time. When they were close to the bed, Colonel Dewey stopped and allowed Admiral Strayker to continue till he stood next to the bed and across from Lieutenant Lee. He held a small box in his hands but never looked at it, instead focusing his attention on the sergeant who lay before him.

"Sergeant Lindsey Russ," he said in his best military-style voice.

"Yes, sir," she responded, trying to bring her body to attention as best she could.

"As the commanding officer of Fort Patton, it is my distinct pleasure to present you with this box that contains the new insignia

THE QUILL CONSPIRACY

of your new rank. You are no longer a sergeant in the Service. From this moment on, you are now a lieutenant, with all the benefits befitting your new rank. Congratulations," he told her as he held out the box for her.

"You're promoting me?" she asked as she received the box. "Why?"

"Based on reports I've read from the majors in this sector, along with Colonel Dewey's reports and with the recommendation from General Jordan Schmidt, I've come to the conclusion that your rank as sergeant is no longer valid and that you should be promoted as soon as possible," he informed her.

"Don't argue, Lindsey," Colonel Dewey told her. "You've more than earned this promotion. It does, however, have a sticking point that may be hard to overcome."

"What's that?" asked Lieutenant Lee without giving the new lieutenant a chance to ask the same question.

"Because of the damage inflicted by one Lincoln Jacobson, who is no longer with us, your injuries are too much to allow you stay on frontline duty. You are being transferred back to Earth and assigned to Service headquarters. When you a discharged from here, you will report to General of the Service Jordan Schmidt."

"She's retired. I was there when word came down from Devlin Shaw's office. How did she get reinstated?" Lieutenant Russ wondered.

"President Hoss had Vice President Cologne look into Devlin Shaw's affairs before Cologne passed away. He had presented the president with his findings, and President Hoss was furious, but before he could remove Shaw, this little thing with the Quill broke out, and he was distracted. Now that the Quill gun has been taken out, and reconnaissance flights have failed to find any sign of the Quill in around Saturn, the president returned to matters that had mattered more, and Devlin Shaw has been arrested and turned over to the Service for trial. He's currently being held on Mars with a trial to commence early next year," Admiral Strayker explained with a smile on his face. "To tell you the truth, I never liked the man."

"If you remember, President Hoss is the one who promoted General Schmidt in the first place and never hid the fact that he trusted her opinion above everyone else's," Colonel Dewey further explained.

"So I'm back to where I was before this all started. I work once again for General Schmidt, only this time as a lieutenant instead of a corporal," she said as she lay back in bed and turned her attention from the admiral and colonel to Lieutenant Lee. "What do you think?"

"Kind of like going home," he told her. "I don't know if I can get used to living on Earth again. Been a long time."

"Whatever are you talking about?" she asked with a puzzled look on her face.

"It has dawned on me that I'm happier when I'm with you than when I'm anywhere else. If you're going back to Earth, then I'm going with you, either as a lieutenant or a civilian. Either way, I intend to stay at your side," he told her with a look of pride on his face.

"What makes you think I want you at my side? You tried to get yourself killed a while ago. You seriously think I want a man like that around me?" she said in a harsh voice.

"Just think how boring life would be without me. Who else would go on a suicide mission and live?" he asked with a smile.

"So you are a failure, and you want me to take up with a failure. Let's try this again, why would I want you by my side?" she insisted with a straight face.

"I love you," he said softly. "I LOVE YOU!" he yelled as loud as he could.

"Now that's the sound of the man I want by my side," she said as she reached up and pulled him closer and kissed his lips.

Admiral Strayker and Colonel Dewey erupted into applause and moved as close as they could to the bed and joined together for a group hug. Congratulations were exchanged. Nurses and doctors who had been treating other patients in other rooms came running in to see what had happened and were roped into the excitement. A female patient in a wheelchair appeared at the door and shouted her congratulations to the couple, which made Lieutenant Lee stop what he was doing and look in her direction. His face turned from excitement to surprise.

"Annabelle Bishop," he said softly.

"Jason," she replied. "Good to see you again. Congrats on the love announcement."

"What happened?" he asked after a second as he pointed to the wheelchair.

"Caught some flack out there, and it took them a while to locate me. Doc says I'll be able to return to active in a few days."

"Good for you," he told her as he moved closer. "You plan on staying out here or going back home?"

"That's up to Karl Cregg. He's the one that had me replace you in the first place. I work for him. He trusted me just a little bit more than he trusted you, so when he found out that Devlin Shaw was looking to replace you, he leaked out word that I would be perfect for the position, and Shaw bit on it and put me in your place. He then told General Schmidt to have one of her people take you in and give you a position as a civilian. Then things got a little hairy back on Earth, and General Schmidt changed the orders slightly, and you were reinstated working for her. Seems that worked out pretty well for you," she said, looking past Lieutenant Lee toward Lieutenant Russ. "Congrats."

"Karl planned all this?" Lieutenant Lee asked as he turned to face Colonel Dewey.

"Not all of it. He suspected something was coming, and he took the necessary actions needed. His people had to be in the right place at the right time, and you weren't the right person to be out here. He didn't know you enough. All he had was your file. He had never seen you face-to-face. His instincts told him to go with someone else, and when you were retired, he made sure that someone he knew and trusted was put in your place. I was more than thrilled to get you onto my fort and keep you here. I knew you, I trusted you. I would do it all over again if I had to," Colonel Dewey told him in a firm voice.

"It all worked out, son," Admiral Strayker put in. "For some, it worked out better than for others," he said as he watched a body of a fallen Service being removed from a room across the hall.

"Attention," called out Colonel Dewey when she saw the body. It caught everyone off guard slightly, but they quickly responded and came to attention as ordered and saluted their fallen comrade.

"You're right, Admiral. I came out of this better than when I went into it," Lieutenant Lee said as he moved back to the bed and took hold of Lieutenant Russ's hand.

"Thankfully it's over," Lieutenant Russ said as she took hold of his hand.

"Not yet," Colonel Dewey said.

*****

The medical room on a different deck was partially lit. The lights near the door weren't yet operational, while the ones in the rear were on and doing their best to light the room. The hallway lights were doing double duty, lighting both the hall and the front of the medical room. The bed closest to the hall was occupied by an unmoving Service member who was hooked up to what appeared to be every possible machine ever created to save a human life. The machines had a life of their own, and their noise echoed throughout the room. The only other sign of life was a bed that was occupied in the rear of the room with a female that was desperately trying to sleep. Every now and then, she would lift her head up and send a curse to the front of the room for the machines to be quiet. They never listened, and she would allow her head to drop back down.

Into this darkened room walked four men in silence. They crept into the room, keeping one eye on the near bed and the other on the hallway they had just exited. Once totally into the room, they split up so that one was at the foot of the bed, two others were on either side of it, and the fourth kept vigil on the female in the rear bed. Once they were at the bed, they stopped and watched the man on the bed for a minute before taking the final step, which brought them as close as possible to their prey. Each looked toward the others and gave a nod of their head before reaching in and laying their hands on the body before them.

"Far enough," came the words from the doorway.

Spinning, they saw the body of Admiral Strayker in the doorway and a team of ten Service members with weapons drawn and aimed on either side of him. The men entertained thoughts about finishing what they had come here to do. Their eyes went from the admiral to the person lying in the bed. They quickly calculated their chances of finishing the deed. They allowed their eyes to seek each other out, and each gave a nod of the head.

"You won't make it," the admiral said. "You'll each be dead before you even touch the bed."

"I would rather you listen to the admiral," Karl Cregg told them as he sat up in the bed and removed the tubes that were connected to his body. "He really does mean what he says, and he has given you the opportunity to surrender rather than be in a pine box."

The man at the foot of the bed seemed surprised, if only for a few seconds, by Karl Cregg's sudden recovery. Once the surprise subsided, he gave a smile and a nod to Karl. He understood that they had been lured onto a trap and that the exit was closed. There was no way out. The only options they had was to surrender and be put on trial for attempted murder of a Service member, which carried a life sentence on Mars, or try to shoot their way out, which would end their lives. He glanced at his colleagues and closed his eyes while nodding his head. Then he pulled a weapon that had been well hidden under his shirt and took aim at Karl, as did the other three. The room suddenly lit up with the fire of Service weapons. Each of the Service members in the doorway let go at the same time, and each shot found its target. The four men did a strange kind of dance and dropped their weapons in the process. Each took no less than three shots to the chest and were lifeless before falling to the floor. For his part, Karl simply sat there and watched them fall one by one. When it was over, he rolled onto his side and touched a button on the bed console, and a low hum filled the room as his protective shield rose from its position on the bed to its home spot in the ceiling.

"Next time, one of you can lie here and hope the silly thing works," he told the admiral and Colonel Dewey, who had been standing in the hallway, waiting for the event to end before entering.

"You were never in any danger," the colonel told him. "It's made of weapons-proof glass, and with lighting like this, you can barely tell it's there. The chance of you getting hurt, even a little, is pretty slim. As long as you did as you were told and stayed behind the glass, you were going to come out of this without a scratch."

"Perfectly safe," Admiral Strayker told him. "Never seen anybody get hurt using that."

"How many people have you seen use it? Not counting me," Karl asked as he rose from the bed and stepped over the body next to it.

"You're the first. You didn't get hurt, did you?" he asked.

"Only my wits. Otherwise it worked like a charm," Karl said with a smile.

"What about me?" Amber Jameson asked from the back bed. "What if one of those shots had found its way back here and killed me? What would you do then?"

"Didn't I tell you that there was one of those things between you and the door?" Colonel Dewey told her as she strolled to the wall panel and touched a small button. Once again, a low hum filled the room, and everyone knew that another panel had been raised.

"What if that thing had failed?" she yelled out from the bed as she raised herself up onto her elbows.

"It didn't, did it?" asked Admiral Strayker with a sly smile. Then he gasped slightly. His eyes opened wide, and he pointed at her so that the others would turn and see what he was seeing.

The others focused their attention on the woman in the bed and indeed saw what the admiral was seeing. Each, in turn, started walking toward her with a smile on their face. Each was excited about the vision in front of them, none more so than Karl Cregg. After a few steps, he ran to her bedside and scooped her into his arms and applied a big bear hug to her while, at the same time, kissing her cheek over and over again. Tears began to roll down his cheek.

"You're moving," he told her in between the sobs.

"No, I'm not," she told him while trying to gently push him away.

"If you're not moving, then how is it that you're pushing him away?" inquired Colonel Dewey. "And *why* would you push him away?"

"Because," she told the colonel, "he's getting me all wet with his tears."

"When did you find out you could move like this? And how much can you move?" asked Admiral Strayker, moving to her bedside and reaching out a hand to touch her gently on the shoulder.

"I can move some things a little, and I just found out that I could before all the shooting started," she informed them. "I didn't want to yell out and wreck all your plans with my excitement about the ability to move. Besides it isn't like I'm going to get out of bed and walk around the fort. I have *some* movement, not a lot," she told them as she grasped Karl's hand and squeezed it tightly.

"I'll take it," Karl told her. "I would take you if you couldn't move at all."

"But you like me better now, don't you?" she asked.

"I love you. I always have, and I always will. Whether you can walk or not. Whether you can move a little or not at all. None of that matters as long as you're with me, and I'm with you," Karl told her, then leaned in and kissed her cheek.

"So now what?" Amber asked him. "Things are back to the way they should be. What do we do now?"

"Not yet," Colonel Dewey told her. "We still have the matter of one Allison Lisa Morrisonn with two *N*s. She is still at large, and God only knows what she has planned. She has to be stopped as quickly as possible."

"I've already seen to that," Karl told her flatly.

*****

The mess hall, even for this time of day, was near capacity. The only real remaining tables were the ones farthest from the door. Half of the occupants wore Service uniforms; the other half came from the crippled liner and were awaiting transportation back to Earth. Word had it that they would be transferred back within the next few days. Morale was high among the civilians, and each one was talking about life back home and what they would tell their friends and family about this ordeal. The Service members simply sat and ate and chatted about the upcoming day.

Into this area came a young, heavily made-up, fancy-dressed woman with an escort of no less than ten muscular men. She was dressed in the latest style, and every head turned as she made her way to the counter to find something for breakfast. She paid no mind to those she walked past; the only thing on her mind was food and leaving this godforsaken place and never returning. In her mind, she cursed the day she stepped foot onto the liner. The men who accompanied her focused all their attention on those in the mess hall. They watched every move that every individual made. Their job was to keep her safe, and they took that very seriously.

Once they found an open table, the fancy-dressed woman sat down with four of her men, while the rest went to the counter to prepare their plates, plus one for her. She was being treated like royalty, though she was, in reality, not related to any royal that anyone could find. Her family had struck it rich, and she intended to act on it and insisted on being treated like royalty. One of the men returned to the table and placed her plate in front of her, then went back and prepared another for himself.

From a table close by, five people dressed as civilians rose and disposed of their garbage. They looked toward the doorway, then decided on a different direction. Turning, they headed toward the table that the fancy-dressed woman and her guards were seated at. They spread out, and an older gray-haired African American woman took the center spot and seemed to lead the way. She stopped only when she was deemed too close to the fancy woman, and two of the guards stood up and stepped between the two women.

"Allison Lisa Morrisonn?" the gray-haired woman asked.

"And you are?" Allison asked.

"General of the Service Jordan Schmidt, and you are under arrest."

"You forget you were retired. You have no authority here anymore," Allison informed her.

"I guess you're not up on current events. President Hoss reinstated me and promoted me to General of the Service. The only people I answer to now are the secretary and the president. That gives me all the authority I need to arrest you and charge you with treason," General Schmidt informed her in a voice that made it sound as if she was enjoying herself.

"I don't pay attention to that boob. Cologne was the intelligent one, and he died of natural causes, and the new VP is just as dimwitted as Hoss," Allison Morrisonn explained. "Now if you will excuse me, I'm famished, and this food is getting cold."

"There is no excuse for you, and just so you are aware, Vice President Cologne informed President Hoss of the activities of your family and friends before getting sick. President Hoss has taken all necessary actions in correcting the harm that Devlin Shaw, your husband, has done. Shaw is now in custody, while his handyman, Lincoln Jacobson, your brother, is dead. The last of the main characters—you—will now come with me, and I'll even make sure your meal accompanies you. Your men are free to go, and they will be escorted off the fort on the next transport. If they try anything between now and their departure time, I can assure them that they will not see the next sunrise," General Schmidt told the group with the firmest voice she had. She eyed them up, making sure they understood what she was saying.

"You're bluffing. Devlin and Lincoln are both perfectly fine and roaming free," Allison gloated gladly.

"You really aren't up on current affairs, are you? Check the morning affairs, and you'll see that everything I have told you is true. Now get up and come peacefully, or my people will drag you by your hair, screaming from here to the brig."

Allison Lisa Morrisonn looked up from her meal and glared at the woman in front of her. Her men took a step to the side so that the two women could look at each other without obstruction. General Schmidt's people stepped into their places and placed their hands on top of their sidearms. Neither woman made another move; both waited for the other. Allison Lisa Morrisonn reached for her drink and took a long sip. Picking up her napkin, she dabbed her lips and returned it to its resting spot next to her plate. Slowly she rose to her feet and looked the general in the eyes, as if she was still trying to figure out if she was telling the truth or not. In the end, she concluded that it was best if she accompanied her rather than to start a commotion in an area that was half filled with Service members who were paying attention to every word that was being said.

"Lead the way," she said with a smile that made it appear that it was all still a mistake and that she would be freed in the end.

"Make sure these gentlemen finish their meal without incident, then escort them to Commander Kung, who will make sure they get seated on the next ship back to Earth," General Schmidt told her people before she and three of her people escorted Allison Lisa Morrisonn out of the mess hall and to the brig.

20

The day was sunny and more than a little warm. The waves crashed ashore, while the seagulls flew overhead and screamed down at the people sitting in the clearing. They sat at a table with a large umbrella to shield them from the oppressive sun. A party was in full swing, and nothing was left to want. There was plenty of both food and drink. Good conversation could be found no matter where one sat. The island had come alive in the past few days as the celebrants came from all over the system. This had been in the planning stage since the arrests and trial of Devlin Shaw and Allison Lisa Morrisonn. The Quill were gone, and the system was back to where it should be. The forts had been ordered to stand at ease, and repairs had begun. Cruise liners were running weekly excursions to Saturn and beyond for the first time in decades. Now for the first time, the main characters could get together with old friends and celebrate their hard-fought victory.

"What about all those people in the Service who were loyal to Mr. Shaw? What will become of them?" Amber Jameson asked Karl Cregg, whom she was standing close to.

"General Schmidt has already found a few of them, and they are awaiting trial on Mars for treason. I imagine in the coming months, more will be found, and they will face the same fate. Those that manage to evade the good general won't be showing their heads for a long time to come. Remember, the punishment for treason is life imprisonment in a maximum-security prison on Mars. Not exactly the kind of place one wants to spend the rest of their life," Karl said with a slight chuckle.

"What became of those rogue fighters that we encountered on more than one occasion?" asked Colonel Ruth Dewey of Karl Cregg.

She had seen them several times throughout the past few months, but with all the excitement of the Quill gun, she had forgotten about them until now.

"Admiral Strayker had sent several small ships in search of them and found them hiding just out of range of the Martian scans. Turns out, Devlin Shaw and Lincoln Jacobson had some real close friends in the Service who were more than happy to help them. Once those friends saw the firepower headed their way, and they had no way out, they surrendered without firing a shot. They're enjoying Martian hospitality as we speak," Karl told her with a smile on his face. "Hand looks pretty good, Kevin. How does it feel?" Karl asked his old friend. He gave a wink to Angela, who was seated by her husband's side.

"It will never be as good as it was," Kevin told him as he held it up for everyone to see. "Smashed it so bad the doctors were afraid I would lose it. Three bones actually broke the skin. I shattered four others."

"Whatever made you want to punch the wall in the first place?" questioned Amber Jameson, who was still in a wheelchair, even though most of her movement had returned.

"Seemed like the thing to do at the moment," he told her with a laugh. "I can still use it, just not like I used to. For that I thank the good doctors," he said, raising a glass and taking a long drink.

"Hear! Hear!" agreed Colonel Dewey as she raised hers and did the same.

"And you, Amber, what do the good doctors say about you?" asked Lieutenant Jason Lee, who was standing off to the side with Lieutenant Russ by his side. A walking stick was in her hand to steady her.

"I should have all my abilities back before this time next year. For now, I have to use this chair to get around. I have movements in my legs, but they're still not strong enough to support me for any distance. Karl has assured me, though, that I can stay here as long as I want with him, and I'm thinking I could use a long vacation. People back at the shop know their jobs and won't even miss me," she told everybody with a large smile on her face. She looked up and pulled Karl down to her level and planted a kiss on his lips.

"I would love it if you would never leave my side," he whispered.

"I wasn't the one who left in the first place," she told him.

"Let me rephrase then. I would love to stay by your side, if you'll have me," he told her before removing a small package from his pocket and holding it up in front of her.

"I thought you were never going to do it," called General Schmidt.

"So did I," agreed Amber.

She placed both hands on the arms of the wheelchair and pushed herself to her feet. Karl reached out suddenly, afraid she might fall and hurt herself more. Gently she pushed him away and stood on her own feet, unaided. She faced him and put on her sternest face. She felt her temper boiling. She had been holding it all in for so long she wasn't sure if she could get it all out without falling over.

"You want to know if it's okay to stay by my side for the foreseeable future?" she asked with a touch of anger in her voice. "After all these years? After all we've been through? All the time apart? *Now* you want to be by *my* side. Why? Because I'm in a wheelchair and expect to be there for at least the next year? Because the Quill have finally left, and you have nothing else to do with your time? Think again, mister."

The place was stunned. Everything came to a stop, and all eyes found their way to Amber Jameson, who stood there, shaking slightly and breathing heavily. No one had seen this coming. Everyone had expected her to say yes and leap into his arms. Yet here she was, ripping him up one side and down the other and showing very little sign that she was going to stop anytime soon. The partygoers began to look around for some place to sneak off to and avoid what was going to come. They became uncomfortable with just being in the area of Amber and Karl.

"Well, don't just stand there like a strategist who just found out that he was wrong on everything, answer the questions. Do you expect me to just say yes and allow you to stay by my side because I'm going to be stuck in a wheelchair for the next year?" she demanded.

"No," he said softly while taking a step toward her. "I expect you to say yes because I'm madly and passionately in love with you, and I'm really sorry about all the time we spent apart because my job took me far away from you. I promise, that if you give me another chance, I'll make everything up to you."

Amber stood there in silence. She didn't make a move. She barely breathed. She began to sway slightly and caught herself by taking hold of the wheelchair. Steadying herself, she raised her body up as far as she could and cleared her throat. She peered at Karl and thought about what she wanted to tell him. She wanted him to know how she felt. To know about how she felt about all those lost years. She looked at him and fumed.

Then she saw him. Saw the man he was and how much he really cared about her. How dedicated he was to her and would be in the future. He was the man that made her laugh. The man that inhabited her dreams every night. The man she had always dreamed of marrying. The man her father had told her was perfect for her. She saw the man for what he really was, and her anger fell away, and she smiled at him.

"I'm just a shipbuilder," she told him.

"No, you're not. You're the best damned shipbuilder on the planet, and I'm madly in love with you and want to be by your side."

"And I would love nothing else," she told him before falling into his arms. They embraced and kissed, and all their friends broke into applause and rushed to be by their side. Everyone congratulated the couple and patted them on the back, telling them that the future was looking brighter now.

When everything had settled down, and Amber and Karl were sitting close to each other and holding hands, Kevin stood up and walked over to his old friend. He had the look of someone who needed to know something but was afraid, for some reason, to ask. He stood before Karl and Amber and moved a couple of small stones with his feet.

"Tell me something, Karl," he began. "How did you find out about Devlin, Lincoln, and Allison? It seems as if you had the answer all along. That you knew about them before this whole thing even began. How did you find out?"

"Well," Karl began slowly. "What did you think I was doing on that Alaskan island all by myself? I spent almost every waking hour searching the web for any signs of the three of them. One day, I came across a small insignificant article and almost overlooked it. After reading it, everything became clear. Everything made sense, but before I could do anything, that Tracker landed on my shore, then you came, and everything else started."

"Good to see that the second island came in handy for something other than hiding on," Kevin told him with a laugh. "I did wonder what you were doing up there for those couple of weeks."

"You're just glad that I'm not hosting this up there. Can you imagine swimming in those waters instead of these? Cold!" Karl told him, then both men erupted into laughter, and Karl rose up and gave him a big hug before sitting down and laughing even harder as he watched Kevin walk back to his wife and grabbed her by the hand and led her over to the shoreline so the two could swim in the Pacific.

About the Author

Joseph R. Mullen was born and raised in Northeastern Pennsylvania, where he still resides today with his wife and son. He retired in 2019 and decided to pursue his dream of being a published author. His first book is titled *Four Cowboys*.

CPSIA information can be obtained
at www.ICGtesting.com
Printed in the USA
BVHW060917310323
661518BV00004B/129